"The novel centers on two truths: life is complicated, and it can change in an instant. Karen Uhlmann captures the intersection of now and then with this story of loss, grief, love, and redemption. Readers are plunged right into the messy and human world of the characters, and we can't stop reading."

—LIAN DOLAN, author of *The Sweeny Sisters*
and *The Marriage Sabbatical*

"In this intriguing debut, *Intersections* offers a contemporary eye on family, infidelity, and fertility, illuminating both the burdens and blessings of mistakes, and the sometimes-messy path to grace. Karen Uhlmann's sharp-eyed take on the complicated lives of two Chicago families illustrates effectively the intersection between truth-telling, justice, and the power of love. In every chapter, Uhlmann brings to the page a cross-cut of voices from the Windy City, rendering tension with care and precision that keeps you guessing until the very end."

—ERICA PLOUFFE LAZURE,
author of *Proof of Me and Other Stories*

"*Intersections* takes you on a journey that begins with a heart-breaking death and ends with a whole new life. Along the way, secrets force surprising detours that make the reader wrestle with questions of true moral complexity, even as they turn the pages faster and faster. I was left marveling at Karen Uhlmann's ability to transport me so completely into the lives of her flawed but heroic characters."

— LORNA GRAHAM, author of *Where You Once Belonged*

INTER SECTIONS

A Novel

INTER SECTIONS

A Novel

Karen F. Uhlmann

SHE WRITES PRESS

Published 2025

Printed in the United States of America

Print ISBN: 978-1-64742-889-1
E-ISBN: 978-1-64742-890-7
Library of Congress Control Number: 2025900950

For information, address:
She Writes Press
1569 Solano Ave #546
Berkeley, CA 94707

Interior design and typeset by Katherine Lloyd, The DESK

She Writes Press is a division of SparkPoint Studio, LLC.

For my boys:
Tom, Alexander, Evan, and Gregory

ONE  CHARLOTTE

Black Friday, November 2018

Charlotte Oakes hurried through Lincoln Park on a bright, chilly November afternoon. She was running late and should have taken a cab, but Chicago had so few perfect days that she had wanted to walk. It was nearly three o'clock, time to drive her daughter to the dentist. Libby was home for Thanksgiving, and the visit was not going well. Libby's visits rarely did. This was Charlotte's failing. Only bad mothers had troubled kids. Good mothers had children who grew up to be artists, investment bankers, or owners of craft breweries.

Libby was twenty-three and less than two months out of rehab. She worked at J. Crew in Manhattan while she waited to become famous. Perhaps a TV star . . . It was all a little vague. She watched TMZ and hung out in trendy hotel lobbies drinking cappuccinos, hoping to be discovered like Lana Turner sipping a Coke at the Top Hat Malt Shop. Fame was the main point. Libby had refused to move back home after treatment. "Infantilizing" was the word she had used. Libby had learned plenty of lingo in rehab to throw at her mother. "Enabler" was another.

Charlotte was late because she had gone to see Emory. She did not like the word "lover," but that was the closest she could come to describing him. She was still basking in the afterglow of her visit, replaying the way he had kissed her, scooped her up, and carried her to his couch. Maybe, just maybe, they could have a life together someday.

She was, of course, being ridiculous.

It was all a fantasy. She kicked at some of the red and gold leaves littering the path. Emory would never leave his wife, who was Chicago aristocracy—which was the difference between Charlotte and Emory. One of many. He claimed he was happy with his wife, but happy people didn't have affairs. She knew that much. She would leave her unhappy marriage for a shot at happiness—selfish though it might be. And she had been selfish. She should have been home with Libby. Then she wouldn't be rushing.

As she approached the corner, a small girl dressed in a fairy costume darted into the crosswalk. A woman, balancing a toddler on her hip, dashed into the street after her. The woman lunged for the girl's hand as a familiar-looking car flew through the intersection. Was that her car? Charlotte heard a thump. The girl tumbled to the ground, her pink tutu billowing. Her gold foil crown glinted in the gutter, squashed. The woman and her toddler were splayed across the curb.

The girl's head lay in a puddle of blood. So much blood. This couldn't be real, but a crow cawed in a tree. There was a runner in the distance. She was in Lincoln Park on the corner. The accident was real, but children weren't supposed to get hit by cars and die. This child would surely die. Charlotte froze for a second before her instincts kicked in, and she ran toward the child. A dark-haired man, who must have been her father, got there first and began CPR. Charlotte rushed to the woman on the curb. She was badly bruised, bleeding, and cradling a small, sobbing girl. Charlotte started punching 911 into her cell phone.

"I called. Stay with me. Please." The woman's skin was pale and bluish, the color of shock, and her eyes were wide and glazed. Her blonde bob was matted with blood. She pulled her toddler closer, and the child howled in pain. Her arm dangled at her side—broken.

"Are you hurt?" Charlotte asked, before she realized this was a stupid question.

"My daughter." The woman's eyes were locked on the child lying still in the street and the man bent over her. "My husband." Blood still streamed from the girl's head. It soaked the father's gray parka and his jeans. Charlotte willed herself not to vomit. She knew she would never unsee this. Worse, the parents and sister would never unsee the small body in the street. A family had been destroyed in a second.

"I'm here," she said. That was all she could do, though not nearly enough. The two women sat on the cold curb. The father continued CPR. The city went silent. The only sounds were the father's breaths, and the toddler's sobs. Time stood still as if this moment, this nightmare, would last forever.

A cop arrived. He sprinted toward the child. He was heavyset with silver hair and a slight limp, but he was fast. Within minutes, four squad cars and three ambulances crowded the street. Traffic was blocked off, and she had a moment to think.

How much had the cop seen? The accident? The car? How much had she really seen?

The speeding car had looked like her Prius, but she could be wrong. She'd only spotted it out of the corner of her eye—a navy-blue blur. Still, she thought she'd seen an orange daisy decal on the back windshield, like the one she'd been gifted at the Botanical Gardens fundraiser. She had never before put a decal on her car. But daisies, the Danish national flower, reminded her of her Danish friend Kari who wore a small gold daisy on a delicate chain. Daisies also symbolized childbirth and motherhood as well as love, fertility, and sensuality. She liked that.

It couldn't have been her car. Libby wouldn't have been driving. She'd let her license expire, although this kind of technicality had never stopped her before.

A male and a female EMT hopped out of an ambulance, opened the back door, grabbed the stretcher, and dashed into the street.

"We'll take it from here, sir." The female EMT's voice was serious and calm, as she motioned to the father to step aside.

The father stood up. His face was distorted with panic and confusion as he rushed over to his wife, kissed her, then hurried back to his daughter and the EMTs.

"No cervical collar," the female EMT told her partner. "She's not breathing." She held the girl's head while the male EMT rolled the girl onto her side and onto the stretcher. They quickly strapped her in, beckoned to the father to come, and carried her into the ambulance. Within seconds, they were speeding down the street, siren blaring.

Charlotte watched as the next set of EMTs lifted the smaller girl onto a stretcher. The mother shooed away the EMTs trying to assist her and climbed into the ambulance with her daughter.

Charlotte left before anyone could question her, but she couldn't remember her walk home, only that she arrived at their house. She could not stop picturing the girl. Her hand shook as she put the key in the front door of their Lincoln Park brownstone. She walked through the foyer into the warm living room. It seemed as if everything and nothing had changed. There was the white couch, the pale gray chairs, and white roses on the coffee table.

"Libby, I'm home. We can still make it to the dentist."

No answer.

She rushed upstairs and opened Libby's door. Her bed was made, and a glass of water sat on the nightstand. Her suitcase was open on the floor, but Libby was gone. She went back downstairs. The bowl on the kitchen counter where she kept her keys was empty. She paced around the first floor of the house, her thoughts jumbled. Libby must have gone on her own to the dentist. Perhaps she'd taken a cab. Of course she had. The car keys must be in her purse, which was on the kitchen table. She upended her purse and shook it. She checked the side pockets. No keys. She went outside to the garage. Her car was gone. Panic beat in her chest.

She called Libby's phone. It went straight to voicemail. She thought of the girl. Of death. She texted Libby. No response. Lowering herself into a chair in the family room, she called and texted nonstop. She left messages.

Where are you?
Answer me.
I'm worried.
Call me back.

She clutched her phone, shut her eyes, and attempted to magically project her worry through space to Libby. It didn't work. Her phone remained silent.

She dialed again. "Hey, it's Libby. Leave me a message."

Charlotte threw her phone onto the side table. This was better than hurling it across the room, which is what she really wanted to do.

Somehow dinner was made. She managed to boil water for the farfalle pasta, set out saffron and cream for the sauce, and tossed an arugula salad with toasted pine nuts and parmesan.

At seven, her husband Daniel walked in from his investment job at Bainbridge Capital, handsome in his gray pinstripes.

"Smells good."

He went upstairs to change from his suit into jeans. When he came down, he poured a Scotch and turned on the news in the family room. Charlotte sat down on the couch with him.

There was the girl. Her picture was splashed across the screen along with the headline *Hit-and-Run Killing in Lincoln Park*.

She had been five and died on the way to the hospital. Charlotte's breath caught in her throat. Her palms began to sweat.

"The police need witnesses to come forward. Anyone with any information should call this hotline." A number ran across the screen.

"Whoever did that should be shot." Daniel took a swig of his Scotch. "Or even better, run over."

"I was walking by. I saw all the police cars and ambulances."

"That must have been awful."

"I couldn't really see the accident, but it shook me up."

She hadn't meant to tell him anything. The words slipped out. It was an odd secret to keep, but there was the car . . . the car that looked like her car. And Libby. Libby drove Daniel crazy. Her alcohol abuse, lack of direction, and sullenness were difficult for him. There was no need to plant unfounded suspicion in Daniel's mind. Libby was still not home and still not answering her phone. Worry grew in the pit of Charlotte's stomach and spread through her veins.

The news photo of the dead child looked like a school picture, overly lit with an artificial blue-sky background. She was smiling the goofy, wide smile of a five-year-old. Her eyes were large, a pale clear gray. She had blonde hair like her mother's. Her name was Sarah Caldwell. After a visit to the park, she had been crossing the street with her family, holding her mother's hand. Even though Charlotte knew this was not true, it was somehow the worst part—the image of the hands. The split second in which someone could lose a child. Charlotte surreptitiously wiped her palms on her jeans as the news continued. She was not normally a sweaty person. Daniel was watching TV and did not seem to notice. He didn't notice a lot about her, which was part of the problem. She had become invisible, something she had longed for as a child. Now she didn't like it.

"The girl's mother and two-year-old sister suffered broken bones, cuts, and bruises. The two-year-old had a broken arm, the mother broken ribs."

Charlotte looked up at Libby's unsmiling eighth-grade photo on the bookcase. She had always been an unhappy child, a worrisome one, even if it wasn't her fault. Well, not all of it. She had a trifecta of issues: obsessive-compulsive disorder, ADHD, and learning disabilities. Life had been difficult for her, but she had never done anything to hurt anyone. Only herself.

The news droned on. "The father watched, helpless, as his daughter was hit by the car. There was only one other witness. A police officer on paid leave. Neither man was able to identify the driver. The car may have been a dark-colored Prius."

She exhaled and glanced at Daniel, who did not react.

The cop. The man she'd seen. Tall, blue uniform, silver hair. Her mind whirled. The car, the girl, Libby.

The news anchor did not mention the sister's name. Was it as timeless as Sarah? She had been careful not to choose the name of the moment when she was pregnant. Names, like clothing and certain kinds of art, could seem dated. Charlotte was particular about the classic. Elizabeth was a good, solid name. She wished Libby would go back to it. Her daughter had started using Libby when she stopped eating at thirteen, as if shedding letters could also make her thinner.

Libby did not show up for dinner.

"I'm sure she's out with a friend." Daniel had switched from Scotch to red wine. "Would you like a glass?" He poured one and pushed it across the table toward her. She did not like red wine.

"She didn't answer when I texted and called." What if something had happened to Libby? What if she had crashed the car? Charlotte fingered the phone on her lap.

Daniel dug into his saffron pasta. "Does this have cream in it? I'm trying to cut back on fat."

"Yes, sorry. I didn't know." She was having trouble chewing and swallowing. She reached for the glass of wine. If she took small sips, it wasn't so bad.

After she did the dishes, she poured a glass of white wine from an open bottle in the fridge. Daniel, who had finished the red, went upstairs to his office. In the past, his disappearances had made her lonely. It was sad to live with someone who ignored her. Who often didn't bother to answer her questions. Who never wanted to have sex. Her days of trying to tempt him with lacy lingerie and skimpy nightgowns were over. He'd expressed no interest, which only made her feel aging and ugly. Eventually, she gave up.

She thought she'd put that part of her life behind her, until she met Emory and became an adulterer.

If she'd not gone to see Emory, she would have been here with Libby and driven her to the dentist. True, Libby was old enough to get to the dentist on her own. But Libby struggled, and Libby was all she had. She had tried for years to get pregnant again. Daniel had not wanted IVF, and she had finally given up. Now, at nearly forty-five, she was too old.

She took the wine and lay on the family room couch. She propped *Circe* on her stomach, but instead of reading, she pressed Libby's number over and over again. She finished the wine. It did nothing to calm her. Around eight, the back door opened. Libby stood in the hall removing her bright yellow down jacket. Her long dark hair was tangled. Her lips looked chapped, her eyes unfocused.

"Where have you been?" She tried to ask this as if she was only inquiring about her evening. This took a lot of self-control.

"Dinner with a friend." Was there a slight slur to her voice? Having a child who has been through rehab hypersensitizes a person, but she didn't smell alcohol.

"Did you get to your dentist appointment? I know I was late."

"Yeah, my teeth are fine."

"How did you get there? A cab?"

Libby did not answer.

"I hope you didn't take my car. Your license is expired. Unless you got a new one in New York?"

This was met with silence.

"Libby, I'm asking you a question."

Libby headed upstairs to her room. Charlotte sat for a minute, unnerved and angry, before she got up. She opened the door to the backyard. It took a minute for the outdoor lights to brighten. She walked down the back stairs and into the dark garage. Her car was back. She flipped the light on, but it was too weak to see much. Stooping down, she ran her hand over the bumper. She felt a divot and fished her phone out of her pocket. The flashlight clicked on. There was a small dent on the bumper.

TWO  ED

Black Friday, November 2018

I t was a sunny November day, brisk and clear for the throngs of Black Friday shoppers still dazed from their enormous dinners the night before. The first Christmas carols played on radios all over town, and no one was sick of them yet. The white lights were strung along the Magnificent Mile. The tree in front of the John Hancock building was being decorated. Chicago was readying for the holidays.

It was the sort of day that made Police Officer Ed Kelly think that nothing bad could happen, though he knew better. It already had.

On his way to work, his first day back since he'd been released from the hospital, he had been the first on the scene of a hit-and-run. He'd pulled his Jeep over near an intersection adjacent to Lincoln Park after he'd noticed a car weaving. He saw a child dart into the street and heard the screech of brakes. Watched the car flee. The girl was so tiny, he had almost mistaken her for a sweater in the street. She had died on the way to the hospital.

He'd seen kids die, but he would never be okay with it. Each one was worse than the last. This one was unbearable, with the girl's mangled head and the stricken faces of her parents embedded in his mind. His whole body hurt with what must have been sorrow.

This was the same anguish he'd felt when his best friend and work partner, Tommy, was killed. Both Tommy and Ed had been shot by a small-time drug dealer during a narcotics raid. Tommy had died instantly.

After the accident, Ed had to wipe tears from his face in the parking lot before he could go into work. It was unlike him to weep, but witnessing two such devastating deaths within a month was too much. It was as if he'd been cracked open. Maybe his wife, Maggie, was right. Maybe it was time to retire.

He pushed the district's heavy glass door and was hit with the familiar smell of stale coffee and perspiration mixed with cleaning solution. It was disorienting being here without Tommy. Mike Walsh, his deputy chief, was waiting for him near the front.

"Ed, could you come in here, please?" Mike motioned for Ed to follow him and sit on one of the hard folding chairs in an empty office. "It's good to see you. Feeling better?"

"Yes, still a bit of pain now and then but much better."

"I know how close you were to Tommy."

Ed nodded, looking at Mike's doughy, bland face.

"I hate to have to tell you this. The forensics department determined that the bullet that killed Tommy came from your gun."

"What?" This couldn't be right.

"Unfortunately, I have to put you on paid suspension until we complete an internal investigation."

"I . . . I understand." But he didn't.

"I'm sorry, Ed. Hopefully, it will be quick."

"Thank you." Stunned, Ed went to get his car from the lot.

Now, on top of losing his best friend, it seemed the fatal bullet had come from his gun. How this had happened, he didn't know. They had both been aiming for the drug dealer. But he did know it would be a heavy, despairing weight he would carry for the rest of his life. Tommy was the kind of cop who kept snacks and sodas at the district for juvenile detainees, and who organized basketball games and barbeques for kids on the beat, most of whom lived way below the poverty line and without fathers. He was dead. Ed kept forgetting he would never see or talk to him again or never share coffee in the squad car or go for a beer.

He drove back to the park to take a walk and try to make sense of all that had just happened. He needed to keep moving and not think. There was the majestic, but worn, Café Brauer, the Farm in the Zoo, and the seals. He bought a hamburger at the zoo's snack stand, sat outside, and fed part of the bun to the ducks that had gathered as soon as they saw him.

By the time he headed home during rush hour, it was dark and cold. The highway was crowded with workers and shoppers returning home from the Mag Mile. It was then that he remembered the woman. There had been a woman sitting next to the mother and toddler at the accident—the only other witness besides the father. She had disappeared into the crowd, and he couldn't recall her face, which was something he was trained to do. Another fail. The day had been a blur.

"You're late. I was worried." His wife, Maggie, came to the door dressed in her favorite pink sweatsuit. The house smelled of dinner. Tomatoes and beef, maybe meatloaf. She loved cooking comfort foods like spaghetti and meatballs, corned beef and cabbage, and fried pork chops. The food he loved. The food she knew. The food his doctor told him to cut back on—along with his whiskey.

"I lost track of time. There was an accident."

"I'm sorry." She raked her hand through her fine white hair. "I'm beat."

He poured himself a large whiskey and sat down at the table, which was already set with a meatloaf, lima beans, and mashed potatoes.

"Why are you still in your uniform?"

Ed had forgotten about that. Usually, he drove back to the district, dropped off his squad car, and changed into street clothes before he drove home. He resisted the urge to tell Maggie about his suspension, about Tommy, especially since Maggie was already pushing for retirement. Ed was fifty-nine with PTSD and a bad heart. Maggie pointed out that if he had free time, he could work off some of his weight; they could take a cruise. She'd been mentioning Alaska and had brought home brochures from a travel agency. He could start walking and use the pedometer she'd given him last Christmas. He could work out on the deck of a cruise ship. The Princess Cruise pictures showed happy couples exercising on the decks with Windex-blue glaciers in the background.

"It was late, and I wanted to get home. Dinner looks delicious."

"Thanks, Ed." Maggie bowed her head. "Bless us O Lord, and these thy gifts, which we are about to receive from thy bounty. Through Christ our Lord. Amen."

Ed never prayed with her. He was no longer a believer. After Maggie crossed herself, Ed picked up his fork. He was always ravenous, but not tonight. He played with his mashed potatoes, ate a crumb of meatloaf, trying to hide from Maggie how much was wrong. While she concentrated on her food, he took a big gulp of whiskey. He would not tell her about the suspension. He could not. It was humiliating. How could they think he would kill his best friend on purpose? How long would the investigation take? It could be a while; the CPD did not move fast.

He helped Maggie with the dishes, poured himself another whiskey, and they sat on the couch to watch the Chicago news. The girl's picture flashed across the screen. *Hit-and-Run Killing in Lincoln Park.* Her name was Sarah Caldwell. Tears sprang to his eyes. He took another gulp of whiskey. His gut twisted. There was one witness. Him. Thank God the newscaster did not say his name. Yes, another secret from Maggie, but if he told her, he would break down. He kept quiet and drank his whiskey.

The next morning, he got up at six, as usual, said goodbye to Maggie, and pretended to head to work. The day was gray, and the air promised snow. Traffic was still light as he merged onto the highway and drove toward the district. He couldn't go there, but the habit was hard to break. When he was two blocks away on Larrabee, he turned and drove to the intersection where the girl had been killed. He parked. It wasn't planned. He had nothing else to do . . . nowhere to go.

Dr. Phil had talked on his show about cleansing breaths. In for four, out for four. He tried it but wasn't sure it helped. He couldn't get the accident out of his mind. The girl's head. The way her small palm had fluttered and dropped onto the street. He breathed deeply again and smelled woodsmoke through his open window. Someone was sitting in front of a fire. It was that time of year again in Chicago. The intersection was quiet now, blanketed with a light coat of snow that barely covered the leaves. A pile of tributes had sprung up on the median overnight. There were flowers, dolls, stuffed bears, and photos of the girl. Sarah.

He shut his eyes and saw the car swerving, heard brakes squealing, and glimpsed the orange thing . . . the decal. He could see it now. It was a daisy.

He called his newly assigned partner, Frank. "Hey, I just

remembered something. There was a decal. I think it was a daisy on the back window of the car."

"Thanks, Ed, but we've got it covered." Frank hung up. Ed felt the sting.

He would find the girl's killer and bring him to justice. It could easily be someone in the neighborhood who would travel this way again. There would be damage to the bumper. He got out of his car and walked over to the tribute pile. A school photo of Sarah, the same one that had been on the news, lay on top. He slipped it into the pocket of his coat. He would have stickers made. When he could ticket again, he would use them at the intersection and paste them on driver's licenses.

In the Staples parking lot, he sat and thought about what he wanted to say on the stickers.

"May I help you?" A young man with green hair was behind the print desk.

"Do you print stickers?"

"We print anything."

Ed handed him the photo. "Copy this photo, please. Underneath I want it to say *Remember Sarah, 2013 to 2018.*" The clerk wrote this down.

"Come back after two, okay?"

Ed left and drove slowly to Starbucks. He sat at a small table and read the *Sun-Times* he'd brought. There was the funeral notice: St. Clement Church, Thursday at ten in the morning. It was in two days.

He stood in the back of the crowded church filled with families with small children. Two rows up, a familiar-looking woman quietly wiped tears from her face. The kids were talking, kicking the pews, and squirming—oblivious, of course, to the reality of death.

"Sarah loved art and show-and-tell." The priest's voice resonated over the noise. "She loved swimming lessons and gummy bears, her parents and her sister. In her short life, she brought joy to her family and friends. When you leave here today, carry that joy with you."

The children's choir began singing "Bridge Over Troubled Water." Their high reedy voices stilled the crowd.

Ed called Maggie that afternoon. "Don't make dinner tonight. We'll go to the Chop Shop."

It was their favorite steakhouse, a good place to tell her about the investigation. The secrecy was killing him. He would tell Maggie what happened, and that he planned to stay on the force until he was proven innocent.

"What fun, Ed. We haven't been there for ages. I'm in the mood for a good steak."

She met him at the restaurant wearing her best dress, a green pleated silk she'd bought to wear to their daughter Dawn's wedding four years ago. She clearly thought this was a festive occasion. He'd unfairly tricked her.

Ed ordered a J&B on the rocks for himself and ginger ale for Maggie. He took a sip and admired her fine features: the upturned nose, and angled cheekbones with their scatter of freckles. She'd been a true Irish redhead. Her hair had started to fade in her late thirties. The deep red had turned a beautiful copper and then a pale apricot. Now it was pure white. Recently, she'd cut it short, which was too bad. It was lovely, silky hair.

She nodded, mouth downturned, while he told her about the investigation and his plans. She barely touched her steak and baked potato, and she shoved the salad, with Thousand Island dressing, around the plate. She adored Thousand Island dressing.

"Soon. I'll retire soon." He waved for the check.

"I hope so. It must break your heart that anyone could think you would purposely kill Tommy." She looked tired. So was he. Ed reached across the table and placed his left hand on top of hers, their wedding rings clinking, their hands warm.

After he signed the check, Maggie rose to leave. He followed the swing of her dress, the back of her delicate head. He was making her unhappy, but it couldn't be helped. He knew in his head that he'd done as much as he could to prevent Tommy's death and that Sarah's was out of his control, but not in his heart. He needed to clear his name in the investigation and find whoever killed Sarah.

THREE  CHARLOTTE

December 2018

They were late, and it was her fault.

A tray of smoked salmon and caviar blinis was balanced on Charlotte's lap. Another platter with eggplant bruschetta was tucked at her feet. She had taken too long to decide what to wear to the Hamiltons' holiday party. Daniel, driving, glared through the windshield, giving her the silent treatment.

He whipped around a car turning left.

Charlotte, thrown to the side, gripped the seat with one hand and the platter with the other. "Please don't drive like that. You know it makes me nervous."

The street shifted as they headed west from residential row houses to restaurants and boutiques. It was snowing again. Fat white flakes clouded the windshield.

"I'm not going that fast." Daniel's gloved finger tapped the wheel. He looked straight ahead at the street.

He probably thought she was a pain in the ass. Maybe she was. She wondered if he'd had a pre-party drink at home, as he glided through another intersection.

"You just coasted through that stop sign. It's icy, and you're going forty on a city street." She hated to sound like a nag on the way to a party, but he was scaring her.

It was a Saturday in December. She normally loved this time

of year, but not now. Libby and the hit-and-run were always on her mind. Libby had never answered her question about the car. She should have pursued it further, but she didn't really want to know the answer. She didn't want to believe Libby could do something so heinous.

They drove down one of her favorite shopping streets. The stores were lit and decorated, open late for holiday shoppers, and festooned with signs.

Come in for Cider, Hot Chocolate, Mulled Wine.

The sidewalks teemed. Parents pushed bundled babies in strollers. Couples holding steaming cups wandered in and out of stores. People meandered through streets, carrying gifts, paying little attention to the traffic speeding by, even people with small children and strollers. They had no idea how fast an accident could happen. *Be careful!* she wanted to shout out the window. *Please be careful.*

"You're too high-strung." Daniel's jaw was locked into an annoyed position. It was a jaw most women would love . . . that she had loved. His profile was strong with a perfect nose and chiseled cheekbones. The beauty of his face sometimes took her by surprise. At a certain point, they had stopped looking at each other.

"There's a reason you keep getting tickets and people flip you off." An acidy fury rose from her stomach. She could taste it, bitter in her mouth. "And I'm still upset about that little girl who was killed. You know that. Slow down."

"Would you like to drive?" He sped up.

Asshole.

"Yes."

But he didn't pull over. Her fury shifted into heaviness, the sink of defeat. Next time, when they were not late, she would make him pull over and she would get out and take a taxi. Driving safely was a small thing to ask. She should not put up with this. She should not be here in this car with him . . . in this marriage. This was all a horrible mistake.

Exhausted by the time they parked, she was sweating underneath her wool coat, which was uncomfortably tight across her breasts. The car smelled of smoked salmon and garlic. It was slightly nauseating. She slid off the leather seat and into the cold. The snow and ice on the sidewalk had to be navigated in her four-inch pumps while she steadied the blinis. The shoes had been a stupid choice—an extravagant purchase—not meant for Chicago winters or walking.

"Could you grab the bruschetta?" She could not handle two trays.

The Hamiltons' house was an unremarkable yellow frame house strung with colored lights. Through the window, she saw a glittery tree and a man in a blue sweater fingering an ornament that looked like a fried egg. That's right. Allison Hamilton collected food ornaments.

The man plucked the egg off the tree and showed it to a woman who turned it gently over in her hand before placing it back. She should have brought Allison an ornament as a hostess gift. A pickle or a hamburger. All she had to offer were the appetizers. There was probably a pile of gifts near the front door. Daniel and Mike worked together at Bainbridge Capital. Daniel enjoyed parties. She did not. It was the small talk that got to her.

Standing on the stoop, she heard laughter and voices. She did not want to go in. She wanted the soft light of the lamp in her bedroom, her stack of books, the quiet. She wanted to pull back one of her white linen sheets, climb into bed, and shut her eyes.

"Welcome." Allison opened the door. "Let me help you with those." She took Charlotte's tray. Allison was originally from downstate, and Charlotte liked the little twang in her accent. When Allison smiled, Charlotte relaxed a little. They followed their hostess to the kitchen where the counter was already crammed with plates of cheeses, olives, and pâté. How silly to worry about being late.

"Coats are piled in there." Allison pointed to a small den off the kitchen. "Mike is making drinks, showing off. He just finished a mixology class."

Charlotte walked into the den, removed her coat, and put it with the others on the couch. It was an ugly couch, covered in pilling blue-and-yellow plaid. What a snob she'd become. It was hard not to be one in her line of work, where everything was Instagrammable. Daniel, behind her, placed his coat on top of hers. They were a couple again—here at the party. He looked hip in his subtly wrinkled charcoal-gray shirt, jeans, and soft-brown driving shoes. He was in good shape. So many men his age were sporting stomachs, big ones that jutted out under T-shirts and hung over belts.

She wandered back and got a better glimpse of the guests. She was overdressed in her black sheath sprinkled with tiny sparkles. The other women, including Allison, wore silky shirts and jeans, sensible shoes, and bright makeup. Their cheeks were peachy, their lashes spiky with mascara. Charlotte's pale angular face was bare. Her only makeup was a deep red lipstick, a trick that complemented her other features and accented her eyes and the delicacy of her long, thin nose. Her dramatic lips and party dress made her feel old, from a time when a party and a dress went together, although most of the guests looked as if they were also in their mid-forties.

"You need a drink. You have to try one of these pomegranate martinis." Mike poured a drink from the shaker nearest him. An assortment of shakers, bottles, and glasses were set up like a lab.

"This is perfect." She held up the glass. "What a pretty color." She took a sip and tried not to wince at its sweetness. "Delicious." She disliked cocktails, especially syrupy ones. She would discreetly put it down later and pour herself a glass of white wine.

Snatches of conversation about preschool and potty training floated over from a group of women to her right. She did not want to join them and possibly have to talk about being the mother of a twenty-three-year-old. People with small children—and there seemed to be more and more her age—liked to ask about drugs and alcohol in schools, already anticipating the evils against which their babies would need protecting. She didn't want to be the one to tell them they couldn't protect their children . . . or worse, smile and lie.

Libby was probably relaxing now on the gray couch in her studio apartment on Ludlow Street. Charlotte had bought the couch in a fit of guilt-fueled generosity. Libby would still be wearing makeup and clothing from work, including one of those ornate J. Crew rhinestone necklaces, a large white shirt, and her "toothpick" jeans. She might be eating a take-out salad, no dressing, on one of the six cream-colored plates Charlotte had purchased so Libby could have company for dinner or at least, the fantasy of company. Her boots would be on the floor, and her feet covered with heavy socks because Libby was always cold. It came with her thinness, and she was still too thin.

She looked around for Daniel and saw him chatting with some men from work. This was his crowd . . . finance guys. The only person she knew at all, and barely, was Allison, who was busy opening the door, greeting guests, and taking coats.

She popped a piece of Camembert into her mouth and was suddenly self-conscious, standing alone near the cheese. She wandered over to Daniel. The Hamiltons' beagle, Henry, followed her. His stomach grazed the carpet as he walked. He was wearing a green velvet Christmas collar.

Pictures of nieces and nephews were framed all over the living room. The Hamiltons had no children. She sensed sadness here. That this was not by choice.

Two men stood with Daniel. One of them gestured, his pinkish hands poking out of a thick navy sweater. "Sea lions are everywhere in the Galapagos. You have to be careful not to step on them." He wore large, tortoiseshell Cary Grant glasses—fabulous glasses.

The other man was in a shrunken-looking suit and a skinny tie. He scanned the party as if he were bored.

"Sounds like the trip of a lifetime," Daniel said. "Did you do a lot of snorkeling?"

Charlotte put her hand on his arm, trying to remember the difference between a sea lion and a seal.

Daniel glanced at her. "Stuart, Gregory, this is my wife, Charlotte, our jack of all trades."

This was an annoying introduction, but she was relieved to no longer be standing alone.

She had been a well-known food writer until the food magazines were caught in the downward economic spiral after 2008. Her beloved *Gourmet* had closed its doors, and *Bon Appétit* had been forced to cut way back. No more trips to Paris in search of incredible new patisseries or hunting down the most delicious roast chicken in New York. Her journalism and culinary degrees were useless after the financial crash, but she'd been able to parlay her taste and style—and her ability to intuit what people wanted—into a career. And she needed a career. They needed the income.

"What Daniel means is I'm a lifestylist."

"What's that?" Stuart, the Galapagos guy, asked. "Like for movie stars? Do you buy their clothes?"

"No. No movie stars. I do buy clothes for regular people. But I help my clients with much more than clothes."

"She's in high demand. She's an influencer," Daniel said.

"How much help do people need? Shoes? Hair?" Stuart seemed confused.

"My wife and I use a personal shopper at Barney's. I love it. She brings clothes to the house. I never have to shop. She picked what I'm wearing tonight." Gregory did a little shuffle and turned around.

"That's not what I do. But I like your suit."

She was a liar. She hated his suit.

"How do you style a life?" Gregory asked. "It sounds like something out of a reality show. Like *Queer Eye*. I love that show."

"I help people choose whatever they're looking for: art, furniture, vacations. I still buy clothes, but now it's pieces from all over the world. My clients want unique looks." She blushed even though this was true. It sounded silly when she said it out loud . . . shallow and elitist. Chicago had a sky-high murder rate. People were living under overpasses. Children went hungry. And her job was to help wealthy people look good and feel better about themselves.

"Do you work for a company?" Stuart asked.

"No, on my own. I created this job. It's a niche. I work with people who want the whole package: house, art, travel. Things they may not be able to envision themselves."

"You guide people toward good taste," Gregory said.

"Exactly." She'd become a commodity when her clients began wanting more than clothes and took her into their confidence, admitting their insecurities and desires.

First, they asked if she knew a talented florist or a creative caterer. And then they asked for advice on furniture, fabrics, and art. After that, an inquiry about a discreet plastic surgeon or expert dermatologist often followed. Then they wanted her to dress their husbands and smooth out their rough edges. She'd become a personal curator, skilled at coddling the wealthy without being obsequious.

She had no training, but she had an excellent eye. She bought for her clients what she would have purchased if she had endless funds. Her Instagram was filled with enticing photos: a young couple haloed in golden Parisian light at Café Flore; two boys waving from a scooter in Rome; sunsets in Positano; elephants, gazelles, and giraffes from safaris. People loved animals and romance. In her personal photos, she was perfectly groomed and wore outrageously expensive outfits lent to her by high-end stores. Then there were English kitchens with green cupboards and marble backsplashes, antique tables laden with food and flowers, and artwork from galleries around the world. No one needed to know her drawers were messy or that she suffered an assortment of anxiety-driven ailments like insomnia and acid reflux. She projected confidence. People trusted her.

"Well, you certainly like nice things." Stuart gave her a quick up-and-down look. "Those are sexy shoes, Charlotte."

"Thank you." She instantly disliked him. He stared at her feet, which did, in fact, have toe cleavage. Would Daniel ever hit someone who made a pass at her? She doubted it.

Her feet throbbed. They were probably at least a third of the way through the party and could leave by ten. The men resumed their conversation. She bent over to pet Henry, who had been looking up at her hopefully. He sniffed her hand and then swiped her face with his tongue. Her head felt fuzzy. The leafy wallpaper rippled as if being blown by a breeze. She blinked to steady it. When she stood back up, the room dimmed, then disappeared.

She tilted and fell to the floor, her still-full martini splashing across the carpet.

A pair of hands shook her. Daniel? Her stomach churned. Sweat beaded on her upper lip. She kept her eyes shut for a moment longer. She didn't know what had happened. How had she ended up on the floor?

"Is she drunk?"

"No." That was Daniel's voice. "Charlotte doesn't drink cocktails. She just carries one around."

"I think you should stop shaking her," a woman, who sounded like Allison, said. "We don't know if she has a head injury."

Charlotte opened her eyes to shadows that swayed and drifted. A denim leg. A hand near her shoulder. Allison squatting. A group had gathered around, all eyes downcast on her. If only she could sink into the carpet and disappear.

"Are you okay?" Allison was by her side. "Should I call an ambulance?"

Her stomach was roiling. *Please do not let me throw up in front of all these people.* They probably thought she was drunk. Maybe she had a brain tumor. Maybe she'd had a stroke. She couldn't remember the stroke signs.

"Fainting is an awful feeling. It's happened to me. I'll get you a cold cloth." Allison stood up and went to get a towel.

At that moment, Charlotte loved Allison. She wanted to tell her, but she was too sick to talk. Daniel sat down beside her on the floor and took her hand. Allison returned and gently wiped the sweat off Charlotte's face. She placed the towel on her forehead.

"Your color is coming back." Daniel leaned over her, his

brow furrowed with worry. The fuzziness was gone. Her arm was sticky. *The drink. Pomegranate*, she remembered, *stains*.

Monday morning, she wandered from lab to lab at Northwestern Hospital to be pricked and scanned, and to pee in a cup. When she finished, a receptionist told her to wait for her results in the colorless waiting room. The only available seat was between an elderly lady attached to a portable oxygen tank and a man who looked as if he had a terrible virus. Both patients were hacking.

Charlotte tried to read but instead nervously studied the educational posters on the wall. Stroke signs. CPR instructions. BMI charts. Above the water cooler was one of those insufferable "Keep Calm and Get a Flu Shot" posters.

A nurse finally brought her into the office of Dr. Lee, Charlotte's internist of eighteen years. She was seated behind her desk with Charlotte's medical file open before her.

"Hi, Charlotte. The good news is that the CAT scan, EKG, and blood tests are all normal." Dr. Lee studied Charlotte's face and shifted in her chair. It was a shift that made Charlotte hold her breath.

"I don't know how you feel about this, but you're pregnant. Have you missed a period yet?"

"Pregnant?" She felt the blood drain from her face. She leaned forward. She needed to hold onto something. She put a hand on Dr. Lee's desk, next to the silver-framed portrait of her husband and three kids. They were all smiling and had dark, sleek hair. "You're sure? I don't pay much attention to my period." Any of the minimal fertility she might have possessed must have passed her by now that she was nearly forty-five.

"Positive." Dr. Lee made a little chapel with her hands. "And women your age are extremely high-risk pregnancies. It's more common to miscarry than to go to term. Any pregnancy over the age of thirty-five is considered geriatric."

"Geriatric?"

"Yes, so it would be wise to have an ultrasound to see how many weeks you are. If you need to, you can make a decision."

"You mean an abortion?" She tried to focus on Dr. Lee's face. She was looking back at Charlotte, her perfect pink mouth twisted into a small frown. As if she knew Charlotte and Daniel had not had sex for over a year. That Daniel would leave her if she had this baby. If he even knew about this baby. Charlotte took a deep breath and inhaled the sharp, sterile air of the office.

"Yes, a D&C. Or a CVS test to identify any abnormalities if you decide to go through with it. I can write you a script for the ultrasound, but then you need to see your OB-GYN."

"No amnio?" Her voice was shaky. The nausea was back. For a moment, she intensely disliked Dr. Lee, whom she'd chosen many years ago, thinking a female doctor would be more intimate and understanding. She had been wrong.

"CVS can be done between ten and twelve weeks. That's much earlier than amnio, and it would be good to know the results. Chromosomal risks go way up with age."

The ultrasound indicated she was about nine weeks pregnant. She'd attributed her slightly thickened waist to menopause, thinking her high metabolism had finally quit. She was tall, and there was only a small swell.

At first, the image on the screen appeared to be a black-and-white blob, but when Charlotte looked closely, the blob resembled a small child's drawing of a baby. The technician zoomed in on a white, pulsing dot.

"This is the heart." There was a whoosh and a thump when the technician turned up the sound. The loud beat of a heart filled the room. It was astonishing. The beginnings of a baby. Emory's baby. Emory, whom she had not seen for over a month. Whom she planned on never seeing again. Emory had helped create this new heart. Here was physical proof. She studied the tiny curl and felt a rush of unexpected tears.

The tech handed her a Kleenex, smiled, and pointed to the screen. "What you are seeing is good news. A healthy heartbeat." The picture on the machine resembled a fiddlehead fern with a white spot glowing in its center.

"Here's your fetus," she said, printing out a strip of photos and handing them to Charlotte, who slipped the pictures into her purse before the tiny black-and-white image could make her cry again.

FOUR  CHARLOTTE

May 2017

Emory Blaine knew how to appeal to women in a soft, almost feminine, self-effacing way that made women feel both sexy and interesting. He listened. He asked questions. It was his way of flirting. He risked nothing with his low-key, charming ways. No one could accuse him of being anything but a thoughtful, nice guy.

Victor, one of Charlotte's clients, had introduced her to his best friend, Emory, as his personal expert, his very own know-it-all.

Charlotte was at Saks to help Victor, at his wife's request, shop for spring and summer clothes. Emory was there for moral support. Victor, who was an economist at the University of Chicago, hated shopping.

Charlotte perused shirts and sports jackets. Victor, who was completely uninterested in the clothing, described to Emory the trip to Sicily he and his wife, Lucy Ellen, had recently booked for June. The trip, designed by Charlotte, focused on both the ruins and luxuries of Sicily and included a side trip to Positano on the Amalfi Coast. They would stay at the exquisite Le Sirenuse in a room with a balcony that opened directly over the sea. Victor showed Emory a photo of a room on his phone. The balcony table was set with a breakfast of cappuccinos, scrambled eggs, a basket of pastries, and a bowl of peaches, plums, and cherries. The water below was a brilliant blue.

Victor disappeared into a dressing room. Emory sunk into the plush armchair next to where Charlotte stood. He ran his hand through his messy, light blond hair. He was quiet for a moment, staring at the three bottles of Perrier that a manager had set down on the table next to him. He seemed to be thinking.

"I can't believe how jealous I am." Emory glanced up at her as she was about to wander over to a rack of sports jackets. "I want to go on Victor's trip. I mean a trip like Victor's. Is it too late for this summer?"

Emory's voice didn't fit his face. It was higher than she had expected and did not go with his square jaw or the firm way in which his mouth was set. He was slightly disheveled and earnest in an old flannel shirt with ink stains on one pocket. He could have used a good haircut and some sprucing up, but for some reason his messiness seemed endearing rather than sloppy. This was puzzling. She thought of sloppiness as a form of entitlement, a kind of "fuck you" to those who were required to dress for work. She had harbored a years-long grudge against the mothers in workout clothes who stood around drinking coffee in front of Libby's school. Perhaps it was an energy Emory gave off or his open, hopeful face. He studied her a beat too long. Something passed between them. She felt it.

"Probably not too late. I'd have to check hotels. How many rooms will you need?"

"At least two. I have three kids. Three rooms might be better. My son could get away from my girls."

Victor appeared in a gray T-shirt, cashmere lavender sweater, and gray jeans. "What do you think?"

"You look exactly like an Italian. I can see you sitting in a square having coffee. It's perfect." She meant every word. Victor was a slight man with salt-and-pepper shaggy hair. It made her happy to think of him at a little table with the elegant Lucy Ellen, surrounded by the churchgoers, the apéritif drinkers, and the kids racing around on bikes.

"Nice, Vic." Emory gave him a thumbs-up.

"Be right back." Victor left and then appeared a few minutes later in seersucker pants and a navy polo. He did a little twirl, and Emory whistled.

"That's another keeper. You have one more." This was miraculous. She was actually finding stylish clothes for Victor that he liked. Victor preferred to dress like a penniless professor, which drove his wife crazy, especially when they traveled. She was here to please Lucy Ellen, who was one of her biggest clients.

"I saved my favorite for last." Victor ducked back into the dressing room.

"You're really considering Italy?" Charlotte turned to Emory who was still in the chair.

"Totally. Any chance you could meet later for coffee or a drink to talk about an itinerary? I want to get this trip rolling."

"I guess so." It struck her as an unusual request. It didn't displease her, though she disliked his use of "totally" and "rolling." She'd put all assumptions aside after years of working with people. Most everyone had a few quirks. Would his wife be there? Were they still married?

Daniel was in New Orleans at a conference. She had the evening free, so there was no reason not to work.

Victor reappeared in burnt-orange cotton pants and a cream polo.

"That's fabulous on you, Victor. You'll make Lucy Ellen proud."

"You really do this for a living?" Emory unscrewed a Perrier and poured some into a glass.

"Yep."

"Are we on for later?"

"Sure."

"Can you meet at The Continental Bar around eight thirty? It's a few blocks from here."

"Sounds good." The thought of seeing him again later made her weirdly happy. She reached into her bag. "Here's my card in case anything changes for you."

Emory was funny and handsome in a slightly overbred sort of way. But it was not his attractiveness that caught her; it was the dazzling way he looked at her . . . took her in. His gaze traveled through her organs and arteries into her heart.

The sun was beginning to fade when Charlotte walked past the red tulip beds planted along Michigan Avenue. She had changed into a coffee-colored dress with a full skirt and leopard print flats. It was warm enough so that she only needed a cardigan. The air smelled earthy and green, even in the middle of the city. Homeless people camped in front of Neiman Marcus, Tiffany's, and Saks holding cardboard signs that read, "Please Help" or "Army Vet" or "Domestic Violence Sucks." She stopped and gave five dollars to the woman with the domestic violence sign.

"Giving money to the homeless goes straight toward drugs or booze." Daniel's voice echoed in her ears.

She found Emory sitting at a small, round table. No wife. He was far enough away from the piano player so that they would be able to talk. The musician, a handsome man in a tux, was playing classics. As she sat down, he was on "Moon River," a romantic, old-fashioned song that was perfect for this woody, dark bar.

"What would you like to drink?" Emory handed her the drinks menu. He wore an ill-fitting, navy-blue sports jacket. His hair appeared to be brushed. She had to squint to see the menu in the dark room. She was not about to put on her reading glasses.

"The white burgundy."

A waiter appeared with small bowls of nuts, cheese crackers, and olives.

"Two white burgundies, please." He sat back in his chair and studied her. "Tell me about Sicily. What's your favorite place there?"

"My favorite? That's hard. Do you like mosaics?"

"That's one of the reasons I want to go."

"The Roman mosaics in Villa del Casale are gorgeous. There's a wonderful wall called the Bikini Girls in one of the baths. Girls in red bikinis throwing balls, running, and weightlifting. Pretty amazing, considering it's from the fourth century." The waiter placed a glass of wine in front of her, and she wrapped her fingers around the stem. "Sicily is very different than the rest of Italy, almost as if it's another country."

Emory studied the bowl of cheese crackers with a serious expression, then spun it slightly with the tip of his finger. "Could you put together an itinerary for me? In July? With sights and hotels?"

"Of course." She took a sip of the wine. "Are you open to driving? It's the best way to get around Sicily. But you need nerves of steel."

"I can handle it. It would be better than taking trains with my teenagers."

There was no mention of his wife.

"Would you like to spend a couple days on the Amalfi Coast like Victor? It's touristy and crowded in the summer, but the views alone are worth it."

"How do you know so much about Italy?" Emory leaned forward and brushed her hand with his, leaving a trail of warmth.

A mistake or intentional?

"My mother's parents lived in Milan and had a summer house in Ravello. It originally belonged to my great-grandparents. We visited in the summer."

"They were Italian?"

"Yes. My mother's Italian. An Italian Jew. My grandparents lived in New York during the war to escape the Nazis."

"That's terrifying. It was lucky they got out." His forehead creased with concern. Her heart melted a little.

"It was lucky. Something like eight thousand Italian Jews were deported and killed in the camps."

"Was the rest of your family safe?" He chewed on his lip.

"They were. The part of my family who stayed in Italy were hidden in a monastery."

"Fascinating."

"I guess, but when I was little, I used to have nightmares about hiding from the Nazis. My grandparents talked about the war a lot. It was the biggest crisis of their lives, but at least they lived to talk about it."

"And they went back to Italy?"

"They considered themselves Italians above all else, so they did go back, and they were able to reclaim their house in Ravello."

"Ravello's on the Amalfi Coast where Victor is going, right?"

"It's on the coast, but Victor is going to Positano, which is much more crowded but also a lot livelier. I love Ravello, it's quiet. There's not much to do at night other than dinner and a walk. There are two wonderful hotels there. The Caruso and Palazzo Avino."

"I think I'd like it. I prefer quiet."

"The best part is the town square right below the church. I learned to ride a bike and roller skate there. At night, the entire town goes to the square to eat ice cream, meet friends, and gossip. It's filled with kids and dogs and parents and grand-parents."

Emory leaned back in his chair with the blissful air of a child anticipating a story.

The waiter brought over two more glasses of wine, which she didn't remember ordering. She was already feeling a pleas-ant buzz from the first glass.

"Pretty idyllic." Emory smiled. He had a good smile.

"It's a wonderful childhood memory. Do you have a place that's part of you?"

He shut his eyes for a second. "It would have to be Paris. Eating a croissant and having café au lait in a hotel garden. A garden with potted fruit trees."

"That sounds lovely." She adored potted fruit trees and Paris, which she'd visited many times. "Paris is my favorite city."

"I hope to get back soon. Maybe it will be the next trip after Italy."

For a few moments, she imagined sitting with him in that garden, on a sunny morning in June, with a big café crème and a buttery croissant.

"I love wandering the streets." He was staring at her intently. "All those tiny restaurants and boutiques. You never know what you'll find. There's a store that only sells bookmarks."

"It's lovely." She tried to force thoughts of a tiny hotel room and a rumpled bed out of her mind.

"I can totally see you there walking down the street with a scarf and a little dog."

She laughed and felt an odd sensation. As if something important was happening. It was as if she were being willingly stripped of her defenses and sense of order. She wanted to reach across the table, take his hand, and trace his lips with her finger. What would it be like to kiss them?

What was wrong with her? He had children and probably a wife. She was married. This was a business meeting. She excused herself to go to the bathroom to compose herself. When she was done, she stood before the mirror and carefully reapplied her lipstick.

Emory paid, and they left walking side by side, close enough to feel each other's heat but not touching. It was late. A few taxis trolled the streets. On the corner, he gave her a look that would become familiar—one filled with lust and promise. He stroked her cheek and kissed her. It was a graceful move. He was a good kisser, not too hard and not too sloppy. It had been a long time since she'd been kissed like that. She needed this kiss. It was like a drug.

He hailed her a cab and murmured in her ear that he wanted to see her again.

Soon.

She was still warm from the kiss, slightly tipsy, and completely undone when she got home. She had crossed the line into unfaithful, done something entirely out of character. Something morally corrupt. She hated herself, yet she was bursting with joy. She got into bed with her laptop and googled Emory. Pages and pages popped up.

He was married. There was her picture. Meredith Blaine was blonde with a Mayflower face, blue eyes, and a small, upturned nose. Her family was one of the oldest and wealthiest in Chicago. Art Institute wing, University of Chicago hospital wing, every kind of wing.

He ran a well-known literacy foundation, funded by his wife's family foundation, which provided reading specialists and books to underserved schools. He and his wife threw fundraisers for liberal politicians and hosted visiting dignitaries. Stunned, she scrolled through photo after photo. She had never met anyone so far out of her orbit, which she had always considered a sophisticated one. She must have been a weak moment in his full life. She would probably not hear from him again, which was just as well.

The bed seemed too big with Daniel away. Even though they stuck to their own sides, she was not used to sleeping alone. She had a night of fitful sleep with disjointed dreams she could almost, but not quite, remember.

When she opened her email in the morning, Emory's name was in her inbox. It gave her a little shock of pleasure. She read his note quickly.

He'd written that he'd had *fun* with her last night. What did that mean? Was fun some sort of code or an accurate description of the way he felt? She'd certainly felt something more than fun. Perhaps she'd misjudged him. Maybe he kissed women all the time and thought little of it. He wrote that he'd forgotten the name of the hotel in Taormina and asked if she could send it so he could look it up. The email was signed, "Your friend, Emory." She wrote back with the names of several hotels along with the one she'd described last night. She signed, "All the best."

She did not hear from Emory over the next few days. She tried to forget about him and concentrate on the online art gallery and auction sites she was searching. A client had purchased a suburban home on the lake and wanted to fill it with art. Charlotte had seen an exciting work by a young photographer who took photos of people near or in bodies of water. Now, she was on the hunt for a similar piece. The search was not going well.

She was distracted, her mind wandering toward Emory. One minute she was light and elated, the next guilt-ridden, the next lonely. She rearranged the swatches on her corkboards. She stared out the window into the garden where the hydrangeas were beginning to bud. She got up twice to make tea.

"What's wrong with you?" Daniel held up the kitchen scissors he had just retrieved from the fridge.

"It's Libby. She called obsessively this afternoon after she finished work. Eleven calls in a row. I can't think."

Libby had called, but that's not what was really wrong. What was really wrong was that she was a terrible person.

When she opened her inbox the next day, there was a new email from Emory officially asking her to plan the trip for him. He sent her dates for the end of July and asked if she would draw up an itinerary and meet with him at his office. They arranged a time for the following Tuesday. She set to work. It was easy enough to plan. In ten days, he could drive to the important sights where his family would meet guides in the morning and spend afternoons cooling off, lounging in pools at charming hotels. On the way home they could stop in Ravello and stay at the Palazzo Avino for a couple of days. The kids would like the hotel's beach club. She checked availability. The hotels in Ravello were nearly full. She called and held three rooms to be safe. One had a sea view, and the other two faced the hotel's lush gardens. He would need to commit when she saw him if he wanted to go this summer.

INTERSECTIONS

She tried to pretend it was only a business meeting. She put it in her calendar. They would meet in his office at the literacy foundation.

On Tuesday, Charlotte dressed professionally as if she were seeing any new client—a white silk shirt, fitted black skirt, one baroque pearl on a thin chain around her neck, and small coral flowers from Ravello in her ears. She swirled her hair into a topknot instead of her usual tight ballerina bun.

Emory's office was in a brownstone on State Street in one of the fanciest parts of town. She left early enough to find a parking place without panicking over time (she was a stickler for punctuality). On the way, she attempted to focus on the Sicily trip and not on seeing him.

She ignored the noisy beat of her heart as she walked up the steps and pressed the bell next to the glossy red door.

A pretty young woman with a peroxided pixie and large fashionable black glasses greeted her. "You must be Charlotte. Come in. I'm Jen, Emory's assistant."

She led Charlotte down a hallway to an office lined with books. Emory sat behind a large, black-lacquered desk with stacks of papers spread across it. A plate of shortbread cookies sat on a coffee table. Paintings and pictures lined the walls; a faded Persian rug covered the floor. The room, which smelled faintly of leather and spice, was overloaded and sumptuous . . . the kind of room Charlotte loved.

Emory stood up. He was dressed in baggy dad jeans and a nubby gray sweater. "Thanks for coming. Please sit down." He motioned to one of the two brown leather club chairs next to the fireplace.

"I'm going to my class now, Emory." Jen waved. "See you tomorrow. Nice meeting you, Charlotte."

"Nice to meet you, Jen." Charlotte worried her heartbeat was audible in the quiet room and that Emory might hear it. He glanced at her for a second before he walked over to the far side of the room and popped open a cabinet, revealing a small fridge. It was very James Bond for a man wearing dad jeans.

"Would you like a drink? There's white wine, and I'm going to have some."

She hesitated. He was her last appointment, but it was only three-thirty, and she was not a day drinker. She also did not want to be rude.

"Why not? You're my last appointment today."

Emory busied himself with uncorking and pouring the wine into two glasses. She was confused. Did he want to go on a trip or seduce her or both? He had kissed her, after all. And he was married, too. Maybe he was nervous, but what if he was a Lothario and she was a sucker? The backs of her legs began to sweat and stick to his leather chair.

"To Sicily." He brought the glasses over and raised his to clink. "Cheers."

The wine was delicious. Dry and cold. She would have liked to hold it to her face. The folder with his itineraries was on her lap. She opened it, reached over, and handed the pages to him as he settled into the matching chair.

"These are simply ideas. You should look to see if there is anything you want to add or subtract. I've included small descriptions and photos. I can give you restaurant recommendations later."

He studied the pages in the folder.

She concentrated on not looking at him, sipping her wine,

and taking in the room. She glanced at the framed picture on the side table next to her. There he was with President and Michelle Obama. She noted the Dexter Dalwood painting above the desk. It was of an otherworldly stairwell. There was a Cy Twombly over the fireplace, and two Diane Arbus photos next to the door. This man, or his wife, had excellent taste in art.

"The trip seems pretty perfect." He put the pages back and shut the folder.

"If you're interested, you need to book it soon. I'm not trying to pressure you. The hotels are filling up."

He put the folder down. He looked her in the eyes. There it was. The want. "I feel like I'm sixteen."

"Me too."

He stood up, leaned over, and then his arms went around her, pulling her into him, holding her tight.

FIVE  CHARLOTTE

November 2018

The night after the hit-and-run, the cell phone on Charlotte's nightstand woke her. It was around eleven-thirty, and she had been drifting into the place that is neither asleep nor awake. She had been roaming somewhere, perhaps a hall, when she heard the ring from afar and then nearby. Startled, she sat up and grabbed the phone in the dark. Daniel moved as if he'd heard it and then settled back into sleep.

It was Libby's former college roommate, Melissa, who had moved back to Chicago. Libby was still visiting, and the two had gone out for dinner.

"Libby OD'd. Going to the ER at Northwestern." Melissa was speaking fast and scrambling words. Charlotte, groggy, had trouble understanding her.

"Libby overdosed? Where is she? Is she okay?"

"We're in an ambulance. She's okay now. Meet us in the ER."

Charlotte was suddenly wide awake and in full panic mode. This was the phone call she had always dreaded. "She's really all right?"

"Sick, but she'll be fine."

Charlotte had begun frantically pulling on her clothes before she realized she needed to wake Daniel. "Libby's in the hospital. We have to go." She shook him awake.

"What? How?"

"An overdose. Get up. Now."

"Overdose!" Daniel leapt out of bed. "Oh my God!"

"Come on. We need to leave."

In the garage, Charlotte turned on the weak overhead light and hurried to get into Daniel's car, hoping he wouldn't notice the dent in her bumper. Or that she'd removed the daisy decal which had left a sticky outline. He didn't mention either and sped all the way to the hospital on the empty Outer Drive. Charlotte did not tell him to slow down. She wanted to get to Libby so badly, she had trouble sitting still. She wanted to get out and run. He exited onto Michigan Avenue and zipped past the darkened stores.

"I'm dropping you off and going to park in the garage." He pulled up to the ER entrance behind an ambulance. "Be there in a few."

The waiting room was packed. A man's head was bleeding through a towel. A woman was passed out, lying across three chairs. Groups of people clustered together, waiting. Some were eating. It smelled like Doritos.

"Gunshot wound," a voice behind Charlotte called out. She stepped aside, and a teenage boy, clutching a bloody shirt, was quickly wheeled past. She grabbed the edge of a chair for a second, dizzy.

"My daughter's here." She was at the triage desk. "Libby Oakes. She's inside. I need to see her."

The nurse, expressionless, pressed a button and the doors behind her opened. "Go on."

Inside, a group of nurses stood looking at a computer behind a desk.

"Libby Oakes, please?" Charlotte's head pounded.

"Right down that hall." A nurse pointed. "A doctor will come in and talk to you soon. She's stable."

Charlotte tore down the hall and found Libby and Melissa behind a half-open curtain. Libby was on a cot, pale, sweaty, and holding a plastic kidney-shaped basin. A man to her left was talking loudly on his cell phone. A woman on her right was moaning.

"She's been throwing up." Melissa was sitting in a chair beside the bed.

"Libby." Charlotte rushed over and hugged her. She pressed her face into Libby's shoulder. Her skin was cold and damp.

"Too nauseous." Libby shrugged her mother away.

Charlotte let herself fall into a chair now that she could see Libby was in one piece. "Daddy's coming. He's parking the car."

Libby looked at her with glassy eyes. Charlotte wanted to ask questions. What had Libby been taking and why? She wanted to hug her again. But she didn't dare. She sat still until Daniel burst through the curtain.

"Libby!" Daniel rushed to her bed.

Libby dry-heaved into the trough.

"What happened?" Daniel turned to Melissa.

"I went into my room to get a magazine to show her. When I got back, she was unconscious. Not breathing. I called 911, and they used two shots on her. To counteract the drugs. Then they brought us here."

"Shit." Daniel's face went white. "What did she take?"

"Oxy, but I don't know how much. I thought she was dead." Melissa hunched over and clutched her knees. "I was terrified. She was actually dead for a minute."

Dead for a minute.

The room wobbled. Charlotte felt for the edge of the bed.

Yellow spots exploded and danced in the darkness of her lids.

"Mr. and Mrs. Oakes?" The voice sounded as if it was underwater to Charlotte. "I'm Dr. Parker. We need to talk about the next steps for Libby. Ma'am, are you okay?"

Charlotte smelled something like ammonia underneath her nose. She opened her eyes. The room came back into focus. A young woman in a white coat stood beside her.

"Smelling salts. You looked as if you were going to pass out."

"Sorry." Charlotte was embarrassed. "I'm okay now."

"Good. We need to talk about Libby." Dr. Parker looked at the file. "As you know by now, she was resuscitated by the EMTs with two shots of Naloxone. If help had arrived a minute later, she would have died. She wasn't breathing and barely had a pulse." She looked up and at Libby. "Do you know how close you came? What you're going through now is withdrawal."

"I feel awful."

The doctor's eyes narrowed. "You are lucky you can feel anything at all."

Charlotte intervened. "She was in rehab two months ago. For alcohol."

"What's important now is to get her back to rehab. She needs to go immediately."

"We'll try and get her into one in the morning."

The doctor nodded. "I'm discharging her with three days of medication to ease withdrawal. But she must be completely supervised until she's in rehab. I have a list of rehabs for you. Call around until you find a bed. The next time, she may not be as lucky." And with that, she walked out.

The room was silent for what, to Charlotte, seemed like an hour.

"I want to go home." Libby threw off her sheet.

"You'll come home tonight with us." Charlotte brought Libby her shoes. "Tomorrow it's rehab."

"I want to pick the rehab."

"There may not be a choice. You heard the doctor."

At home, Charlotte lay in Libby's bed with her. Libby was turned away toward the wall, her legs splayed and her hair trailing all the way to Charlotte's shoulder.

"Did you take my car yesterday, Libby? Is that why you relapsed?" Charlotte was terrified to ask this question.

"I don't know why I relapsed, but I didn't take your car."

Charlotte, not at all convinced, lay awake for a long time. She listened to Libby's soft snores, experiencing alternating pangs of terror over her daughter's near death and relief that she was beside her living, breathing daughter. They had been given another chance—something Sarah Caldwell would not get.

SIX  CHARLOTTE

December 2018

She did not want to go home after the ultrasound. At the same time, she couldn't tolerate another second in the hospital building. Its overpowering antibacterial scent and gray corporate furniture reinforced her idea of medicine as a big business. The hospital had grown into a sprawling complex over the years.

Nerves jangling, she hurried through the enormous lobby past the coffee shop, gift shop, bookstore, and the chairs set in strategic places near the entrance so patients could rest or wait comfortably for a ride. It looked like a mall.

The abundance of wheelchairs was what she usually noticed. Today, pregnant women and strollers were everywhere. This awareness was the curse, or blessing, of the pregnant. When she'd been pregnant with Libby, twenty-four years ago, the world had seemed full of babies. Today, these women looked so young, fresh-faced, and innocent. They weren't thinking about rehab or self-starvation. Charlotte had trouble believing she was one of them, even though her pants seemed tight, as if her belly had grown with her knowledge.

The wind hit her as she emerged from the revolving door into the seventeen-degree day. She wrapped the crimson-colored cashmere scarf, last year's Christmas present from

Daniel, over the lower part of her face. The snow was filthy, tinged with black and yellow. The tall hospital buildings cast a shadow darkening the street, even though it was only two in the afternoon.

She climbed into the taxi that was at the head of the line. The driver, who was talking to someone, speakerphone on, did not look at her when she opened the door and gave him her address. She sat back and listened to him chat in an indecipherable foreign language. He was wearing a leather jacket despite the cold, and the heat in the cab was stifling.

As the taxi headed toward the Outer Drive, Charlotte googled "nine-week-old baby" on her phone. She read: "Your baby is the size of a cherry. He or she is now a fetus and no longer an embryo. During the embryonic phase, the major organs form. These include the brain, heart, and lungs, plus the arms and legs. In your fetus, those organs and parts are now growing and developing. The pregnancy hormone HCG is at its peak level at nine weeks. Chances are you're experiencing fatigue, morning sickness, headaches, and mood swings. It will get better in the next few weeks as your hormones level out."

The diagram of the baby in its various phases filled her with dread. Daniel would know this wasn't his child. She had no idea how or what to tell him. He would see this as not only a betrayal but a scandal, despite the fact that no one would really have to know. But the truth was she should have already left the marriage. She'd made too many excuses and held onto something that was not real, not only with Daniel but also with Emory.

Emory. She did not need to tell him about the baby. There would be no gain other than financial, which would feel dirty, as if she had been after his money and tried to trap him. At the same time, it seemed cruel not to let him know and bring up a baby completely without a father. She also had no grasp of her legal rights with Daniel. Would she get any alimony or a divorce settlement if she was pregnant by another man?

An abortion could solve this. She firmly believed in the right to have an abortion, but she didn't know if she could bear to have one, especially since the father was Emory, whom she should hate, but she didn't—at least not all the time.

A baby would, no doubt, be difficult for Libby. She detested change and loved the attention that came with being an only child. Still, a baby could be a hedge against her future. A sibling would be able to help if Libby needed care after Charlotte and Daniel were dead. Libby existing on her own was something Charlotte worried about on a regular basis. A sibling could manage her finances, her meds, and the doctor's appointments for her depression and OCD. Libby would not be helpless and alone on this earth. A sibling was insurance.

It was selfish reasoning—to bring a baby into the world to take care of Libby—a baby with a preordained job.

Charlotte looked up and saw that the driver was not slowing down as he approached her street. She interrupted his call to ask him to turn before it was too late.

"Okay, okay," he said, waving one hand in the air and sounding annoyed. When they arrived, he reached his hand back, still talking, for the money.

Rude, she thought, and then felt guilty. This man might have fled violence in a war-torn country and seen family members murdered. Perhaps he could no longer cope or engage in normal pleasantries. She handed him a more-than-decent tip, even though, in all likelihood, he was simply rude. She was a pushover.

She'd left the lights on in the family room. A domestic still-life glowed inside. Books lined the shelves. The gray flannel armchairs waited with their hot-pink pillows. A Kiki Smith painting of a fawn hung over the couch. It was inviting, but she did not want to go in and look at the life she had created with Daniel. The life she would be leaving behind. It was hard to imagine being alone after all these years. Admittedly, many of them had been unhappy, filled with fights over Libby's treatments, career letdowns, and loneliness. Sometimes she found it exhausting to even try and talk to Daniel, who frequently did not respond. His silences gnawed away at her and made her wonder whether she somehow did not deserve a response. Still, she'd had a long marriage and a certain amount of security. Soon she would have no husband and no house. She felt a tightening in her head—a headache coming on.

Charlotte took two Tylenol from her purse and swallowed them with the dregs of a water bottle. She lingered, trying to figure out what to do and where to go. She wandered into the garage. She could talk to Claire, her sister-in-law and best friend, but then Claire would tell the whole story to her brother, Sandro, who would tell their parents. No one in her family, except Charlotte, was good at keeping secrets. No, she did not want to involve her family until she had a better grip on this dilemma.

In the garage, she studied her car. She'd had the dent fixed at a body shop on the South Side, far away from her neighborhood, and made up a story about hitting a dumpster in a lot. She paid in cash. Yes, she questioned her motive, but she figured no matter what had happened, it was better to fix it. She was only being prudent.

She started the car and pulled out, maneuvered through the snowy alley, and drove to Costco, a place Daniel found revolting. Under Costco's fluorescent lights, she pushed a big shopping cart that she did not need. Daniel only ate organic and insisted on Whole Foods. All she bought here were white roses and paper products, but she found the full shelves tranquilizing. Occasionally, when she was pressed for time and feeling a little bit wicked, she bought the store's excellent chicken noodle soup, dumped it in a pot, and said it was from Whole Foods.

She wandered the aisles, eyeing gallons of olive oil and mayonnaise, sampling a new brand of frozen stuffed mushrooms and a chunk of toxically orange cheddar. The cheese was especially delicious.

The next aisle was diapers. Stacks and stacks. Preemie diapers. Pull-on diapers. Overnight diapers.

She was surrounded. It had been a long time since she'd even thought about diapers. Now she might need them. If she had this baby, she would use real diapers and not contribute to the landfill. She could almost see the nursery, hear a cooing baby, smell the slightly stinky diaper bucket. It suddenly occurred to her that it could be a boy. She didn't know about boys. Her brothers' wives joked about the dangers of changing a boy and being sprayed in the face. And then there was the whole circumcision thing.

She picked up a package of Pampers just to feel them, and then she put the package back. She examined diaper creams, four to a pack.

A toddler yelled, "Mine!" The word echoed down the long aisle.

An exhausted-looking woman with a curly-haired boy seated in her cart walked over to study the section with pull-up diapers. The boy was eating something purple, and it was smeared all over his face. Charlotte saw a Pop-Tart in his hand. It had been years since she'd seen a Pop-Tart.

"Mine!" he yelled again, pointing at a toy truck he had dropped on the floor. The mother bent over to pick it up, and he let out a loud, high shriek as if he were being murdered.

Maybe this was a sign that she should not have a baby.

Charlotte retreated to the floral department where she grabbed two large bunches of plastic-wrapped roses. On her way to check out, she plucked a gold box of Godiva chocolates from a display. She would leave flowers on a makeshift memorial to Sarah. She had been bringing flowers since the accident, and she still had time to go to the intersection before dinner. It was only three-thirty.

At home, she stripped both bunches of leaves and thorns and arranged one bunch in a bowl for the coffee table. She buried her face in the other and sniffed before she wrapped the roses with a green, gauzy ribbon. The flowers had no scent, but she always hoped they would. She'd read somewhere that in creating a sturdy, long-lasting rose that could withstand cheap transport from Colombia, the scent had been bred away. They were perfect-looking but soulless.

She tucked the flowers and the chocolates into a shopping bag, put her coat back on, and headed on foot to the intersection. The memorial items were piled onto a large median abutting the intersection. Charlotte set her flowers down next to the other tributes.

A man was there today aiming his phone at the intersection and videotaping, which was strange. He looked familiar, and with a jolt she realized he was the cop at the accident dressed in street clothes. He was tall with a good head of silver hair. He reminded her of the Marlboro Man from her childhood and the television commercials. Kind of handsome, but why was he here? Was he looking for her car? She shivered as he lowered his phone. He gave her a quick nod and pursed his lips as if about to speak.

No, no talking. She smiled, nodded back, and hurried away. She cut over to Geneva Street, so she could pass the house where Sarah's family lived. She had googled the address and was surprised at how close the house was to hers. She walked quietly to their front door and left the box of chocolates outside.

The house had become a magnet since the accident. Charlotte was unable to stop herself from going by it both on foot and in the car. It was a large Chicago red brick with an entrance on the garden level.

Evergreen branches and berries filled the planters flanking the door. The house was two blocks from where Charlotte lived, and she observed it whenever she could. Dark and empty-looking during the day, lively and lit up at night. She had seen the younger sister go in and out with her parents. Sarah's mother raking leaves. UPS deliveries. The dad going to work. Life went on. She wanted to know how. She wasn't sure she would have been capable of it had Libby died. The shades were open, and she paused for a second to look in the window.

Sarah's mother was sitting on the floor with the younger girl, whose arm was in a cast. They were playing a game that looked like Candyland. Charlotte stood transfixed for a few seconds before she could tear herself away. She knew this was wrong. It was like an itch you know you shouldn't be scratching, and yet you do.

She had not admitted to anyone that she lurked there and left a few small gifts on the doorstep: a box of cookies from Bittersweet Bakery; small bouquets of wildflowers in Ball jars that she bought at Whole Foods; a change purse in the shape of a monkey's head for the little girl who, she could now see, did not look much like her sister.

SEVEN

 ED

November 2018

Three days after Sarah's death, Ed had bought an expensive new iPhone. It was the smallest phone he'd ever owned, which was good because he held the phone for hours at a time. He was looking for any damage on passing cars, especially ones that ran the stop sign. He drove to the corner where Sarah had been hit and filmed cars for three hours, hoping that the proof—drivers running the stop sign—would also help Maggie understand that by not retiring, he could save lives. And, at the same time, he could hunt for the killer. He could no longer ticket, so this was all he could do. For now, it was better than nothing.

But Maggie refused to look at the footage. She said she knew people ran stops all the time, and he would never find the car. She didn't understand what he was doing and even suggested he was a little cracked.

He kept filming anyway. He liked tracking the world through that tiny lens.

He had a speech prepared for when he could ticket again. "Did you know a little girl was killed here by a driver doing exactly what you did?" he would say to each errant driver, as soon as they lowered their windows. Most, he knew, would look horrified. People didn't think of themselves as killers. Ed

believed a ticket could be a teachable moment. People needed
to remember how quickly a life could end. The stickers would
help. He believed in the power of putting a face to a name, and
he wanted people to drive with the image he carried of a child
dying on this street.

He had learned from his years on the force that unlike
most criminals, the people who ran stop signs were remarkably
diverse. There was no way to predict who would brake and who
would roll.

That day, he'd noticed the lady with the flowers and her
tentativeness as she put down a bunch of white roses on the
makeshift memorial on the median. She hesitated, holding the
flowers midair, and then placed them slightly off to the side,
not touching the other flowers or stuffed animals. He felt as if
he'd seen this woman before, but he couldn't place her. Had she
been coming here all along? Perhaps he'd missed her while he
focused on the intersection.

She glanced up, as if she felt him staring. He couldn't tell
the color of her eyes at this distance, but they looked startled. He was embarrassed when she hurried away. At least it
wasn't because he was a cop. She couldn't know that. And
so many people hated cops. Especially in Chicago. Especially
these days.

On Friday, she was back. She wore a different coat, this one a
long black wool, and her hair was piled on top of her head. At
first, Ed wasn't sure if it was the same woman. She didn't look
his way as she placed a bunch of roses to the side of the memorial again. She picked up her last bunch, now brown and dead,
and threw them into a nearby garbage can. But he saw her face
as she hurried away. The same face. A lovely face with striking

features like he'd seen in paintings. He wondered if she would show up next week. Perhaps she was a friend of the family.

The following Tuesday, Ed waited, a little anxiously, and the woman appeared. He watched through his cell phone camera as she placed her flowers on the grass. The pile was disappearing as it grew colder. He'd seen park workers clear away the dead flowers and dirty toys. Except for this woman, people had stopped bringing tributes. People had short memories. Nothing was left at the memorial but her withered roses. This time, she wore a black parka, tossed the dead flowers into the city garbage can, and replaced them with a new bunch. He knew she knew he was watching. She nodded in his direction. It was getting a little weird.

And then, she smiled. Her smile was closed but nice. She was attractive in an elongated way that reminded him of those Afghan dogs. Long and sleek. She dressed like many of the neighborhood women, in leather boots and skinny jeans. Tiny earrings caught the light and sparkled on her ears. But he recognized desperation in her face. Skittishness in her movements.

The next day, she stopped and looked directly at Ed. He was standing beside his car, and he lowered his phone. She crossed the street. The way she held herself reminded him of movie stars from the 1950s—the elegant women with pearls and white gloves. In the sun, her eyes were gold like the eyes of cats he'd seen. An odd color.

"Charlotte." She held out a leather-gloved hand.

"Ed." He shook her hand. "Pleased to meet you."

"Pleased to meet you, too." She offered him a tight smile.

"Are you a friend of the girl's family?" It was the only reason he could think of that she would be here so often.

"No." Charlotte fished her sunglasses out of her bag and put them on before she turned to walk away.

"Oh." Ed didn't know what to say, but she was already gone. It was strange she was here so much with no familial connection. He kept trying to remember where he'd seen her before.

The following day, Charlotte brought two coffees. Starbucks. "I didn't know if you took cream or sugar." She offered him a packet of sugar from her coat pocket. "I couldn't bring the cream. They might have called the police if I walked away with the pitcher." She gave him a side-eye, and Ed laughed.

"Thanks, only sugar. That was awfully nice of you." How did she know he was a cop?

"We seem to be keeping the same vigil. No one knows I do this. How about you?"

"Just my wife. She thinks I'm crazy."

"Are you here every day?"

"Yes, I film cars to document how many people go through this stop."

"Are you looking for suspects?"

"Yes, I was the only witness at the hit-and-run, but I wasn't able to see the driver."

"Do you think it does any good to be here?"

"I like to think so. I see quite a few sliders. And I have videos as proof. I'm looking for a car that has some damage. I had stickers with the girl's—Sarah's—face made for when I can ticket again."

"Again?"

"I'm a cop, but I'm on paid leave right now." He didn't want to go into it. "Do you want to see the stickers?"

She followed him to the car. He opened the glove compartment and handed her a sticker. She studied Sarah's picture and the dates for her short life, holding it up to the light. She set her coffee on the ground. Ed watched as she removed her gloves, found her driver's license, and pressed the sticker neatly onto the bottom half of her license. She had long fingers, like a piano player, and wore an expensive-looking diamond wedding band.

"She had such an adorable face." She put her license back. "Those beautiful eyes. I can't imagine losing her."

"Do you have children?" The picture seemed to have shaken her.

She hesitated. "A daughter. She's twenty-three and living in New York. Do you have kids?"

"Two. Also grown. A boy and a girl. Would you like to sit in the car and warm up for a minute? You look like you're freezing." It was four-fifty. The sun was setting, and the wind had picked up.

She walked over and stopped near the door, frowning as she peered through the window. Was she worried about getting into a stranger's car? He didn't blame her. It was a bad idea.

"If you'd rather, I can bring some of my wife's chocolate chip cookies outside to have with our coffee."

"No. I'd like some heat. I'm freezing."

Ed walked around and opened the passenger door for her.

EIGHT  CHARLOTTE

December 2018

Sitting in Ed's car, sweat prickled at her temples underneath her hat. Had he seen her Prius? She did not tell him she had been there, too. That there was another witness. She had to be careful and not be too friendly. There was also a chance she was being foolish and getting into the car of a psycho. Why was he on paid leave? Her mother's favorite warning to Charlotte as a teenager was "Remember Ted Bundy." Ed looked more like Ed Asner on *The Mary Tyler Moore* show. She'd always had a soft spot for Ed Asner: his shrugs, the little twinkle in his eye, even his rumpled look.

"Have a cookie." He reached for a large Ziploc bag in the back.

She noted the gracious way he offered up the cookies and the gentleness in his eyes. His wife baked for him. He was not, she was sure, a psycho. She relaxed, taking in the car. A *Sun-Times* was creased and folded on the console between them. A can of Diet Coke was in the drink holder, and the remains of his lunch sat in a small portable garbage in the back.

"I wish my car were a little neater. I wasn't expecting company," he said.

"It looks tidy to me. Tell me about your kids." She took a sip of her coffee. "What do they do?"

"Paul's the oldest, thirty-four. He manages the Foot Locker stores for the Midwest. Paul and his wife, Ashley, have two boys. My daughter, Dawn, who's thirty-two, is a lawyer. An assistant state's attorney."

Charlotte finished a bite of her cookie. "They sound very accomplished. And these cookies are delicious."

"My wife, Maggie, is a great baker."

"She is, and you must be thrilled to have grandchildren."

"Yes, but Dawn hasn't been able to have a baby. And she's dying to have one. She and her husband, Jake, are paying up the wazoo for fertility treatments and so far, nothing but heartbreak. She gets pregnant and miscarries. The worst was the baby girl she miscarried last year at six months."

"How awful."

"It's really been hard for her."

"Probably for all of you."

"Yeah, but I mainly worry about her. And a bit about Maggie."

"Why Maggie?"

"She's a devout Catholic, and she quit the church because it prohibits in vitro. I'm sure that's left a big hole in her life. It was her community."

"That must have been hard for her. Lonely."

"Do you worry about your daughter?" Ed faced her. "She's so far away."

She was caught off guard and remained quiet for a few seconds, not wanting to talk about Libby. "Yes. She's lost. In life, I mean. Untethered."

She imagined Libby rising from the street and blowing like a balloon through the New York City sky. For a moment, she forgot where she was and careened alongside her daughter.

"I worry about my kids, too," Ed said.

His voice brought her back. They sat, comfortably silent,

eating, sipping their coffees, and watching the cars as they stopped. Every car stopped at the sign. The only sound was faint music, maybe Dylan, from his radio.

When she finally left the car, it was dark. She walked home, moving quickly up to Clark Street and then Webster, past Libby's old school. She cut down Grant Avenue. The dog walkers were hurrying along. The houses were lit and welcoming. People were making dinner, pouring wine, and feeding toddlers. She felt a buzz of happiness. Her mouth was still filled with the sweetness of the cookie.

NINE  ED

December 2018

As Ed drove home, a good feeling, a warmth, spread across his chest and lingered until he thought about home and Maggie. Between her obsession with Dawn's fertility treatments and her nagging him to retire, he'd begun to find it trying to be around her. It didn't help that he missed Tommy so much—missed having a buddy to talk to and confide in. That's why he'd overshared with Charlotte, whom he had just met.

Maggie's enthusiasm for the fertility treatments was a surprise, considering the church's position. When Dawn and Jake had started at the fertility clinic, Maggie was worried and consulted their priest, Father McCann. She'd thought of Father McCann as kind, wise, and practical, figuring he'd provide guidance and compassion, and help her navigate through this emotional process, increased by its contradictions to the church's principles. She was torn and so worried about Dawn that Ed went with her to Saint Celestine.

"Being a mother has been my life," she told the priest in his small, dark office where he was seated behind a desk. "I don't want Dawn to miss out on having kids. The doctor says there's no chance for her without in vitro. I don't understand why the church is against it. Can you help explain this? I'm confused."

"A child is a gift, not a right." He nodded to Ed and Maggie as though he were imparting great wisdom. "The church considers in vitro immoral. Conception should take place in a woman's body, not a petri dish. And there are the extra embryos that are discarded. Life is being discarded."

"I can't believe wanting to be a parent is a sin." It was unusual for Maggie to say something like this. Ed watched her as she let the priest's words sink in, seeing her cheeks heat in anger.

"We understand the pain of infertility." Father McCann added this in a toneless voice that made Ed clench his fist. "But the church doesn't condone artificial insemination, in vitro, or surrogacy." He gave Maggie a sheet on the church's stance on conception, which she folded neatly and put in her purse.

"Thank you, Father." She was trying to mask her disappointment with a vague smile.

In the car, she told Ed that she was sorry she had trusted Father McCann with her confessions, petty as they might have been.

Later, she sat at the kitchen table and read and reread the paper.

"Who has the right to tell a couple they can't have a baby? To call it immoral? Even artificial insemination is a sin. I had no idea, and I don't get it."

Ed shrugged. He had never been much of a Catholic. He attended church to please Maggie. But he thought its rules were archaic, begging to be broken. No birth control in this day and age? No support if you needed help getting pregnant? "Dawn and Jake don't care what Father McCann thinks. And you shouldn't, either. He's a jerk. Hopefully, the treatments will take. And, if not, you hear all the time about people who stop trying and *poof!* A baby."

"I still can't help but be upset. Fertility treatment should not be a sin."

"I know, Maggie, and if it helps, it's not your sin. It's Dawn and Jake's. And, anyway, I think it's bull. Killing someone is a sin. Wanting a baby is not."

"That doesn't help." She tore Father McCann's paper into bits. "I'd like to think that no one is sinning. And you know what? Besides your health and safety, grandbabies are a great reason for you to retire. You love being a grandpa, and you certainly enjoy spending time with the ones we have. If you were home, we could pick up Teddy and Liam at school together. You could take them to Cubs games and Dairy Queen. Play checkers or one of those Wii games. You should enjoy them while you can."

"Maggie, you know I don't want to retire yet."

Maggie crumpled up the paper and did not answer.

That was the end of Maggie and Saint Celestine Church. She even abandoned the bridge group and the Wednesday potluck dinners.

Ed was hoping she'd take some college classes, since she'd never had the chance. Maybe meet new people. But she spent her days at home or with Dawn, monitoring her treatments with a despairing fanaticism that made it hard for Ed to be around her. This was something he didn't know how to help her with. When he pulled onto the highway, instead of listening to his usual Dr. Phil show, he slid in one of the CDs the kids had given him for one of his birthdays and sang along with Neil Young about searching for a heart of gold. As he drove, he felt as if he were searching, too, and he thought of Charlotte again. What was she searching for at that intersection?

TEN  CHARLOTTE

December 2018

After coffee with Ed, Charlotte climbed the snow-covered stairs to her house. Remembering she was pregnant—a fact that kept slipping in and out of her mind—she held onto the handrail. Midway up, she saw a flash of movement behind the French doors. She froze for a second, then realized it was Daniel. He was usually still at work now.

He'd seen her and opened the door. "Hey, where were you?"

"Out for a walk."

"Was today your doctor's appointment?"

"I went to see her on Monday." Just saying the words made her heart race. "What are you doing home? You scared me."

"The markets were slow; I decided to come home and eat a late lunch. And I promised Libby I would ship her an iPod in rehab. They're allowed to listen for good behavior. What did your doc say about fainting?"

"She couldn't find anything wrong. Maybe it was those ridiculous shoes." She hoped she sounded cheerful, as if it had all been a silly worry.

"Are you coming in? It's freezing out here." Daniel stood on the porch in a T-shirt, shorts, and socks. She walked the rest of the way up the stairs, and he ducked back inside.

His yoga mat was spread in the middle of the living room floor. Daniel had taken up yoga last month and was diligent about practicing the poses. He got on the mat and perched on one leg, wobbling madly.

"Tree pose."

"Nice." He looked ridiculous, but she wanted to be encouraging. A small box was beside the mat. He put his leg down on the mat and picked it up.

"Is this the box you're sending to Libby?" She wondered again how Libby would take the pregnancy, and how she would break the news to Daniel. It seemed even more daunting now that she was home with him.

"Could you hold the edges together while I tape?" He picked up the box and a roll of packing tape sitting on the table nearby.

Charlotte squatted on the floor hyperaware of both the small belly hidden under her coat and the familiar musty smell of Daniel's sweat.

"Do you have a marker?" He'd managed to tape the box.

She went into the kitchen and retrieved a Sharpie from the mess drawer.

"I had a bite of the soup in the fridge. Is it for dinner? It's delicious."

"Thanks. Yeah, I made it earlier. Also, a salad." Her mouth was dry with anxiety.

"You're fine? The doctor said that?"

"Uh-huh. She did some tests and couldn't find anything wrong. Said that if it ever happens again, I should lie down on the floor."

This story, this untruth, flew out of Charlotte's mouth. She turned away from Daniel for a second to hide her guilty face. With her back to him, she busied herself gathering sections of a

Chicago Tribune scattered on the couch. Even during her affair, she had never mastered the art of lying . . . only lying by omission. Now she seemed to be lying to everyone.

"Why?"

"Why what?"

"Why should you lie on the floor?"

She wished he would stop asking questions. "I guess . . . I guess so I won't hit my head."

"Hmm, aren't you taking off your coat?"

She'd forgotten she had her coat on. She did not want to take it off, but she did.

The kitchen still smelled of thyme and tomato from the soup Charlotte had made earlier. The butter lettuce, olive oil, and crunchy multigrain rolls waited on the counter. She walked through the kitchen back into the family room. Daniel had turned the news on. His Scotch sat nearby on the end table.

A suicide bomber had driven a bomb-laden car into a hospital in Yemen. This was followed by a coordinated militant attack. At least twenty-five people had been killed, including six doctors and four patients. There was footage of bodies strewn in hallways. Bloody people on stretchers. Mothers crying, searching for their children.

How could they show this? This ultimate breach of privacy. Nausea rolled through her. She wondered if the world had become more brutal, or if it only seemed that way because they were privy to every tragedy. "Barbaric. All those innocent people."

Daniel didn't respond. Next up was Trump having a tantrum about Michael Cohen. She couldn't look at his face or listen to his tirade. She went back into the kitchen and leaned against the sink. Had she ever been this tired before? Between the atrocities in war-torn countries and Trump, she felt as if humanity had hit a new low. But then, there was slavery, the World Trade

Center, World War II. And was it in ancient Rome where all
those Christians were thrown to the lions? She took a bite from
one of the rolls, hoping it would stem her nausea. Then she
remembered hearing during her first pregnancy that nausea was
a healthy sign. She had not had any when she was pregnant with
Libby and had worried about it.

If this baby did not have a monstrous deformity, if it was by
some miracle viable and wanted to hang in there and be born,
she did not want to say no to it. She would be sixty-eight when
the baby was Libby's age, but she would probably make it to sixty-eight and get the chance to be a mother to this baby. Besides
being overwhelmed, she was excited. Maybe she would be a better mother to this baby than she had been to Libby . . . or at least
a different kind of mother. In order to do that, she had to know
where she had gone wrong and figure out how she had failed to
help Libby overcome her unhappiness—and now—her destruc-
tive and possibly murderous behavior.

She loved Libby, but it had been hard to be her mother.
Hard to watch her struggle first with OCD and then alcohol
and drugs. Hard to feel helpless, and sometimes, frustrated and
angry about the addictions. What if Libby's issues were a colli-
sion of circumstance and genetics that would not repeat itself?
This time, Charlotte would be an older and wiser mother. And
this baby's father would probably not be involved, even if he
eventually knew about her. Charlotte could raise her as she
wished, which was both thrilling and terrifying.

She stood by the sink, roll in hand, trying to figure out how
she would get through this evening with her secret. With Daniel. Still, there was an indisputable nugget of happiness at the
thought of the baby. Emory's baby. A piece of him that was hers
forever. A prize she'd won.

The nausea subsided and she set the table, washed the lettuce, and toasted pecans for the salad. She mixed the salad together, adding blue cheese, olive oil, and lemon. She got a plate for the rolls and bowls for the soup. She was on automatic pilot as she turned on the wireless music system. A little Nina Simone. Too melancholy. She switched to Spanish classical guitar. Listened as it drifted through the house. She dimmed the lights, tried to empty her mind of Emory. Love. Pregnancy. She failed. She stayed busy ladling the soup into bowls while her mind went wild.

She was on the ultrasound table. With Libby in detox. Being kissed by Emory. A baby girl sat in a high chair in a white room. A blank of a room. Emory walked into the room with a bowl of raspberries, which he put on the tray. The baby rolled the berries and put them in her mouth. They stained her lips deep pink. Tiny hands reached out to be picked up. Charlotte was in the room but on the edge watching.

"I'm starving." Daniel sat down at the table, moving the vase of yellow and orange poppies out of the way with a clunk.

Her mind snapped back to dinner. She sat down and put her napkin in her lap.

Daniel drizzled a little olive oil into his soup. Charlotte did the same. She didn't trust herself to talk. They ate in silence. Luckily, they rarely talked during dinner, first getting over the business of eating. Daniel had always been quiet whether eating or not. That had been one of the things she'd first found attractive about him. Unlike most guys she had known, he didn't go on about himself.

"Cheers." Daniel raised his glass.

Charlotte was momentarily thrown. Daniel had poured her a glass of the cold white wine that she must have put on the table along with glasses. A glass of wine or two was her habit, and she could really have used one now.

"I have a headache tonight. I think I should stick with water."

"Did you take an Advil?"

"Tylenol."

"I hope it goes away soon. Is it one of your migraines?"

"No. It's not that bad."

"What do you think about going to the Amalfi Coast next summer?" Daniel had finished his soup. "Maybe in August. Airfares are great now. Really low. We should book if you're interested. Maybe stay near Ravello. Walk by your grandparents' old house. I wonder if the same couple still owns it?"

Their one luxury had always been traveling. It was something they both loved, and they did it well together. Daniel was at his most relaxed on trips. He said he liked having time to wander and read. He enjoyed sitting around pools and ordering lunch from his chair. She loved being a foreigner. Newness sharpened sensations and etched them into her memory: the delight of that first plunge into the ocean, a bite of a warm ripe peach at an outdoor market, a walk under a leafy arch of branches on a cobblestone street.

It was odd for him to be bringing up a trip. He never planned their trips, but he did know how much she loved Ravello, and that it held a family history for her. It was always Charlotte who mapped out their vacations, and Daniel paid little attention to where they were going until they arrived. What had brought about this offering? Did he sense something? By next August, she might have a new baby. She took a sip of the wine she'd said she didn't want. "Can we afford that trip?"

She knew he did not like this question, and she felt bad for asking, even though it was a deflection. Daniel made less and less every year. After the crash in 2008, the turbulent financial markets became too unpredictable for him. He was no longer a big producer in his company. He played more golf, had more long lunches. They could barely afford this house. Their days of luxury travel were certainly over, and she missed them. Maybe he knew that and was trying to please her, which was touching even if it was terrible timing.

"The airfare is cheap. We can easily do it if we don't go overboard on the hotels or fancy restaurants." He sounded excited. "We could try an Airbnb. Maybe there are some in that town below Ravello. What's it called?"

"You mean the town with Palazzo Avino's beach club?"

"Yes, the one down those millions of steps."

Palazzo Avino was Charlotte's favorite place in the world. The hotel was at the very top of Ravello and had gracious, old-fashioned common rooms overlooking the sea. She had always booked the cheapest room with no view, which was still expensive. Every night they'd have a drink on the terrace, which had its own spectacular view of the coast and was scented with lemons, lavender, and rosemary. Along with the drinks, tuxedoed waiters served plates filled with little sandwiches and savory pastries, fat green olives, and nuts. It was a pure luxury of the senses that Charlotte had felt in every cell of her body.

The hotel's beach club was in a different town and was accessed by following a steep, winding road in the hotel van or by taking a ninety-minute hike down the time-worn stone stairs. Once a guest arrived at the beach club, another four sets of steep stairs had to be climbed to get either up or down from the ocean to the clubhouse. Nico, the man who served lunch and drinks, had the most muscular legs Charlotte had ever seen.

"I think it's Marmorata. I loved hiking down all those old steps."

On the stairs, climbing down to the beach, they would pass house after house. Water and bread deliveries sat in some of the doorways. About halfway down, there was a square with a small church that was always empty. It was cool and dark inside, and Charlotte liked to rest on a pew for a few minutes. Before they left, she would put a euro in a small wooden box and light a candle. Lighting a candle could never hurt.

Charlotte suddenly felt hot and realized she was about to be sick. She bolted from the table and made it to the powder room before she threw up. She sat on the floor and rested her forehead on the cool toilet seat. This baby was making itself known. Somehow, this made her feel more pregnant than the ultrasound.

"You okay?" Daniel was calling from his chair. Charlotte rinsed her face and mouth, which still tasted like acidy lentils. She went back and stood at the table. The smell of the soup was making her feel sick again.

"You never throw up."

"I think it's a stomach flu. Everyone has it."

"You should go upstairs and lie down. Do you want to take some tea up?"

"No. Going to rest."

Upstairs, she peeled back the quilt. She already felt better but now had to pretend she was sick. There was no way she could keep up this charade. She had to decide.

She took off her jeans and sweater, glanced at her belly, and pulled a cotton nightgown over her head. Exhausted, she opened the book on her bedside table. *The Flame Throwers*, which she liked because it was about Italy and New York in the '70s. The letters blurred. Her eyes closed and the book lay heavy on her chest. She was vaguely aware of Daniel coming to bed, turning out the lights, and pulling up the quilt.

Without looking, she knew he had already turned toward the wall.

It had been nearly two years since Charlotte had reached the point where she realized she was surprised by touch. She startled when a hand or shoulder, even Daniel's, brushed against her. If anyone had asked, she would have said she missed touch and warmth. But no one had. She did not look as if she were suffering in any way. She'd hung onto her looks, her thick hair, and smooth skin. And, sure, she invested in Botox, fillers, and the occasional laser treatment. She dressed well in flattering jeans and sweaters. Part of it was vanity, but it was also her job. She had to be her own best advertisement.

No one knew about the constant ache in the pit of her stomach. It occasionally threatened to knock her off her feet with a swift stabbing pain that might, she knew, be soothed by arms wrapped around her, soft kisses down her neck, or a hand stroking her hair.

Neither Daniel nor she—it was her fault, too—kissed each other hello anymore. At night, they both read before turning their lamps off to sleep in the far corners of the bed. A world between them. Was he as lonely as she was?

They had become a couple who existed in silence. They had no more questions. By now, they knew each other's opinions and tastes. They performed the rituals. Dinner at Naha on their anniversary. Soft shell crabs and champagne.

This is my life. This is who I am now, she had thought. *A sexless, middle-aged woman. Now, I'm a pregnant, middle-aged woman.*

When it was her birthday, Daniel bought Charlotte one of the hammered gold bangles she loved adding to the collection that jangled on her right arm. It grew heavier each year. When it was Daniel's birthday, Charlotte searched for leather messenger bags, cashmere sweaters, and herbal aftershaves. She presented these presents sumptuously wrapped in handprinted paper.

Both were grateful for these gifts.

ELEVEN  ED

December 2018

Still singing in the car along with Neil Young—now to "Old Man"—still happy about sharing cookies and conversation with Charlotte, Ed turned down his street and passed two kids building a snowman. He slowed. A little boy bundled in a blue snowsuit pressed two prunes for eyes into the snowman's face. The boy's cheeks were red from the cold, and even from the car, Ed could see his nose was running.

It seemed like only yesterday he was building snowmen with Paul and Dawn. In those days, they'd used coal for eyes. He could still see their frozen little faces and snow-encrusted suits. Maggie would have them take their coats and pants off in the back hall, where the snow melted into puddles on the linoleum. Then she served hot chocolate to thaw them out— marshmallows and all. He missed those days.

Dawn lived three blocks away and drove this same street. She was always on his mind; he worried about her. Each miscarriage seemed to sink her further into depression. He wondered if, every time she saw these kids or a new mother with a baby, she felt devastated not to have one of her own.

Ed wondered if couples got hooked on the trying. He got that, but at what point would they stop? Part of him wished Dawn had reached that point. She had used up the IVF allowed by her insurance but kept plowing money and hope into treatments that might never work. They were talking now about taking out a second mortgage. Did doctors ever say, "Enough is enough. Face the possibility of failure"?

They really should adopt. Once they had that baby in their arms, they'd be happy.

It couldn't help Dawn's state of mind that she worked in the criminal court building on Twenty-Sixth and California, the most depressing place on earth. A place entirely populated by murderers, drug dealers, thieves, cops, and lawyers. If Sarah's killer was caught, Dawn could potentially be one of the prosecutors. He would like to see Dawn get out of that hellhole and go to work for a small private practice, with or without having children. She said she would make the switch after she had a baby. Not "if." He should mention adoption or get Maggie to mention it. It killed him to see her heart pummeled again and again.

Cook County Jail loomed behind the court building, spanning eight blocks. It was one of the largest jails in the country, as well as one of the most notorious. Al Capone, John Wayne Gacy, and Richard Speck had all been inmates there. Ed got the shivers when he thought of Gacy in his clown costume, his yard filled with the bodies of the young boys he'd raped and strangled. He was glad Gacy had been in another part of town, and that he'd never had to witness anything like that backyard.

He pulled into the driveway of their well-tended bungalow. Three bedrooms and two bathrooms. The house's neat, solid appearance always gave him a rush of pride, even though it looked like most of the others on the block—small brick houses with tiny front yards and driveways on the side. Most were owned by police officers and firefighters. While the neighborhood appeared suburban, it was within city limits. To work for the city meant you had to live in the city.

He'd grown up in a house nearby, similar to this one, and attended the same high school as his kids. His son and wife lived with their two sons, Liam and Teddy, less than a half mile away. Maggie picked up the boys from school a few times a week and walked them home.

He found this continuity reassuring, even though he had not been particularly close to his own parents. His father had died when Ed, the youngest of three boys, was thirteen. It was back in the day of the belt, and the boys got it plenty. Ed and his brothers didn't exactly miss their father or his temper, but his death still left an empty space in their lives.

Widowhood transformed their mother, already a meek woman, into a frail one.

She abandoned her vigorous house-cleaning rituals and let dust bunnies and dirty laundry gather while she watched soaps and sitcoms. The stews, tuna casseroles, and lasagnas that the boys grew up eating were replaced by frozen dinners served on TV trays while she sat sipping sherry. The sound of *The Flying Nun* or *Get Smart* distracted from the silence. The boys escaped to their rooms or out to friends' houses after dinner, leaving her alone in front of the TV. Ed wondered if she truly watched the shows or was lost in thought or sherry-induced daydreams.

His mother shrank and faded until she was hardly there at all. Ed had been relieved when, shortly after Maggie and he married, she moved down to Florida to be with her cousins. It helped to think of her getting some sunshine. He called her on Sundays, and they talked about the kids or the Cubs. She was more lucid now and seemed to have kicked her sherry habit.

He and Maggie visited her every March as a break from the snow. It wasn't much of a break, though. Ed ended up fixing all the loose latches, broken tiles, and appliances in her small ranch house. Maggie cooked. She made stews and soups they could eat for dinner rather than his mother's collection of Banquet frozen meals. Maggie packed up the leftovers to freeze for his mother, so she would have something decent to eat when they left, even though Ed was sure she preferred her microwaved Banquet fried chicken and turkey and gravy dinners.

He was surprised to see Dawn's car on the street. He hadn't known she was coming for dinner. Despite living a few blocks away, his daughter and her husband, Jake, worked late hours and rarely joined them for their early meals. Maybe this was perfect timing for a talk about adoption. He wanted to get a private minute with Maggie. She was better at bringing these things up. He was embarrassed talking about fertility and women's issues. And Dawn had a short fuse, especially on all the hormones she was taking.

He walked into the living room and found Jake sitting on the well-worn brown couch, watching the news, whiskey in hand.

Jake stood up to greet Ed. "Let me make you a drink. The girls are cooking." The overly warm house smelled like pot roast.

"You got away from work early." Jake worked as a construction manager for a successful developer in Lincoln Park and had ridiculously long hours. Jake mixed his drink, standing at the liquor cabinet across the room. He was still in his work clothes—chinos and a blue button-down shirt.

"I got lucky today." Jake grinned. "One of our big projects finished up and sold. Four million."

Ed whistled and took his drink. Jake knew exactly how he liked it. Two fingers and a splash of soda. "Thanks. Smells good in here." Had he somehow missed a special occasion? A birthday or anniversary? "I'm going to say hi to the girls."

Jake's smooth forehead furrowed as he nodded.

"Hey, hon." Maggie was removing the pot roast from the oven. A plate of baked potatoes, Parker House rolls, and bowl of green beans sat on the counter. Dawn was sitting at the small kitchen table where they ate dinner when they were alone. It was covered with pamphlets.

Maggie put down the pan. Her back was still to him. "Ed, can you help carry the food to the dining room table?"

He carried the beans and potatoes. Dawn picked up the rolls and retrieved butter from the fridge. Jake wandered in, and they all sat. Maggie arrived with the pot roast. There was a nervous skew to her mouth and an avoidance of his eyes. They bowed heads and Maggie said grace, a habit they had not given up despite Maggie's new views on the church. Food was passed in silence. Ed waited. Was someone sick? He was having trouble chewing and swallowing.

"Dad." Dawn pushed back her plate. "We have a question for you." She brushed her thick red hair away from her face. She had gained weight from all the hormones, and her cheeks were as chubby as they were when she was little. "My doctor thinks I can never carry a baby to term. I have what's called an incompetent cervix, and I'll keep having miscarriages. Mom offered . . . well, she offered to help."

"Yes, I want to help them." Maggie turned to look at him.

"Of course, Dawn. We have some savings. We're happy to help."

"Ed, that's not what I meant. I want to carry the baby for them."

"What? How?" He chewed a tough piece of meat, gave up, and swallowed it whole. *Carry? What about a stroller?*

"In me, Ed. As their surrogate."

The room went quiet.

Words choked at the back of his throat. "Christ, you're fifty-two." Maggie winced, and he felt awful. He didn't know anything about surrogacy, except that it was something celebrities and rich people did, probably so they didn't have to be bothered with carrying their own babies or ruining their figures. "What about Ashley? I'm sure Paul would be okay with it. She's had two healthy boys. She's much younger."

"Her uterus can't take another pregnancy," Dawn said. "Her doctor said it would be life-threatening. He tied her tubes after Teddy was born." Dawn took a slow sip of water and turned back to her mother.

"I went for an exam at Dawn's clinic," Maggie said. "It's not a problem. I've already had some tests. I'm healthy and not too old to be a surrogate. It would be Dawn's egg and Jake's sperm. Like IVF but implanted in me."

"You went to the clinic without telling me?" Ed realized this evening had been planned for his benefit. A cloud of anger, the kind he had not felt for a long time, swirled in his head. He could have used another drink, but he didn't want to get up. "Jake, would you mind pouring me another one?" He was stalling for time without leaving the scene.

"Me too, Jake." Dawn held out her water glass. "I can drink now." She began cutting her meat into tiny pieces to avoid looking at anyone.

"I went to make sure this was possible before I told you, Ed. They could have said to forget it. I've already started on hormones."

"You've already started? Without discussing it with me?" Ed realized he was yelling. He saw how Maggie, in her excitement, looked younger. Her eyes were bright, her cheeks pink. "This could be dangerous at your age."

"Stop getting so worked up. Risks for certain things like

high blood pressure and diabetes go up with age, but I'd be closely monitored. My blood pressure is very low."

"How does it even work?" Ed blurted. Jake, who was bringing in the drinks, reddened.

"Dawn's been giving me hormone shots. And they do the implant the same way they did with Dawn."

To Ed, this seemed like science fiction or a nightmare. Did she say something about hormones? "Dawn's been giving you hormone shots and you didn't bother to tell me?"

"That's right." Maggie looked him straight in the eye. "It's not a big deal. Surrogates are common."

Ed was tongue-tied. He imagined his wife blowing up like the girl who turned into a blueberry in *Charlie and the Chocolate Factory*, which he had recently watched (and liked) with Liam and Teddy. Maggie with a tiny head, swollen limbs, and a huge belly. This upset him. He would like to take his Scotch, go upstairs, and lie down.

"It's not that strange, Dad." Dawn sipped her whiskey but didn't meet Ed's eyes. "She's healthy. Her body can take it."

"How do you know that? You're thirty-two, not fifty-two." His voice sounded too sharp, but he wished Dawn would pipe down.

"The doctor said Mom will be an excellent surrogate. She won't be the first grandmother to do this."

"Look, Ed, since I had no trouble with my pregnancies, the chance of success is pretty high. The doctor said old eggs are a problem, not an old uterus."

Ed swallowed too much of his whiskey and coughed.

"I don't know." He wished the alcohol would do its work faster. "You guys took me by surprise. You've had time to think it over, and I haven't. Of course, I want Dawn and Jake to have a baby, but I'm worried about your mother carrying it."

"What exactly are you worried about?" Maggie had stopped eating.

"Safety. I don't want to lose you. How do we know it's safe?"

"I don't think we know that anything is totally safe. A little girl recently died crossing the street with her parents. Right? That's what you've had your head wrapped around lately. I've weighed the risks, and I want to do this."

"I need to think it over." Ed couldn't believe Maggie mentioned the girl. It sounded mean. She was never mean. And the truth was, he was being told, not asked.

He couldn't sleep that night. He lay in bed staring at the ceiling. Was he being unreasonable about this? He was worried about Maggie. Then he was furious with her, and then furious with Dawn.

Around two in the morning, he convinced himself that he'd left the garage door open. He got up, put on his down coat, and went outside. The door was shut. He stood on the cold driveway for a minute. He wished for a second he still smoked, for the comfort of a cigarette in his hand. Every light on his street was off and for once, he could see the stars. The stars were spectacular, but something about the vastness of the inky sky disturbed him. If only he could believe in Maggie's God and think that Tommy was up there, but he couldn't. Still, he said a small prayer to the stars asking for forgiveness. When he went back in, he poured himself a small whiskey and drank it at the kitchen table. He finally went back to bed but couldn't sleep.

TWELVE  CHARLOTTE

September 2018

She knew, despite her pleasure in him, she should hold Emory at a distance. Not only was he married to one of the wealthiest women in Chicago, but he was also a study in contrasts. He asked to see her but seemed distracted and anxious when she arrived. He was nervous about being caught yet kissed her on the street. He was delighted by the little treats she brought him: fancy chocolates, books, and weird pens, but never surprised her with anything.

Even kissing seemed only to be a means to an end. He began as soon as she walked into his office. First came the soft kisses, the ones she liked the most. Then, the more heated ones and a slow removal of her clothes.

Afterward, he was happy to chat. But it was the sex that came first. This was okay unless she had things she wanted to talk about. Then this direct path annoyed her; it was very "teenage boy." It wasn't that she didn't like the sex. She loved it. It was that she worried he didn't care about her thoughts or her life. But she was too cautious to bring it up, to risk breaking their connection by being what he might consider whiny.

Just as her heart was opening, he began to voice his worries and reservations. Around two months into their relationship, when he still could not keep his hands off her, his car was rear-ended. He had just left his office after meeting Charlotte. The accident was bad enough that his airbags went off and bruised him. His face was black-and-blue and tender when she saw him two days later.

"I feel like this is a sign." He was lying naked and sweaty on the couch. Charlotte's head rested on his chest.

"Like a sign from God?" She sat up. "Why does God want to punish you? And I thought you were an agnostic."

"A lapsed Episcopalian. I'm being punished for you. For seeing you. For cheating. For lusting after you when we're both married."

"You really think that? It's a little crazy."

"I feel bad about myself."

"I don't feel good about deception. But there's not much left of my marriage, and it's not like I don't have guilt. Like I'm amoral."

"You don't seem to feel guilty."

Something inside Charlotte crumbled.

"No one likes being a cheater."

The thing was, it had been addictive to be wanted. At first, simply knowing Emory existed, that she would see him again, thrilled her. Then she began to ache when she had to leave him. The pull of him hovered around her even when he wasn't there.

Had it been the same for him? Had he felt all this newness pricking at him? Did he sense how everything had changed for her? Had it changed for him? These were questions she could not ask. How would it be if he didn't feel the same way? She didn't want that answer.

Emory was a stranger who was no longer a stranger, yet he wasn't familiar, either. They dwelled in a specific space. He kept her there. Charlotte knew little about him or his habits.

What his living room looked like, what they had for dinner, what books were stacked by his bed. She'd learned a little about his kids, whom he seemed to adore, but she would never meet them. She would never go out with his friends. He would never meet Libby.

How was it that she could inhabit a new life, small as it was, and stay the same in another? She wasn't the same. She had been rearranged and put back together as a different person—a person who wanted more than what she had, who wanted him, and now he seemed to regret this. To regret her.

He began to rush her out of his office, saying he was late for a meeting or late for a friend. It pained her to see how eager he was to get rid of her. And that she, pathetically, accepted it. Accepted crumbs. A small dose of him was enough to make her happy. It would carry her through days.

"What's wrong with you?" her friend Nellie asked when she finally had to confide in someone. "He doesn't deserve you. You shouldn't want this." But the problem was, she did.

It was becoming clear that Emory viewed her as the one bad thing in his otherwise perfect life, in which he was an upright citizen and husband who contributed to the city's social welfare.

What she wanted was to be a good thing, beloved. The idea of being viewed otherwise was diminishing. It made her cringe about her frothy romantic fantasies of starting a new life with him in Paris or Rome, far away from everyone. Eating in intimate restaurants, strolling down beautiful streets. In her edited fantasy, they stayed in the United States. Maybe they could buy a small vineyard in Sonoma. The door would be framed with bougainvillea. Libby could swim in a pool out back while they grilled salmon and local vegetables. They would toast each other with their own rosé.

She was an idiot.

Men, she thought, *could smell attachment.* He could taste it on her. The salt and flint of love. The chase and capture were over. She was no longer bright and wonderful. Emory's face lost that look of want. She became a drag. A danger.

Still, he asked to see her, and she went. They met in his office at least twice a week. She played by his rules but could feel her heart beginning to crack.

"Come here, you," he'd say, and draw her to him. He'd shut his eyes and kiss her. Peel off whatever sexy outfit—a tight black T-shirt and black jeans—she was wearing. He'd take a good look at the expensive lingerie she'd begun buying, always with cash, and lead her to his couch.

He began to make excuses not to see her. He used work and family as a shield, canceling on Charlotte last minute with events he should have taken into consideration in the first place. She became last on his long list:

His wife was being honored by a community center she funded on the South Side.

He had to supervise homework.

His boys would be unhappy if he didn't watch the Cubs game with them.

He needed to take out a friend, in the middle of a divorce, and cheer him up.

The dog had a vet appointment for a checkup that he forgot about.

She was less important than his dog. She loved dogs, but this was a hard fact to swallow.

He was phasing her out. Stringing her along just enough to keep her hooked. This was not going to end well. She would be in a great deal of pain.

"I can't give you what you want," he'd say if she complained.

"I never promised you anything." Both were true. He had been careful, stingy even, with his words. There had never been an "I love you" on his part despite the fact that she had once, to her horror, blurted it out. She was met by silence, a kiss on her ear, and a torrent of shame.

It was up to her to leave him. It was the only way to keep at least some of her dignity. She had become discardable.

THIRTEEN  ED

December 2018

Ed, exhausted from not sleeping, waited, hoping Charlotte would show up. He'd checked his hair in the mirror when he parked to make sure he hadn't forgotten to brush it. In his viewfinder, he spied her crossing the intersection, holding a cardboard coffee box along with flowers.

"Hi." She offered him a cup and set the roses on the median.

"Good to see you. And you're in luck. I have some great baklava." He opened the car door for her and instantly felt shy. He hoped he wasn't being presumptuous and was relieved when she smiled, got in, and took off her gloves. Ed reached into the back for a small brown bag and handed her a Saran-wrapped pastry. He thought about telling her the surrogate news that had been sprung on him last night, but it seemed awfully intimate. And even though he was still hurt and angry about being left out of the decision, sharing this with her seemed like a betrayal of Maggie.

Charlotte unwrapped the baklava and took a small bite. "This is delicious. Did your wife make it?"

"No, it's from a convenience store on my beat. I still go there even though I'm on leave. The owner and his family are Syrian. His wife makes the baklava, terrific hummus, and baba ghanoush. Maggie keeps me supplied in cookies, though."

"I used to love to bake, but I've no one to bake for now. My husband is strict about his diet and Libby, my daughter, doesn't live here and doesn't like to eat."

"Why doesn't she like to eat? One of life's greatest pleasures. Still, I could do with a little less." He caught himself as he was about to pat his gut, which really wasn't that bad. More of a pooch. He turned toward Charlotte, who was frowning.

"Anorexia."

"Oh, boy," he exhaled. He wasn't sure what to say. This was unfamiliar territory. "That's tough. Is she doing any better?"

"Well, she's in rehab again, so they will make her talk about it. She still has food issues."

"Has she been treated? In a program?" He'd seen advertisements for places addressing all kinds of disorders.

"Before she went to rehab it was addressed by her therapist, and she had weekly weigh-ins with her pediatrician until she went to college. It was never so bad she had to go into an eating disorder program, so we were lucky in some way."

"Sorry if that was too personal a question." Ed was flustered. Anorexia and rehab. That was a lot and far away from his world. He sipped his coffee and stared out the window to avoid looking at Charlotte.

"Not at all. When you have a kid with issues, you learn not to be embarrassed about them. It would amount to being ashamed of your kid."

"Oh." He'd never thought of it that way.

"Well, the first time, she was gone for five weeks. People knew. And who cares? It's also common. Addiction and anorexia. Not that it makes it any easier. It's awful."

"How did you find out about her addiction, or could you see it?"

"At first, it was alcohol, and very noticeable. It's hard to hide the smell of liquor. This last time, right after Thanksgiving, it was OxyContin. She overdosed. Luckily, she was with a friend who called 911. She's in rehab again." Ed was astonished that her voice was so matter-of-fact.

"That must have been petrifying."

"It was." Her voice softened. "She nearly died. The medics had Narcan and were able to revive her. I carry Narcan now. Do you carry some when you're working?"

"The district gave it out a few months ago. We have the injection form in the squad cars. It seems easy to use, like an EpiPen. And a lifesaver. We got a lesson."

Charlotte rummaged through her shoulder bag and pulled out a cardboard box that said NARCAN in large, hot-pink letters. "I have one at home, too."

"Smart. It's so easy to get opioids. We see them all the time, and it's getting worse. Chicago's one of the top distribution centers. People call the Eisenhower Expressway the Heroin Highway."

"Wow. I didn't know that about the Eisenhower. That's frightening."

"Were you surprised about Libby?" It was getting warm in the car. Their breath fogged the windows. Ed unzipped his coat and turned down the heat. Charlotte kept hers zipped, and he wondered how she could stand it.

"Yes and no. She's had problems since she was little. I guess drugs and alcohol were a good escape."

"Problems?" Was there more than anorexia and drugs? He couldn't help being engrossed.

"OCD." Charlotte turned away from Ed and looked out the car window.

"Oh." Ed realized he was making her nervous, and he wasn't sure what else to say. He only had a sketchy concept of OCD. Obsessive something.

"Bad OCD. Libby has better control now, but she used to tap three times on everything. It was humiliating for her in school. Worse, she had terrible thoughts she couldn't get out of her mind. Like that she'd somehow caused an airline crash. Or that I would die if she didn't lick her light switch before she went into her room. I can understand the appeal of drugs and the escape."

"That's awful. I can't imagine living like that. She's been through a lot. You have, too."

"I guess so. My husband is not a believer in therapy or medication, so we had a lot of disagreements about Libby. He was angry when I went ahead and put her on medication against his wishes. I felt as if I had no choice. Her teacher requested it, and her doctor thought she needed it. She couldn't function."

"Did he want to treat it at all?" He couldn't help but think of Maggie starting on hormones without discussing it with him. But this was different. Charlotte and her husband had talked it over. True, they disagreed, and she went ahead anyway, but it was a serious situation with her child.

"He wasn't completely against therapy as long as he didn't have to participate, which he did. He hated it. The therapy was supposed to keep us on the same page in terms of parenting and addressing things like her tics, but we weren't in sync at all. So that was hard. If Libby didn't get the answer she wanted from me, she would go to him. She played us."

"How did he deal with her drug addiction?"

"He wanted her treated then. Seeing your kid locked up is awful, but dying would be worse. Her overdose terrified both of us. He was behind it for her alcohol addiction, too. The detox from both were miserable for her. The symptoms are agonizing. Nausea, sweating, splitting headaches. With the Oxy she had muscle pain and a lot of anxiety."

"So, the first rehab didn't work?" He noticed Charlotte was slowly crumbling the baklava in her lap. A piece of gooey pistachio stuck to one of her fingers.

She shrugged. "No, but most people relapse. It's some enormous number, like eighty-five percent. It's a shame she picked OxyContin as her new drug of choice."

"I guess you can only do so much, but Oxy is scary."

"Yeah, I worry. I feel as if I'm always waiting for something terrible to happen." She looked down at her lap and the sticky crumbs. "When did I do that?"

"Telling me about Libby. It must be stressful to talk about."

"I guess it is. But no more stressful than living with it." She leaned back in the seat. "I am kind of exhausted."

"Here's a napkin." He reached into the glove compartment. "You're covered with crumbs."

"Thank you." She wiped her hands. "And thanks for listening. I hope I didn't dump too much on you."

"Not at all. As awful as it is, I find it fascinating."

"Addiction?"

"Libby's whole history. It seems as if it could happen to anyone. She has a good family, and still, that couldn't prevent her mental illness or addiction."

"I know, it seems like a roll of the genetic dice." Charlotte carefully brushed the sticky crumbs from her lap into the napkin.

After Charlotte left, Ed looked up OCD on his phone. He wanted to be able to keep talking to Charlotte about Libby. He read about common compulsions—washing, cleaning, checking, rechecking, praying, and counting. Then he scrolled to obsessions, which listed harm (fear of being responsible for something terrible happening to others), perfectionism, excessive concern over right and wrong and offending God, and superstitious ideas about numbers and colors. The list of symptoms was long.

He thought about what it must be like for a small child to believe she had killed everyone on an airplane, and that if she didn't tap on a wall, it could happen again. Living with that fear must have been excruciating.

It *was* all a roll of the genetic dice. Parents didn't know what type of child they were going to end up with. His own family's genetic makeup was no prize. There was his father's heart attack. His mother's sherry drinking after his father's death. He sometimes drank more than he should. He knew that. These genes might lurk, waiting to be sprung into the family pool. He was glad he'd had kids before he was smart enough to be scared, but Maggie was about to have another baby. Technically, the baby would be his grandchild, but Libby's history had unnerved him. Who knew how this science experiment would turn out?

FOURTEEN  CHARLOTTE

December 2018

The young woman behind the desk at the doctor's office wore maroon scrubs and a tag that said *Tiffany*. "You need to sign this consent form." She pushed a paper toward Charlotte. Her gold eyeshadow sparkled under the fluorescent lights.

After the document was signed, Tiffany led Charlotte to a changing room and handed her a maroon hospital gown. "Take everything off. You can put your belongings in one of these lockers. You have a full bladder, right?"

"Yes." That was an understatement. She had been drinking water all morning. Her belly was uncomfortably swollen beneath her loose dress, and all she could think about was peeing.

"I'll see you when you're all set." Tiffany disappeared.

Charlotte pulled off her dress and tights and folded them with her underwear in the middle. She put the pile in a locker and placed her purse on top. Then she took the key, on a plastic band, and slid the band onto her wrist. She was nervous, even though she understood that the miscarriage risk was minimal. What she didn't know were all the risks for chromosomal diseases, except that they increased with age, and she was considered a maternal dinosaur. She had decided she was better off not researching them.

"Ready?" Tiffany reappeared, taking Charlotte into a pale pink waiting room that had a fountain trickling in the corner. This was a blatant calming attempt. "Have a seat. Dr. Logan will come get you."

Charlotte sat in one of the upholstered chairs, as far as away as she could get from two other women and their partners. She stared at the pile of magazines on the rattan table. Next to the magazines was a bowl of wrapped chocolates. Each wrapper read *High-Risk Maternal Health*. She was too nervous to eat or read. The fountain's steady tinkling began to infuriate her as her need to pee grew more urgent. Who puts a fountain in a room filled with women who have been told to drink a lot of water?

One of the couples was holding hands so tightly their knuckles were white. Another woman walked in with a lady who must have been her mother. Charlotte suddenly wanted her mother. "Don't worry, *cara*," she imagined her mother saying in her thick accent. "Everything will be all right."

She aimlessly checked the time on her phone. Her screensaver—a picture of her with Daniel and Libby—popped up, making her feel even worse. She still had not told Daniel.

"Charlotte?"

A tiny woman with a long, dark ponytail appeared in the doorway. She also wore maroon scrubs and looked barely older than Libby.

"I'm Dr. Logan. I'll be doing your procedure."

"Nice to meet you." Charlotte stood up.

"The room is right down the hall. Is there anyone here with you? Someone you would like to bring in?"

"No, I'm alone."

The doctor studied Charlotte's face for a minute before she continued down the hall.

"Here you go." She motioned to the table. Charlotte lay down. It was covered by a thin sheet of paper that crinkled as she settled on it. She realized she was shivering.

"Are you anxious? Cold? I can get you a blanket."

"Both." She was trying to keep her teeth from chattering.

"Everyone gets nervous. It's normal."

"The idea of miscarriage and chromosomal diseases is pretty overwhelming."

"I know. The miscarriage risk is very low, though. But I know the test is not emotionally easy. Any questions?"

"Not really." Charlotte noted Dr. Logan said nothing to reassure her about the chromosomal risks.

The doctor left, then reappeared with a heated blanket.

Charlotte covered herself; it felt luxurious in the frigid room.

The doctor wrapped a blood pressure cuff around Charlotte's arm. "Okay then, your vitals are great." She removed the cuff. She wheeled the ultrasound machine closer to Charlotte. "State your name and date of birth, please."

Charlotte did, and the doctor typed in her information.

"Now, we're going to take a look at this fetus, so the blanket will have to go."

The machine bleeped on. The screen was not facing Charlotte. Perhaps it was considered distressing to see a fetus during this test, to become attached when there could be issues. She had read that the legs, arms, hands, and feet were easily visible by the eleventh week.

"This will be cold." Dr. Logan lifted the blanket and gown to cover Charlotte's belly with gel. She ran the probe over the gel and squinted at the image. "I need you to empty your bladder a little. About two cups. There's a bathroom behind us."

"Is something wrong?"

"No, your bladder is so full it's getting in the way of the picture."

When Charlotte returned, the doctor applied more gel.

"May I see the picture?"

"Are you sure? I usually discourage it during this test."

"I'm sure."

The doctor turned the screen. At first, the black-and-white image looked like a mass of dots. But after a few seconds, Charlotte could make out what looked like a tiny baby with arms and legs.

"There's the head, legs, the cord." Dr. Logan pointed to each. She zoomed in on the baby's head. The machine made little clicks as she measured it. "The fetus is eleven weeks and two days."

"The head looks a little like ET."

Dr. Logan laughed. "It does. I'm used to it, but they look unearthly." The baby opened its mouth. "That's a yawn." It kicked its feet. Waved its hand. It looked as if it were waving at Charlotte.

She felt a flash of love followed by a flash of terror. "Wow, it's really moving. Is that . . . is that normal?"

"Completely. You just can't feel it yet. Now, I'm checking the fetal heart rate."

Charlotte heard the thump of the heartbeat again.

"A strong, healthy heart." The doctor slid the probe over her belly again. "The fetus is in a good position. I'm turning the screen while I do the test. First, I'll give you a shot of local anesthetic. You'll feel this, but it's quick."

Charlotte felt the cold of the antiseptic wipe. There was the sharp smell of alcohol, then a sting and a pinch. She clutched the edge of the table and turned away to avoid looking, remembering that one of the test's risks was the needle hitting and destroying a limb of the fetus.

"What if you hit a limb?" Sweat beaded above her lip.

"That risk is if CVS is done before ten weeks. You're past that. You'll be fine."

Charlotte shut her eyes.

"Take a deep breath and keep breathing. I'm inserting the needle. It draws a sample from the villi." The doctor sounded as if she were reciting from a scientific paper. "These are wisps of placental tissue that contain the fetus's genetic makeup. You may feel some cramping."

Charlotte felt another sting. She held still and tried to distract herself by finding words that rhymed with villi. *Cry, eye, lie.* There was a stirring sensation in her uterus, which must have been the needle, then excruciating cramps that felt like labor. She wanted more than anything for this to be over. "How much longer?" Charlotte realized she had been holding her breath.

"You're cramping? Some women cramp. Others feel little."

"Yes. I didn't think it would hurt this much." She dug her fingernails into her hands.

"Take a deep breath. Four counts in, hold four counts, and four counts out."

The stirring stopped. The cramps let up.

"It's done," the doctor said. "Feeling okay? You're pale."

"I'm glad it's over." She opened her eyes and wiped the sweat from her face with the edge of her gown.

"Take a few more deep breaths while I check the heart rate again."

The beat was loud and strong and not going anywhere. Charlotte went cold again with fear. This was an actual heart in an actual baby. How was it that she was this old and still did not think through consequences? She hadn't thought she needed protection, but even so it was stupid. Reckless. And now she was having a baby alone. She had a lot more in common with Libby than she'd imagined. Not only had she been impetuous, but this baby and Libby would share DNA. She tried to remember the DNA diagrams from school. What if this baby had OCD and was an addict, and she had to go through the past twenty years all over again? What if she was a criminal?

"Excellent." Dr. Logan was done. "You might have a small amount of cramping and vaginal bleeding over the next day. Call if it's excessive or if you have questions. Take it easy for the next day or so. Staying off your feet is a good idea. And no sex or exercise for three to four days. I'll call you with the results in about a week. You can get dressed. Talk to you soon."

"Thank you." Charlotte was eager for the privacy of the dressing room, where she sat for a minute, depleted, and stared at the pristine wall. She gathered her things, got dressed, and then went back out into a world where taxis were still honking, shoppers were carrying armfuls of bags, and the homeless were begging in front of the luxury stores. And yet, everything had changed. She'd seen her baby yawn, wave, and kick. She wished she could tell Emory. She wanted to think that some small part of him would be happy.

She went into a Starbucks, bought a regular coffee and a decaf, and headed to the intersection in a taxi. She didn't want to be alone anymore. She needed some company.

FIFTEEN  ED

December 2018

"Hi, Ed." Charlotte got out of a cab at the intersection.
"Hi," he grinned. "It's Monday. I didn't expect you.
Nice surprise." He had found himself thinking
more and more about Charlotte lately, having discussions with
her in his head and wondering what she would think about
things.

"I felt like chatting. What's new with you?"

"Not much, except Maggie is furious that I come to the
intersection. She wants me home and spending more time with
the grandkids."

"Do you have any pics of your grandkids?"

"Of course." He got out his phone and scrolled through it.
"This is Liam, who's seven, and Teddy, who's five. Here they
are with their parents. My son, Paul, and his wife, Ashley. And
here's one of Dawn and Jake."

"You have such a sweet-looking family. When you retire,
you can spend a lot more time with them."

"Well, I'm still on leave, but Maggie would like that. I
promised her I would retire. That was before Sarah was killed."

"It seems a shame that Sarah's death could keep you from
retiring. Maybe it's time for both of us to let her go."

Ed was quiet.

"Why do you think you hold onto her?" She returned his phone.

He leaned his head on the headrest and shut his eyes for a second. "Sadness, I guess. Watching that little girl die." He opened his eyes and faced Charlotte. "My partner was shot a few months ago. He was my best friend. I watched him die, too. It was the worst thing I've ever been through."

"Oh, Ed, I'm so sorry."

"There's one more thing. The reason that I am on paid leave is that forensics believes the bullet that killed my friend Tommy came from my gun. So, I killed him."

"I'm sure it's some kind of mistake. That can't be right."

"Well, there's an investigation, so we'll see."

"How awful for you."

"It's been rough." He paused. "What about you? Why do you hold on? Bring the flowers?"

Now, it was her turn to pause. "I'm not sure. I started with the flowers when there was a group memorial, and I couldn't stop. I guess Sarah makes me think about Libby. How I would cope if Libby had died, or does die, of an overdose. I'm not sure I could. So, it's more about me than Sarah, I guess."

"Makes sense." He removed his hand and passed over a bag of cookies.

She took one and they sat together, eating their cookies and watching the sun set.

"I'm glad we talked about this."

"Me too, Ed. I'm . . ." She didn't finish.

"Yes?" he said, putting his coffee in the holder.

"Oh, nothing."

But there was something. Her unsaid words swirled in the air and out the door as she left.

The next Tuesday afternoon, Charlotte approached the intersection, roses in hand. Her head was covered by a red knit hat with some sort of pom-pom on top like a kid's hat. He'd seen these hats around. They were sort of silly, but he figured they must be in style. She wore sunglasses to buffer the weak winter sun.

Suddenly, brakes screeched, and Charlotte dropped her flowers. She stood still in the middle of the street. Images of Sarah flashed in his mind. Ed focused on the red of the hat and blinked as dots swam before his eyes. The red fragmented. Blood. Was there blood? He struggled to undo his seat belt, hefted himself out of the car, and ran. A black Volvo station wagon was stopped right in front of the intersection. The car's door was open. Charlotte was in the street with another woman and a large, furry, brown dog. She had one hand on the dog as if to hold it in place.

"Oh my God." The women knelt to touch the dog. "Is he okay?"

"Yes, you stopped just in time." The dog looked up at Charlotte, his eyes brown and enormous.

"I nearly had a heart attack." The woman stood up.

"Well, he doesn't seem the least bit upset." Charlotte stroked the dog's back. The dog leaned into her.

"Everyone okay?" Ed was out of breath by the time he reached the women. There was a roaring in his ears. He couldn't hear. He knew Charlotte wasn't hurt, but despite his training, he was panicking. He saw everyone was okay. The roaring stopped. Both women stared at him. The woman from the car was dressed in a wool coat and heels as if she had come from work.

"We're fine. This is one lucky dog." Charlotte tentatively

felt around the dog's neck, which was a tangle of fur. The dog didn't seem to mind. "There's no collar."

"Maybe he's chipped." Ed glanced down at the dog, who wagged its tail. "We can get him scanned at Animal Care and Control, but let's get out of the street."

They were standing in the middle of the intersection. Cars zipped around them. Charlotte headed back to the curb; the dog and Ed followed her. The woman got into her car with a wave.

"He's such a sweetheart." Charlotte steered the dog by gently tugging the hair on his head. "But his hair is all matted. He's been lost or is a stray. I'm worried he might bolt. I wish he had a collar. I could at least hold onto that."

"Wait a sec." Ed went over to the squad car, grabbed a long scarf from the passenger seat, and wrapped it loosely around the dog's neck. "This will have to do."

She walked the dog over to Ed's Jeep.

"You're coming with me?" Ed opened the door.

"Uh-huh, I need to know how this turns out."

"If he was your dog, what would you name him?" Ed leaned down to rub the floppy ears. The dog stared up at him, snout in air, with appreciation.

She thought for a minute. "Maybe Profiterole."

"Profiterole? What's that?"

"A round pastry with ice cream or whipped cream and a lot of hot fudge sauce. It's my favorite dessert, and he reminds me of one. I don't know why."

"Hmm, maybe it's all his brown fur and the white nose."

The dog jumped into the back seat as soon as Ed opened the door. He had clearly not been a stray all his life and looked out the window as they drove to the shelter.

A heavily tattooed young woman buzzed them in. The dog sat patiently while she scanned him. He did not have a chip.

"What should we do?" Charlotte appeared distressed. "I can't take him home. Daniel's allergic." She bent over and stroked his ears.

"He's a nice boy." The volunteer put away the chip scanner. "I hope we can find him a home. He's large, so he's not as adoptable as a smaller dog."

"There's a chance you'll put him down?" Ed was horrified.

"We're way over our max right now. Let me put a collar and leash on him." She sorted through a large box of donations. "This should fit." She secured the collar around his neck.

"What usually happens to big dogs here?" Charlotte asked.

"Sometimes a rescue steps in and takes them if they're not adopted." The volunteer shrugged. "But there's no guarantee." The dog licked the flower tattoos covering the young woman's arm. "If the shelter won't take them, they're put down. We have no choice."

"I hate to leave him here." Charlotte was worrying the zipper on her parka.

"Me too." Ed bent down for a final pat. "I'll check up on him tomorrow. He'll still be here tomorrow, right?"

"Probably. We're closing in a couple of hours, so nothing should be happening."

"Okay." Ed opened the door to the street. "I'll see you tomorrow."

They walked outside. It had started to snow. "Come on, I'll drop you off."

"You sure you have time? I can take a cab."

"Of course I have time."

The fresh air felt good after the overwhelming stink of urine, fur, and cleaning solution inside the shelter. The car was in front, and Ed opened the door for her. Charlotte got in. When he started the car, snow flurries whirled in the lights.

They went down LaSalle Street. The blue city plows were out scraping the street, their backs piled with salt.

"That was one cute dog." He glanced over at Charlotte.

"Sure was. Wish I could take him home. I'm worried about him."

Ed nodded. He was wondering what Maggie would say if he appeared with a large dog. Probably that it would be too much. She might be afraid he would jump on her when she was pregnant or on the grandchildren. They'd never even owned a cat.

He continued to Lincoln Avenue, which was lined with a mix of pizza parlors, drug stores, and houses. The old hospital had been torn down recently to make room for condos and five new townhouses. The enormous lot was a mess of a construction zone. Backhoes and dumpsters lined the street.

He turned left onto a street with fancy houses. Many of them had massive additions and no backyards. *It's sad to get rid of your yard*, he thought. Still, the houses were beautiful.

"My house is right up the block. The third one from the corner."

Ed pulled up. With its enormous old trees and historic houses, this street was one of the nicest in Lincoln Park. It was ritzy. Charlotte was a little ritzy. Her house was smaller than most of the others, a pretty three-story brick with black shutters. He couldn't tell if there was a backyard. The lights were on inside, and he could make out a white couch and two chairs in the living room.

"Thanks for the ride." She made no move to leave. "How about we meet at Starbucks next Tuesday for coffee? Move away from the intersection."

"Good idea. I feel the same way." He knew he'd still go to the intersection on the other days. He kept believing that somehow the driver would miraculously turn up, run the stop again, and he would see the damage on the car. Maggie called this magical thinking.

Charlotte got out with a wave, and he watched until she slipped into the brightly lit house. He saw her shadow in the window and was instantly lonely. He thought of the big goofy dog. The way he was so easygoing and happy. Those big brown eyes. He couldn't bear it if he went back tomorrow, and his dog had been put down. Maybe he should go back and get him. He could sleep in a dog bed near their bed. Ed could go on long walks with him. That could be his exercise. If Maggie objected, he could get a local kid to walk him while he was at work. He might even be good company for Maggie, who was alone in the house all day.

But she might be furious. And in all fairness, this dog was huge. He could go back and just look.

He texted Maggie.

Running a little late. Eat if ur hungry.

He headed back to the pound. The dog, tail wagging, barked when he saw Ed walking toward his crate. He stuck his hand through the metal bars, and the dog licked him enthusiastically. The surrounding dogs began barking, as if they, too, wanted some love. As if they knew their fates. It was deafening and sad.

He thought of Maggie and made himself walk away from the crate. He passed a beagle, a pit bull, and some kind of terrier mix. They stared at him hopefully. The terrier pawed at its crate as Ed walked back to Profiterole. This was his dog. He knew it.

"I can't leave you here, big guy. Promise to be good?" He could swear the dog smiled at him.

"I changed my mind," he told the volunteer.

"Awesome." The volunteer handed him a clipboard. "You'll have to fill out paperwork, since I've already processed him."

Ed sat down on a folding chair. The application was long, especially when considering that the alternative might have been to put the dog down. The questions were varied. Where will he keep a dog? How many hours will he be with it? What pets had he owned in the past fifteen years? What was the name of his vet? Were there pet allergies in the house? It went on and on.

When he finally finished, the volunteer opened the crate and clipped a leash to the dog's collar. "There's no fee because you brought him in. He needs his shots. You'll have to take him to a vet for an exam and to get chipped. Someone will follow up with you in the next few days to see how it's going."

"Thanks." He led the dog outside and opened the front door of his Jeep. The dog jumped in and sat regally on the passenger seat. "Come on, big guy, let's go home." He climbed in and flipped on Dr. Phil, mid-show, where the discussion was about not being dependent on others but making your own party.

Dr. Phil was probably not talking about getting a dog, but it might be a good omen.

He pulled into the driveway and went in the back door, the dog beside him. From the hallway, he heard the water running in the kitchen. "Hi, Mags." He paused in the doorway with Profiterole. "I got you a present."

"Hold on a sec." Maggie's back was to him as she pulled off her bright green rubber gloves. She turned and stared at the dog. He was wagging his tail. "Lord, you've brought home a bear."

"Meet Profiterole."

"Where on earth did you find him?"

"He was nearly hit by a car. I brought him to a shelter. They said they might have to put him down, so I went back and got him. What do you think?" He let go of the leash and Profiterole bounded over to sniff Maggie's hand.

She backed away. "I think you're nuts, Ed. We can't have a big dog like this. He could jump and hurt someone. One of the kids. Or me if I end up getting pregnant."

Ed felt all the air rush out of him. He put his hand on the dog's fur. He couldn't imagine living without this dog.

She glared at him, turned, and walked away.

He wasn't sure what to do. He locked the dog in the bathroom and went into the kitchen, where he found Maggie furiously washing baking pans. Two coffee cakes sat on the counter.

"Oh, Mags, we don't have to keep him. I'll take him back."

"I don't understand how you thought it was okay to adopt an enormous dog without checking with me. I live here, too."

Well, she'd never checked with him about the surrogacy. But bringing that up was not going to get him anywhere.

"I'm sorry. I knew it might be too much, but I thought, I hoped, you might think he was cute if you saw him." Ed put his arms around her and kissed the top of her head.

"He's cute, Ed. But huge."

"I can return him. Tonight, if you want." His chest ached, and he was glad the dog was out of his sight. He was surprised at how attached he already felt.

Maggie studied his face. "Go get him. Let me meet him again."

Ed opened the bathroom door. Profiterole bounded out, ricocheted off his leg, and continued to Maggie. She bent over to pet him, and Profiterole swiped her face with his tongue. "Blech, but he's growing on me. He's sweet."

"Sweet enough to try out? Can we see if it works? I'll take him back if it doesn't." He sounded like a little kid, but he didn't care.

"Is he trained? Will I be able to walk him?"

"I have no idea. Let's give him a spin. Grab your coat and boots."

Together they walked on the shoveled sidewalks. Profiterole lumbered obediently by Ed's side, even though he had no understanding of the commands "sit" or "stay." He peed on every lamppost.

"He needs his hair cut or brushed or something." Maggie fingered the tangle around his neck. "But he doesn't look undernourished. What do you think he eats?"

Ed silently thanked Dr. Phil and God (if he really was out there). If Maggie was thinking about dog meals, she was getting on board.

"I have no idea. How about I take him to the vet tomorrow? Do we have any frozen hamburger? That should be okay until we get some dog food."

Maggie made a doggie dinner of hamburger and rice, which she placed in a bowl on the floor. She stood beside Ed, smiling. They watched as he gobbled it down and looked at them hopefully for more.

"That's enough, big guy. We don't want any puking."

"Ed, what does Profiterole mean?"

He had a rush of guilt. He still had not told her about Charlotte. He knew why. Maggie would disapprove of the woman with the flowers as much as she disapproved of his videotaping. She believed that his vigil was a waste of time. She would view Charlotte's flower tributes as a waste of money. It also didn't help that Charlotte was a woman and a very pretty one. And while it was true that he had never had a woman friend, he thought of Charlotte as a friend. She was the closest he had felt to someone since Tommy. And now their meetings would be official. In Starbucks. He should tell Maggie because really, he had nothing to hide.

"It's a pastry with ice cream and chocolate sauce. I read about it in a restaurant review."

Now he was lying again, even though he wasn't doing anything that would be considered cheating. The thing was, he was sure Maggie would not like him spending time alone with another woman. Even a friend. It would be a problem.

"Profiterole. That's a mouthful. And one that can't be shortened. Since you seem to call him Big Guy, how about we call him Big."

"That's a good name." Ed hoped that renaming was another good sign. "Come here, Big. We're taking another walk. And I'm bringing a big plastic bag with me. Maybe two. We don't want the neighbors to hate us."

Outside in the dark, he saw Maggie watching through the window. He rounded the corner, walking the dog past the identical houses that stretched down the block. The light from the gas station a half mile away blinked red. Going around the second corner, he passed his friend Jim's house and was tempted to ring the bell and show him the dog. He fought the urge in case he didn't get to keep him. Disappointment was always worse for him if others knew about it, and he had to discuss it or explain it.

The dog did his business. When he returned, Maggie was still in the window waiting. Her face, in the yellow lamplight, looked lit from within. She slipped out of sight to open the door. He came inside. Maggie held out her hand.

"Come here, Big."

The dog raced to her, swiping her face with his tongue, which made her laugh and duck for cover.

SIXTEEN  ED

December 2018

The politically correct term was "gestational host," Ed soon learned. The baby would be a guest in Maggie's womb, a combination of Dawn's egg and Jake's sperm.

"Think of me as a baby B&B." Maggie needed shots to get ready for the egg transfer. Dawn had already started them, but now it was Ed's job to give them. The process was straightforward: she lay down on the couch, pulled up her dress, and slid down her underwear to expose her butt. The first time, he was startled. He rarely saw her undressed, especially in a lighted room. Her body had spread. Or was swollen. Her flesh made him think of taffy that was being pulled. Malleable and soft. Stretched and vulnerable.

If she got pregnant, he would have to give her these shots throughout the first three months. It made him queasy. The needle was almost two inches long. He distracted himself by reciting the steps in his head. Hold the syringe. Place the needle lightly on her flesh. Push it into her, press on the plunger, and watch the liquid flow. Afterward, he had to massage the area, so the medication was fully absorbed.

"I don't think I can do this. It's making me feel sick. Maybe we should call Dawn to come over."

"You need to get used to it, Ed. We can't have her come over every time, and the egg retrieval and implantation are happening soon. Consider it your contribution to this pregnancy."

He hoped it was the hormones making her snappy and not some midlife change to her formerly gentle personality. He thought again of Dr. Phil, who had talked about relationships being worked out together. If someone was dealing with one-sided demands all the time, then they were going to be stuck in a toxic marriage.

"You never asked me about getting pregnant. You went ahead and made the decision yourself. Or with Dawn. I don't really want any part in it, but you've left me no choice."

"Let's not rehash this now." She sighed and stared a little melodramatically into the throw pillow.

He placed the needle against her flesh and pushed it in. Maggie grimaced, twisted, and nearly fell off the couch. He had a rush of satisfaction, and then he felt terrible.

Within days, Maggie was bruised. She started wearing loose dresses, so nothing pressed on her hips or butt.

Ed tried, each time, to find a new patch of unbruised skin. His eyes watered as he shoved in the syringe and pushed the liquid deep into her flesh. He hoped she was not bruising because he was incompetent. He wanted to beg her to let him stop.

Dawn was also taking hormones to produce eggs for harvesting, which—he couldn't help it—reminded him of the chickens his mother had kept in a backyard coop when he was a boy. Dawn was such a pro that she could give herself shots. One in her stomach in the morning, one in her butt at night. When he asked her about the bruising, she said it was normal. That she had it, too. She was scheduled for her egg retrieval. It was her fifth time.

"Does the retrieval hurt?" Maggie was putting Chinese takeout on the table. Dawn and Jake had come over to help finish decorating the tree. Paul and Ashley had brought the boys over earlier to put on ornaments. The children's tree trimming lasted about ten minutes. The boys only put up the ornaments they had made in school from Popsicle sticks, felt, and foil, leaving the rest of the ornaments strewn across the floor. Dawn, who had always loved tree trimming, hung the others.

"I don't feel a thing while they do it. I have twilight sedation. They sort of hoover the eggs and wake me up. I cramp afterward. If it's bad, I have pain pills."

"Can I come with you?" Maggie paused with a plate of egg rolls midair.

Dawn looked at Jake, who nodded. "I could use the break. It's busy at work."

That Tuesday morning, Ed and Maggie drove Dawn to the University of Chicago's Center for Reproductive Medicine, where they sat in the waiting room until Dawn was in recovery. The procedure was quick—about an hour start to finish. Afterward, they drove their groggy daughter back to her house and Maggie settled her on the couch with a heating pad. Ed heated up some canned chicken noodle soup. He put three bowls and crackers on the coffee table, so no one had to get up. Maggie sipped hers. Dawn left hers untouched.

"Are you ready for this, Mom? I feel bad about what you're going to have to go through. The hard part."

"I've been pregnant before. I loved it, and I'll be carrying my grandchild. I could never have imagined it possible."

"You're not nervous at all?"

"Of course I am, but still thrilled to do it."

Dawn dozed off. Ed went into the den to watch a show on the History Channel, about Churchill during World War II. Maggie was settled into a chair and finishing *Gone Girl*.

Later, the fertility nurse called Dawn's cell, which she put on speaker so that Maggie and Ed, who rushed to stand nearby, could hear. Dr. Franklin had been able to collect eleven eggs from Dawn's ovary, which would produce at least three healthy embryos. They would pick two. The nurse scheduled the transfer for Maggie on Friday morning.

"It's really happening." Maggie looked thrilled.

"How do they pick which embryos to use?" This was all new to Ed.

Dawn took a bite out of a saltine and slowly chewed before she answered. "They have a rating system and use the ones likeliest to survive."

"What if they both survive?"

"Twins."

Maggie put her hand over her mouth for a second. "Really? Is that why I see so many more twins these days?"

"A lot of them are IVF babies." Dawn acted as if this was no big deal.

Ed held his face in neutral, a skill he had learned over all the years when he'd had to check his personal reactions. But his mind flooded with images of two red-faced bawling babies emerging from Maggie. He heard the words from a Dr. Seuss book he'd read to Teddy yesterday, while the boy was snuggled up against Big on the couch. *I do not like this, Sam I am.*

When it was time, Ed, Dawn, and Jake accompanied Maggie to the clinic for the transfer. They sat on hard purple chairs in the small waiting room that smelled of stale coffee. No actual coffee was offered. Old magazines—*People*, *Cooking Light*, and *Sports Illustrated*—were piled on an end table along with a box of Kleenex and a bottle of Purell. *It could be a little nicer*, Ed thought, considering what these doctors were charging.

This one treatment alone would cost more than $15,000, and it might not work. Ed knew this because he had insisted on paying, partly to assuage his guilt for his disapproval. Dawn and Jake would have had to borrow money. Maggie and he agreed they would prefer to spend some of their small savings than have the kids feel the financial pressure. They could forfeit a few of their restaurant nights, and if necessary, he could take another job after his retirement to make it up. They didn't want their kids to have a new baby and more debt.

It was mind-boggling to think of handing over this much money time and time again. He tried not to dwell on the success rate—about one in three. Not great odds, and it could also work too well and produce twins.

A nurse emerged from behind a door. She was carrying three bottles of water. "Who's the lucky recipient?"

"Me. The grandmother."

"Drink as much as you possibly can. Your bladder needs to be completely full for the procedure."

It took Maggie about twenty-five minutes to drink two and a half bottles, and Ed knew her bladder must be bursting. She sat stoic, paging through an old *People*, which he was sure she had absolutely no interest in. She didn't even like current gossip magazines.

The nurse reappeared. "Does anyone want to come with me? We'll see if she's ready."

Jake stayed behind. Ed and Dawn followed Maggie. Ed didn't want to watch, but he also didn't want Maggie to be without him. A technician appeared with two pairs of blue scrubs and paper shoe covers.

Dawn thanked the woman. "We need to put these on over our clothes, Dad."

Ed almost tripped as he pulled the scrubs over his khakis and again when he put the shoe covers over his sneakers.

Maggie changed in a bathroom. He and Dawn waited until she appeared, wearing a floppy pink hospital gown tied in front. There was something so exposed about a hospital gown. Maggie's skin looked almost transparent. The veins on her legs were visible and blue.

The technician asked Maggie to get on the table, place her feet in the stirrups, and open her gown. She rubbed gel on Maggie's stomach and pressed into it with the ultrasound's hand piece.

Dawn positioned herself so she could see the screen.

Ed stood next to Maggie.

"How does it look in there?" Maggie strained to see the screen but couldn't.

"Excellent." The technician walked to the phone and pressed a button to page the doctor.

Maggie waved her over. "Will it hurt?"

"No. It will feel a little strange, that's all."

A man in scrubs and a surgical cap appeared. "I'm Dr. Franklin." He shook their hands before he washed up.

He was a little guy, Ed noted, as the doctor turned the screen, beaming the image of Maggie's uterus toward them so they could watch the implantation. Probably the type of guy who was picked on as a kid. The doctor concentrated on the screen. Maggie's uterus looked enormous and dark like a cave.

"The embryos are ready," the technician called from across the room.

Ed turned to watch her carry over a small steel container. He placed his hand on Maggie's shoulder.

"Okay, Maggie." Dr. Franklin guided a tube into her. Ed hoped it really didn't hurt. On the screen, he saw the tube snaking forward and gave Maggie's shoulder a squeeze. "Get ready, here we go," Dr. Franklin said. A white drop flashed, shot through the tube, and disappeared into Maggie. The doctor leaned back, satisfaction on his face. "Perfect landing."

SEVENTEEN  CHARLOTTE

October 2018

Emory opened his office door. He wore a sports jacket, which was odd for him. His eyes skimmed Charlotte. "I only have an hour. A friend from LA came in unexpectedly, and I'm taking him to dinner." His voice sounded brusque, strained—a tone she had not heard him use before.

He moved to let her in. No kiss. No hand offered. Something was wrong. Something, she guessed, that would cause her pain. She followed him down the hallway and into his office. Someone, maybe his assistant, had filled a large black vase with shocking pink anemones and placed it on the coffee table. They must have cost a fortune.

"Wow, those are gorgeous." Despite his chilliness, Charlotte couldn't help herself.

Emory didn't reply. He motioned for her to sit in a chair and lowered himself into its twin across from her. Her jaw clenched. She wanted whatever was going to happen to be over, and she knew it was up to her. He'd had her come here to tell her he had other plans. He was playing some game she didn't understand, and she felt both crushed and duped.

"It's been hectic lately." He glanced past her as if she were a piece of furniture.

"Apparently."

"People expect a lot from me. They count on me."

"I see that. Are you saying I can't count on you?" Her head buzzed.

There was a tense silence. Emory stared out the window, which he usually covered with a linen shade. His eyes looked squinty. Evasive.

"How do you feel about me?" She astonished herself by cutting right to the point.

Her mind sped and bumped as she waited for an answer, which took a long time. With nothing to lose, she'd leapt from asking for too little information to asking for too much.

"I don't know." He sighed.

"You don't know how you feel?" She leaned back in her chair and peered directly at him. He tilted his head away from her gaze.

"I'm attracted to you. I like being with you." His voice flattened.

"Why did you start up with me?" She watched him squirm in his chair. Part of her was beginning to enjoy this; part of her was raging.

"Boredom . . . I guess."

"Really? Boredom?"

"Sex gets routine and boring after all these years. I guess I wanted a little excitement and thought it would be a fling."

"It's been more than a year," Charlotte said. "Not exactly a fling."

Boredom? Excitement? Fling? Her relationship with Emory actually had nothing to do with her at all. It was about Emory and Meredith. Or maybe just Emory. She was being dismissed and in the end, all dismissals are the same.

She sat, propped her feet on an ottoman, and waited. Pale orange light filtered through the window, tinting her bare knees the color of baby aspirin. Inside she was crashing. She had known this was coming and now it was here. "It's not enough. Attraction is not enough."

He was silent. She got up, gathered her things, and walked toward the hall. She heard his steps behind her, walking her to the door, but she did not turn. She would not let him see that he had broken her heart.

She headed toward her parking place. Leaves covered the ground, and burgundy, orange, and yellow mums flanked the stately houses. She passed a few nannies with toddlers returning from the local park. Her legs felt as if they might collapse from under her. She was bursting apart, and she had to keep moving.

The late afternoon air seemed to ripple as she opened her car. When she leaned forward to turn her key, she sensed a minuscule shift in her body, so tiny she placed it in the back of her mind where she would not remember it until later when Dr. Lee told her she was pregnant.

Emory called. He emailed.

"I was just trying to be truthful," he said. "Not make false promises. It doesn't mean I don't care. I care. I care a lot."

She wished she were the kind of person who could toss away letters and delete messages, but she wasn't. Still, she did not answer. She wondered what she had been to him. This would go unanswered. Undefined. She hated that.

Emory kept it up for three weeks. Then he stopped, and she discovered how much she hated being ignored. Her anguish battled with her work—the client trips, new designer seasons, and antique side tables. She was forgetful, no longer interested. Details, her specialty, cluttered her mind, and then escaped it.

Place order with Indian scarf company.
Call hotel in Paris for the Kaufmans.
Emory's hand on her thigh. On her face.
Talk to art broker.
Pick up a chicken for dinner.

While she was driving to Whole Foods to pick up the chicken, a bike appeared out of nowhere and darted in front of her. She slammed on her brakes but nearly hit him. He braked at the same instant, hit a pothole, and was thrown off onto the street where he lay sprawled. It happened in a split second. Sarah. This could have been Sarah. She could have killed someone. She stopped, hands on the wheel, pulled the car over, and ran toward him.

The biker got up and stalked toward her. He was muscular with bulging biceps and legs. A black bandanna covered his head. He did not appear to be hurt.

"Are you okay?" she asked, her heart pounding. "I'm so sorry. I didn't see you. That's no excuse, I know."

"None of you fucking bitches know how to drive." He moved closer. He wore thick silver rings. One, she saw, was a skeleton head. She backed away and ran to get into her car. He followed, pounding his fist on her hood. "Fucking bitch!" he yelled, pulling the bandanna off his head and waving it around like a weapon. "Stupid cunt." As he headed for her open window, she sped away, driving right past Whole Foods and any thoughts of chicken. The world was turning on her.

At home, still shaking, Charlotte lay down on her bed. She knew the close call had not been completely her fault. The biker had cut her off, and his fall was from a pothole, not her car. He was part of an aggressive bike culture in Chicago that broke traffic laws, flew through signs and lights, and then went after drivers and pedestrians. Still, she could not let it go. She should have seen him sooner. The words seemed personal, bored into her.

Bitch. Cunt. Stupid. Maybe he was right.

EIGHTEEN  CHARLOTTE

December 2018

I t was a Thursday night, six days after her CVS test, when Dr. Logan called Charlotte's cell phone. She was washing the dinner dishes. Luckily, Daniel had gone to a seven o'clock yoga class, so she didn't hesitate to answer.

"Charlotte, I have good news. You're carrying a healthy girl."

"Thank you." She was silent for a moment, then had a coughing fit.

"Are you all right?" The doctor sounded concerned.

"Sorry, I didn't realize how nervous I was." This was a lie. She'd been brimming with anxiety since she'd had the test, sure the baby was a chromosomal disaster.

"You're definitely not alone. But it's good news. I hate giving sad news. Congratulations."

"Thanks again." As Charlotte put the phone down, she thought of the tiny waving hand on the ultrasound image and smiled. This baby was real. She might have Emory's curls, his love of art and books. Maybe she would get his adorable dimple. She felt a rush of love, or possibly hormones, for the father of her baby. She let herself wonder what life would be like if they were together. Then she recovered. He'd been so callous during their last conversation. She had sat, stoically listening to him, while she was breaking apart. Using a baby to create a bond was a terrible idea.

The baby was a girl. Like Libby. Possibly a lot like Libby. She sat down hard on a kitchen chair. Libby was in a safe place for now in rehab. At some point, she'd have to know about the pregnancy, but she seemed fragile when Daniel and Charlotte went to the family meetings and visited her on weekends. Charlotte had still not been able to ask her about the car. She seemed unable to ask anyone anything these days. And now, Charlotte was about to further erode Libby's stability by leaving Daniel and having this baby. She hoped the stress wouldn't cause another relapse.

She might be the worst mother in the world.

At the rehab meetings, the families told their stories. It was not optional. Most of the stories were scary. Heroin. Crack. Overdoses. Dead friends. There were boxes of tissues neatly lined up on the tables, as well as plates of chemical-tasting sugar cookies and bitter coffee. The worst part was when people brought their children or grandchildren.

"My mother has a very small voice," said a six-year-old girl who had looked up from the picture she was coloring to talk. "That's why she took heroin. She's here to get her old voice back." Her older brother had refused to speak, and her grandmother reported that she had turned to prayer. That had almost brought Charlotte to tears. All of it had, even when they were all told to hang tough.

Addiction, it seemed, was not for sissies.

The rehab's education director, who led the meetings, had a husband who was a recovering alcoholic. She certainly looked worse for the wear. Most of the participants did. She gave this advice:

"Imagine you're in a boat pulling your loved one behind you in order to save her. If you haven't maintained your boat . . . if the boat is full of holes, you will both sink."

Charlotte felt as if she were already sinking along with Libby.

She finished the dishes and went upstairs to read. She changed into her nightgown, lay on top of the bed, and since she was alone, peeked at her abdomen. She stroked it, letting the full impact of the news sink in. Her baby was healthy. She'd been gearing up for the worst, so this amazed her, and now she wished she had someone with whom she could share this news. Her friend Nellie would be appalled, and she wasn't up for that.

"Hi in there, little girl, can you hear me?" she whispered.

"Hey, Charlotte." Daniel was home, bounding up the stairs to their bedroom.

She quickly pulled her nightgown down. "Did you have fun?"

"I'm exhausted. I'm going to shower and get ready for bed."

Charlotte read until he came to bed and turned out his light. When she finally put her book down, she tossed and turned, distressed and excited about both her baby girl and her big girl.

The next morning, she brought her coffee and buttered toast into her office. From her desk, she had an unobstructed view of the sidewalk. As she ate, she watched a man in jeans and a blue down coat walk a golden retriever. Two children in snowsuits trudged along behind a mother struggling to push a stroller through the snow. Chicago winters were long and hard, especially with small children. It had been difficult with one child. She couldn't imagine shepherding three through all that snow. Poor woman.

She tried to work, but she couldn't settle down, so she paced around the room. A rack of tagged clothes sat in the corner. Sweaters were stacked on a chair. The shelves were lined with her books. A valentine Libby had made for her in kindergarten was propped next to her computer. This was the only place in the house that was completely hers, and usually it was soothing. Not today. She thought of the Italian phrase her mother used. *Non comodo nella tua pelle.* Not comfortable in your own skin. She wanted to jump out of hers.

Finally, she sat down with one of her storyboards. Charlotte built outfits, rooms, and vacations on corkboards. Building a story was her favorite part of work. Head-to-toe ensembles with shoes, dresses, and bags were photographed from the boards, so the clothes were easy for clients to envision wearing. She also created rooms on boards, then put together pamphlets containing snapshots of antiques and art along with swatches of material.

For travel, she made a board for each day with side trips that included museums, cafés, and restaurants and then compiled folders with pictures, hotel brochures, and itinerary options. She knew which clients cared about beds and which clients cared about sea views. She did not waste her clients' time or money. She was specific and quick.

Through her work, Charlotte had come to understand that, while people generally noticed only the outside of things, the superficialities, the external could shift the internal—and vice versa. Clothes could be transforming and a boost for self-esteem. She translated fashion for the older, younger, thinner, or heavier: the flattering trick of a scarf's volume around the face, the pant that was cut to perfection for a wider backside, the swish of an intricately embroidered dress. It was wonderful to watch a woman looking at herself in a mirror, amazement on her face.

Part of Charlotte's job was to bring pleasure.

She had a client who was going to St. Barts, so she perused the online fashion shows. The models were young and gawky-looking in their sunglasses as they strutted down the runway. They made her think of Libby again. She would never completely understand what had happened. How had her sweet baby transformed from a funny toddler into a sullen, troubled girl? A sad and angry girl with whom she had to tread softly. A girl she no longer knew how to reach. One who might be lost to her.

Charlotte's pregnancy with Libby had been easy. When she had felt her first pain one night, she had mistaken it for appendicitis as she doubled over on the bed where Daniel was reading.

He had looked up, his face turning a greenish white. "Charlotte, you're bleeding. There's blood all over."

She was in so much pain, she couldn't speak. Her due date was two days away.

"Come on. We're going to the hospital." He'd jumped out of bed. "I think you're having the baby."

She had tried to get up but could not. Daniel had grabbed two towels, which he placed under her. Then he'd picked her up and carried her to the garage. This could not have been easy. "Do you want to lie down in the back seat?"

She had shaken her head. She wanted the seat belt and was afraid she might have the baby in the back of the car. Daniel helped her into the front seat and belted her.

Charlotte remembered how fast he had driven, how every pothole on the Outer Drive made her want to scream. The pains were right on top of each other. This couldn't be right, she had thought. Labor was supposed to start slowly and build. She didn't know why this was happening, but she was in too much agony to care.

Daniel had left the car in the hospital's driveway and carried her in. She couldn't stand, so she lay on the floor in front of the Labor and Delivery desk.

"I think my wife is having the baby right now. She can't get up."

"I'll page a doctor." The woman behind the desk looked down at Charlotte. "Can you try and stand?"

"No!" Charlotte had screamed.

A female doctor appeared with two male orderlies. They hoisted Charlotte onto a bed they'd wheeled over. The doctor pulled up the nightgown Charlotte was wearing.

"Remove your underwear."

"I can't." The pain was breaking her in two. It was everything. The doctor had huffily bent down to take her underwear, and Charlotte had silently wished this doctor the worst labor in the world.

The doctor tossed Charlotte's underwear on the bed. "The baby's crowning."

A security guard appeared. "Sir, you have to move your car."

"My wife's having a baby. Now."

"It'll only take a minute to pull it into the garage. It's fire code. You can't leave it there."

Daniel sprinted off to move the car. By the time he was back, Libby had been born.

Libby was a small, alert baby with a tuft of dark hair. Daniel and Charlotte had watched, enraptured, as she was cleaned, weighed, and wrapped in a pink blanket. A pink hat covered her head.

"She's beautiful." Daniel carefully ran his finger over Libby's cheek. "She doesn't look smushed like the books said she would."

Charlotte smiled. She was exhausted.

"I'm sorry I missed her birth." Daniel kissed her on the cheek. "That damn security guard."

"You're here now. It all happened so fast."

"The doctor said you're a medical freak. You never felt labor, only transition."

"I didn't know what was going on. She really is a beauty, isn't she?"

Daniel had walked alongside them as his wife and daughter were wheeled to a room. It was nearly midnight. "Will you be okay if I go home and get some sleep?"

"Yes." She really wanted him to stay, and he must have sensed that.

"I bet we can get someone to bring in a chair I can sleep on."

He slept next to her bed, and when she woke in the middle of the night, he was holding her hand.

Libby had been perfect in the hospital. But as soon as she was home, she screamed for hours. Charlotte paced up and down with her while Daniel was at work. She was worried and didn't know what to do. No amount of walking or bouncing seemed to help. There was no escape. Libby cried and cried, her little face turning red, her eyes scrunched shut.

She called her new pediatrician, sure that there was something wrong with either the baby or her. "Colic. It's very common."

"How long does it last?"

"Three to four months," the doctor said.

Charlotte thought she might collapse before then. Daniel held Libby and walked for a few hours each night but said he needed his sleep for work. So, Charlotte went downstairs whenever the baby woke up.

The colic finally did pass, but Libby woke at midnight, at two, and then for the day at four in the morning. Charlotte wondered how mothers had survived all these years. Babies, too. She fantasized about getting a good night's sleep and was actively jealous of anyone who looked well-rested.

It was two years before Libby slept through the night, and when she finally did, Charlotte was elated. They went to the playground, the zoo, and to Moms and Tots class. Libby would only eat peanut butter on Triscuits and wear clothes that were red, but it was okay. Libby laughed, sang, and had an extensive vocabulary for a toddler. They had a good time together.

Libby made it to kindergarten before she started demanding a bath in the morning and another after school. It had to be given in a specific order, starting with hair washing. If a step was skipped, a tantrum with hitting and biting ensued. Charlotte thought she'd never heard a child shriek as loudly as Libby. It sounded as if she were being murdered, and Charlotte half expected the police to show up.

By the time Libby was seven, stairs had to be taken with her right foot first, and sidewalk cracks could never be stepped on. Walls were tapped three times, which was her number. There were times she still giggled and played, but they were becoming less frequent. At night, she lined up her stuffed animals in species groups and got up to check on them repeatedly. Charlotte and Daniel could hear her long after she was supposed to be asleep.

Charlotte feared Libby's behaviors were not those of a happy child. One night, listening to Libby roaming her room, she turned to Daniel, who was reading. "I'm worried about her."

"She'll grow out of it. Children go through phases."

Charlotte thought it was more than a phase and that Libby might need help.

Daniel was skeptical, but Charlotte made an appointment for Libby with a psychiatrist recommended by Libby's pediatrician.

She sat in for the first session while Libby played with toys on the floor. After that, Libby went in alone and Charlotte sat in the small waiting room where a sound machine blocked out all noise. Charlotte strained, unsuccessfully, to hear what was going on. By the sixth session, Libby was diagnosed with OCD and was started on a small amount of medication.

Still, Libby's symptoms worsened over the years, and medication only helped minimally. Daniel began snapping at Charlotte.

"I can't believe you're giving her mind-altering drugs. They're not even helping. I don't like all this psychiatry bullshit."

"Her doctor says she needs them, but I'll make an appointment to talk to her. Would you like to come?"

"No, and that hour will be another three hundred bucks."

"I honestly don't know what I'm supposed to do, Daniel. She needs help." He was frustrated. She understood. She was as well. Still, it was too much. She left the family room and walked upstairs to get as far away from his words as she could.

Charlotte went to her appointment, eager for the doctor to fill her in.

"Libby likes her OCD. She's used to it, and she's afraid of change. She fights the meds, but she still needs to take them. Until she's ready to cooperate with cognitive behavioral therapy, there's not much I can do except continue seeing her and talking about it, especially the thoughts. Those do bother her, particularly when she has them a lot."

"What are the thoughts about?"

"Mostly about you dying if she doesn't do things in exactly the right order. Her rituals, like walking up steps a certain way, relieve the anxiety temporarily. When the thought enters her mind again, she needs relief again, and the tics become repetitive."

"Did I cause this?" It was usually the mother's fault. Or had mother-blaming gone out of style?

The doctor shook her head. "No, this is a neurobiological disorder. It may also be genetic, and certain things at certain times can trigger it. There's still a lot we need to learn about it."

"She's only ten."

"I know. And hopefully we'll learn more. There are various levels of OCD. Libby's is severe. You're in this for the long haul."

"It never goes away?"

"It can be controlled. As she gets older, the tics may bother her enough that she develops the skills to overcome them."

"In the meantime, what should I do?"

"Encourage her not to tic. Ask her to stop. Hold her hand when she's anxious. Keep bringing her in once a week, so I can monitor her."

Charlotte walked home and dreaded having to tell Daniel that this was a lifetime commitment. But all children were lifetime commitments.

NINETEEN  CHARLOTTE

December 2018

For three weeks, Charlotte had done nothing, and now it was almost Christmas. She had not miscarried, nor had she told anyone she was twelve weeks pregnant. She was crossing the first-trimester threshold, and the holidays were upon her.

Libby had made it through rehab and would be coming home for the holidays. Tasks ticked through Charlotte's mind.

Pick up the organic turkey at Whole Foods.
Send an orchid to her in-laws.
Schedule three-month sonogram.
Freshen Libby's bed.
Leave lilies on her nightstand.
Put clean towels in Libby's bathroom.
Tell Daniel she was pregnant.
God, yes, she had to tell him.

Libby would be here soon, staying with them for a few days, before she went back to her apartment and job in New York. There was a good chance she would notice her mother's expanding abdomen. Weight-obsessed Libby was far more observant than Daniel, and if she discovered Charlotte was pregnant before Daniel found out, it would turn this situation into an even bigger disaster.

Last night at dinner, Charlotte had tried to tell Daniel about the baby. She'd made a large pot of saffron and parmesan risotto, one of her favorite meals. It was delicious, and she'd been famished. She was hungry all the time now.

Daniel stared at her as she polished off half her bowl. "You're eating like a trucker."

Charlotte couldn't believe he'd said that. "I'm eating for—"

"What?"

"That's not nice. What you said. The trucker thing." She pushed her plate away.

"You're eating a ton. It's the truth." Daniel went back to delicately cutting his asparagus. He only liked the tips. "And mostly carbs."

She'd wanted to brain him, possibly with the cast-iron risotto pot. Instead, she leaned forward to announce she was pregnant and knocked over the glass of wine that Daniel poured her every night. She was still sneaking the glass into the powder room to pour it out when Daniel got up after dinner. Wine-soaked paper towel in hand, she gave up. She would have one more chance tomorrow morning before Libby arrived.

"Let's watch something on Netflix." The dishes were done, and she didn't want to talk to him anymore. A movie was always a good solution.

"You pick. You always know something good."

Charlotte scrolled through the titles until she found I Am Love, which a couple friends had recommended. The film starred Tilda Swinton, whose ethereal face and ability to morph into parts, including male ones, fascinated Charlotte. To be a complete chameleon must be wonderful. Not to be stuck inside oneself. It would be like getting inside other people's heads and having the chance to inhabit other personalities. She guessed it could be both freeing and disturbing.

They sat, lights off, in the family room. Daniel was in his chair and Charlotte lay on the couch. Her head rested on a pillow, and she covered her legs with a throw. The film was slow, gorgeously shot, and set in a lavish house in Milan, where three generations of an aristocratic family gathered for a birthday party. The camera lingered in rooms and on faces. Charlotte was captivated.

After about fifteen minutes, Daniel started to snore so loudly he woke himself up. "Had enough. Heading upstairs."

"You don't like it?"

"I'm having trouble concentrating on the subtitles. You can understand the Italian, so go ahead and watch."

By the time she went upstairs, Daniel was asleep again. She was glad. She was still angry about his trucker comment and mad at herself for not being able to tell him about the baby. She settled into bed thinking of Tilda Swinton's character, Emma, making love to a young, handsome chef outside in the country. The love scene seemed so unlike the character, who was proper, shy, and reclusive. The movie was a quiet bodice ripper, but Charlotte was touched by the urgency and the happiness Emma radiated with the chef. She missed that.

She thought back to her younger self. How she'd walked with Daniel down the streets of Paris on their honeymoon, their arms wrapped around each other. How, at the beginning, Daniel had made love to her every night. Sometimes twice. How they'd gone to dinner and could hardly wait to talk to each other. Where had that gone? Some of their troubles revolved around their disagreements over Libby. Some around his parents, who'd never liked Charlotte. They used any opportunity they could to criticize her both to her face and behind her back. She was controlling, extravagant, overly indulgent as a mother, and cold. Daniel ignored their meanness, instead of sticking up for her, which never failed to take the wind out of Charlotte.

Charlotte had first met Daniel's family when she was invited, or as Daniel put it, summoned, to swim and have a Fourth of July dinner at the Oakeses' suburban home. Fireworks at their country club would follow. She had never been to a country club or met a guy's parents. She was twenty-one and had just graduated from Vassar with absolutely no idea what she should do with her future. It did not look bright with an art history major and American literature minor. She was temping until she figured it out.

"A country club, really?" Her mother frowned. "They don't like our kind there." She was teaching a summer course on modern Italian literature at the University of Chicago, and Charlotte had interrupted her paper grading to ask what to wear.

"I think it's a Jewish club, Mom. Not that you even know when a Jewish holiday is."

"They still won't like our kind. We're not country club people." She went back to scratching little red comments on the papers. "Those people need to belong to a place that keeps others out to feel important." Her mother, Lucca, was surrounded by abandoned mugs of tea and a plate of browning apple slices. The housekeepers of Charlotte's childhood had retired. Her mother could no longer stand people around, so the large house had settled into a permanent state of disaster.

Charlotte decided not to ask her mother for fashion advice. Lucca usually disapproved of the way Charlotte looked, which made her worry her mother thought she was unattractive. It didn't help that Charlotte was a foot taller than Lucca, who constantly suggested outfits that might make Charlotte look smaller, thinner, and more feminine. This had particularly hurt when Charlotte was a teenager. Despite her academic successes and outward nonchalance, Lucca, a beauty, had always been proud of her looks. Attractiveness was important in the Ellison family. Although she'd eventually grown into herself, Charlotte had trouble believing she was pretty.

She consulted over the phone with her cousin Leah, a college graduate who lived in her own one-bedroom apartment. Leah worked at Saks and knew quite a bit about clothes.

"Country club casual. Who are you going with?"

"This guy, Daniel, who I like a lot."

"You're dating him?"

"Yeah, for about six weeks. He's a friend of my roommate. What does country club casual mean? Shorts?"

"Actually, it's like a trick. It means country club clothes. Not casual at all. It's bright green, pink, or madras pants on men. The women like those awful Lilly Pulitzer dresses. I think you should wear something silky, definitely not shorts."

Charlotte did not own anything silky. Leah loaned her a pair of lavender silk pants and a white shirt with tiny pearl buttons. The pants were slightly short, but they would do. Charlotte put her one bathing suit, a faded black bikini, and a towel into a straw basket she used as a purse.

Daniel picked her up in his Mazda sports car on the Fourth of July. He was wearing wrinkled khaki shorts and a faded red polo shirt. "You look nice. Maybe a little dressy."

"Should I change?" She did not admit to the borrowed clothes.

"Nah, we'll be late. They like to eat early and get good seats for the fireworks."

She wondered what made for a good seat at fireworks, since

they were above everyone's head, but decided not to ask. She rummaged in her basket for her sunglasses and put the towel in the back.

"Why did you bring a towel?"

"We're going swimming."

"My mother has pool towels. You don't need that."

"I thought it was polite. So she doesn't have to do extra laundry."

"Don't worry about that. She doesn't do laundry. Rose, her housekeeper, does everything."

Charlotte realized she didn't know much about his family other than that he had a sister named Kathy. He never talked about his parents. The drive was nearly an hour and Charlotte was jittery, studying the long driveways and green lawns of the North Shore. Her family rarely left the city. Visiting Hyde Park on the South Side for her mother's faculty events seemed suburban.

Her family lived in Uptown in a rambling Queen Anne. They'd bought the house when the area was mostly poor and called Hillbilly Heaven because of all the Appalachians who piled into the subdivided mansions. The house was close to the park, and her parents had liked the idea of being urban pioneers. It had been cheap, but in need of major repairs, and was large enough for a big family. Now the neighborhood was completely changed. The houses were renovated, expensive, and had historic status, despite their street abutting a gritty neighborhood. The house was now worth a fortune.

Driving through the North Shore, no one was out walking on the clean sidewalks, and all she could hear was the occasional lawnmower. The landscapers were the only people outside. Charlotte caught the glint of the lake through tree branches as they whizzed down Sheridan Road past enormous, gated mansions, leftovers from an earlier era. It felt empty.

The Oakeses' house was a medium-sized brown ranch set on a treeless lot. Charlotte noticed that old trees arched over the lawns of surrounding homes. This house seemed bare and sad. Where were their trees? Daniel noticed her glancing around.

"Everything okay?"

"I was wondering about the trees. All the other houses have trees."

"My parents had them cut down. They don't want any bird poop, especially near the pool."

This statement took a minute to sink in. Her parents had bird feeders. These people cut down trees to get rid of birds.

Daniel's mother met them at the door. Mrs. Oakes was dressed for the holiday in white shorts, a blue top with a sparkly American flag pin, and a red belt. Charlotte, who towered over her, had a good view of her perfect blonde bob, which gave off a strong scent of hair spray. She worried again that Leah had misinformed her, and she was dressed completely wrong. Mrs. Oakes grasped her hand but did not shake it. She turned it over in hers as if searching for something. She had glossy peach nails and wore a large, rectangular diamond ring that reminded Charlotte of an ice cube.

"Call me Kiki." Her voice was smooth, her vowels perfectly enunciated. "So nice to meet you. My, you're tall. So statuesque." Charlotte felt a chill of premonition. This woman hated her.

When Charlotte emerged after changing into her bikini in the powder room, Daniel's sister Kathy—it had to be Kathy—was walking down the hall. She had the female version of Daniel's face with hazel eyes, a perfect nose, tanned skin, and wavy blondish-brown hair. Kathy took one look at Charlotte and handed her the slightly damp towel she was carrying. Kathy was on the short side, like her mother, and bottom-heavy in her black one-piece.

"Hi. You must be Charlotte. Nice to meet you. Daniel's so secretive about who he's dating."

Charlotte smiled and nodded.

"He broke up with the last one so fast we only saw her once. She was super tacky. Worked at Barneys' makeup counter."

"Hmmm, nice to meet you." Charlotte was now anxious about how fast Daniel broke up with his last girlfriend and confused about what to do with the towel dangling over her arm. On top of this awkwardness, Kathy was staring at her—running her eyes up and down Charlotte's body.

"FYI, my mother doesn't like bikinis. She thinks they're slutty. Probably because she could never wear one. You look fantastic, by the way."

"Oh." She was at a loss for words. In Italy, even the old fat grandmas with saggy breasts and fleshy stomachs wore bikinis. Her grandmother, who was seventy-six, wore one and looked good. Kathy probably thought Charlotte was tacky like Daniel's last girlfriend.

Charlotte wanted to get away and go outside. She could see the inviting blue pool through the windows and longed to dive in. She loved pools, their still promise, even their chlorine scent.

She wrapped Kathy's towel over her swimsuit and remained like that for the rest of the afternoon, dipping her toes into the water while Daniel and Kathy swam. The rest of the towels, all an identical royal blue, sat perfectly folded in a basket on the flagstone bordering the pool.

Charlotte sweated in the hot sun and dabbed on sunscreen every hour. She pretended to read *Jane Eyre*, her summer project and a requirement for a class, Love and Autonomy, she was taking in the fall. She couldn't concentrate. Daniel and Kathy threw a ball back and forth.

Daniel lobbed the ball at Charlotte. "Come on in. It's like bathwater."

"Later, I need to finish this chapter."

Daniel's father, Henry, a handsome man with a bony nose, appeared and said hello. Henry made no further attempt at conversation. He sat down and read *Time* magazine at a table under an umbrella. Kiki had disappeared. Charlotte finally dropped the towel and slid from the edge into the pool, swimming its length underwater. She emerged dripping, moving quickly to avoid Kathy's gaze, and resumed her covered position.

When Daniel and Kathy got out of the pool to change, Charlotte went back to the powder room to put Leah's clothes back on. No one was around, and she had a few seconds to prowl around the living room. The house, she'd noticed before, did not look lived in. It had no smells, good or bad. Nothing was out of place. Decorative brown pillows were spaced precisely along a tan couch. The coffee table looked as if it had been sculpted from beige paper and had large *National Geographic* types of books stacked in one corner. Blown glass trees, which made her think of a fairy tale gone awry, were displayed in an opposite corner. Two chairs matched the couch and a hairy brown rug rested between them. The abstract art on the walls was equally muted. Muddy. The room had an eerie sparseness. She felt as if she had stepped into a foreign country, a hostile one.

Dinner was hot dogs, potato chips, and coleslaw on paper plates. Charlotte had not been to a party with hot dogs since she was five. Even her mother, who was always working, pulled together a risotto or grilled branzino for company. Maybe she wasn't considered company. Maybe they figured Daniel would break up with her soon. Charlotte was astonished when, after they ate, Kathy folded the four corners of the paper tablecloth around the mess, gathered them and dumped the whole thing in a garbage bag. She had never seen anyone do anything like this.

At the club, they sat on folding chairs on an expansive lawn and faced the darkening lake. Ladies in gray uniforms with white aprons took drink orders from the grown-ups and circled with cotton candy, popcorn, and snow cones for the children.

Women swooped in and air-kissed Kiki. Girls stopped by to greet Daniel. They were clearly the type of girls Daniel was meant to marry—sturdy, tan, tennis-playing girls.

"Drink, Charlotte?"

She nodded, even though she was not used to drinking. Daniel ordered two gin and tonics, and she was thankful for a few sips of alcohol, despite disliking its taste. Soon she heard a sizzle and a gold ball burst in the sky.

"Beautiful." She did love fireworks.

"Just wait." Daniel held her hand.

The drink muddled her head and she watched, mesmerized, as stars, hearts, and flowers exploded in fuchsias, greens, and golds over the lake. She leaned into Daniel. During a red, white, and blue finale, a piece of flaming debris landed on an empty chair nearby, flaring and sparking. Daniel grabbed her arm and pulled her away. Guests screamed. A bartender quickly doused the fire with water from an ice bucket. The air smelled burnt. The crowd was quiet. More drinks were passed on trays. Ice clinked. Charlotte, shaken, accepted a second from Daniel.

"That doesn't usually happen." Daniel examined the burnt chair. "Except once the fireworks guy blew off his hand."

"Is it okay to leave? It's over, right?" Guests were getting up and milling around where the fire had been. No one seemed concerned. She was exhausted from the evening and the drink and wanted to get out of there.

"Let's go say goodnight to my parents."

Charlotte set her still-full drink on a tray, and they gave their goodbyes.

They were comfortably quiet on the car ride home listening to a Bonnie Raitt CD, watching as the dark suburbs gave way to city lights. Daniel drove the long way, so they passed Argyle Street, with its Vietnamese restaurants, and drove by the Aragon Ballroom and the Green Mill, where Charlotte's parents went to listen to jazz. Daniel pulled into a space in front of her mostly dark house.

He kissed her in the doorway, slid his hand underneath her shirt, and she felt a thrill as he inched under her bra. This was the farthest they'd gone, which she was finding frustrating. She could see the light in her parents' bedroom upstairs. Her mother was probably reading while her father slept. "Want to get back in the car? We'd have more privacy. I think my mom's still up." The question of her virginity had not yet come up. It was long gone.

"Nah, we'll continue this later. It'll give me something to look forward to."

She stifled her disappointment, and he gave her a long goodnight kiss that filled her with longing. She wanted more. There was something about him, even though it was still early in their relationship, that made her want him to want her. To choose her. And she was afraid he wouldn't.

"I think your mother would be happier if you were dating one of those girls from the club."

"They're so boring. And she's never really happy about anything."

"She didn't like me." Charlotte stood still, waiting for an answer, but Daniel didn't hear her. He had already turned toward the car.

TWENTY

ED

December 2018

Maggie was not allowed to do an at-home pregnancy test. The nurse at the clinic was adamant about this. "It's very tempting. But the results are often false with in vitro. A blood test is the most reliable." She scheduled Maggie for the test, which would measure the exact amount of HCG pregnancy hormone in her blood. "Take it easy the rest of the week, Maggie. Put your feet up. Order in."

"I hate this waiting." That was her only complaint, but she told Ed at least twice a day. Ed hated it, too.

Time was moving slowly. He was usually happy during the holiday season. He loved Christmas music and the decorations. The white lights strung along Michigan Avenue, which normally cheered him, only reminded him of how early it was getting dark. He was cold all the time, especially outside, where his fingers and feet went numb. He needed an extra nip of whiskey when he got home.

"Don't overdo it." Maggie noticed him pouring another splash into his glass.

"I need a little more. My nerves are acting up."

They sat in silence for a few minutes, while he sipped his drink. "Can I ask you something, Mags?"

"Of course."

"How do you feel with those embryos inside you? I mean, they may not be growing, but they're still in there."

"I don't feel much." She gazed down at her abdomen. "No nausea or anything like the other times. Nothing, actually."

"I just wondered."

"It is weird, isn't it? Maybe it didn't work. With Dawn and Jake, I felt pregnant pretty quickly."

There was a knock on their front door, the sound of a key, and the turn of the knob. Big jumped up, barked, and then leapt on Dawn. The more comfortable Big became, the worse his manners were, as if he had only been polite until he was sure they were going to keep him.

Ed stood up. "Down, Big."

"Get off me, you damn horse!" Dawn was not a fan of Big. "I brought some salad over for Mom. I know she doesn't like making it."

Irritation spiked in Ed. What Dawn meant was that if Maggie was pregnant, she should be eating her vegetables.

"Bad time?" Dawn must have sensed his annoyance.

"Not at all." Maggie stood up and gave her a hug. "Thanks, sweetie. Can you stay and have some supper? There's a meatloaf in the oven. And now some salad. I was counting the ketchup as a veggie tonight. I've been busy."

"Thanks, I can't. Jake's in the car. We're meeting some friends. You're not walking that dog alone, are you, Mom?"

"Your dad walks him, and we have a dog walker when he's not here." She looked hurt by the question.

Dawn rushed out the door, as if she were going to save someone in battle. "See you later." God, she was loud.

That was the end of Ed and Maggie's discussion. They both had grown up in families where feelings were off-limits. If someone asked how you were doing, the expected answer was "Just fine, thank you, and you?" No intimate information was ever revealed.

The next morning, listening to Dr. Phil on the car radio, Ed thought about how little Maggie and he communicated. "Communicate" was one of Dr. Phil's favorite words. Ed liked the feel of the word in his mouth. The way he had to purse his lips for the m's and the way his tongue touched the roof of his mouth for the "cate" part. Dr. Phil had preached to talk to your partner about feelings, even though it could be tough. He said understanding each other's emotions made healthy relationships.

At first, Ed thought all the talk about emotions was silly shrink-speak, but as he mulled over the concept, he could not remember a time when he'd told Maggie he was angry or frightened or sad, not even after he lost Tommy. He'd had so many feelings: grief, powerlessness, rage. He never shared these. He thought it wasn't manly and wanted to shelter his wife from his sorrow and fears.

Maggie, a former chatterbox and lover of church gossip and neighborhood news, had grown quiet over the years. She divulged little these days beyond updates on the kids, what needed fixing in the house, and the dishes she was making for dinner. She never talked about herself. So, Ed didn't know if she was happy. He tried to lighten things up at dinner by telling jokes he'd heard at work. The G-rated ones.

"Mags, what's the difference between a piano and a fish?"

"No idea."

"You can't tune a fish."

"Oh, Ed," she had laughed, spitting a little water out and covering her mouth.

"Okay, got another. Why don't they play poker in the jungle?

"Tell me."

"Too many cheetahs."

"That's really bad." But she had laughed at this joke, too. She was polite that way.

Their sex life wasn't much anymore, either. Once a month, if he was lucky. Lately, it was less. He figured that came with time, but he couldn't remember when their disinterest had started. Was it mutual? Maybe it wasn't. Maybe she wanted more or less or for him to buy her pretty nighties or something. What if she didn't like sex anymore? Or, even worse, sex with him? Should sex be something to let go of?

When they were young, sex was all they thought about, one of the big reasons good Catholic girls like Maggie married early. They'd had many a happy afternoon in bed, before the kids and even when the kids were little and napping. He had been bowled over again and again by her bare skin, her round bottom, her breasts, her red hair on the white pillowcase.

It all seemed foreign now, as if these memories belonged to another life. He missed that life.

Maggie no longer mentioned the cruise, which he supposed they could go on even if she did get pregnant. Perhaps she was angry with him about that. Or hurt. He should ask if she would still like the trip and offer to go. A trip would give them something to look forward to and talk about. Maggie might make one of her scrapbooks. She loved to collect tickets, brochures, and pictures. She called it "capturing memories."

Somehow, he had to start a conversation about feelings. Maybe a cruise was the way to make this happen. He was certain Maggie didn't want to hear about his time at the intersection. He wondered what she would say if he told her about Charlotte and her flowers. Probably that Charlotte was as crazy as he was—one more crackpot—and Ed was wasting time while

Charlotte wasted time and money. Buying flowers and discarding them, even as a memorial, was not something someone as frugal as Maggie would understand.

The two women had completely different backgrounds. He saw many different types of people through police work. Americans didn't talk about class, he remembered hearing on some radio or TV show, but it certainly existed. Education. Homes. Expectations. Class certainly separated Maggie and Charlotte. There was even a physical difference between them. Maggie was adorable. Small and curvy. Cuddly. Her clothes, which she rarely bought, were on the matronly side. She had a thing for matching sweatsuits. Charlotte, who was lanky, dressed like women in magazines, like a woman who was used to getting what she wanted. Even her voice was different. She lacked the Chicago twang. The accent.

It was odd that he felt so comfortable with Charlotte, whom he had first thought of as aloof. There were big differences between them in both age and class. But, somehow, it didn't matter. Perhaps it was their shared sadness, and how they both hung onto it.

He turned off Dr. Phil and switched to a station playing Bob Dylan. "Like a Rolling Stone." It was perfect. Dylan was speaking to him and was frigging brilliant. Ed let the words wash over him. Christ. He was losing it. Of course, Maggie loved him. The sex thing was normal. They were older. It was the uncertainty of this pregnancy that was driving him crazy. He had no idea what their lives would be like if Maggie got pregnant. She might be exhausted and possibly bedridden.

Chances were the implantation would not take the first time. Dawn told them not to be disappointed if the first try failed. Part of him, despite his considerable investment, hoped it would fail. As scientific as it seemed, this whole thing was something of a crapshoot. It just didn't seem right that Maggie could give birth to their grandchild.

He knew pregnancy must have been on Maggie's mind last night, as she baked Christmas cookies for their grandsons and organized the gifts she'd been buying all year. He still had to get her present. Every year he swore he would do it early, but he always waited until the last minute.

He passed the neighborhood florist and parked on a whim. The window was filled with red poinsettias. One of those would look great on the coffee table and be a nice surprise for Maggie. The florist wrapped the plant in cellophane with a big red bow.

He quietly opened the front door and placed it on the table. "Hey, Mags. Come here."

She appeared with Big, wearing a green sweatsuit. He watched her face as she smiled in surprise. The soft wrinkles on her cheeks. Ed flooded with love. He could not imagine life without her.

"Oh, Ed, that's beautiful." She plopped down on the couch and covered her face. She was crying, not the reaction he'd expected. Big took a giant leap, his curly hair flying. He landed next to Maggie, put his head in her lap, and nudged her with his wet nose.

"Honey, what's the matter? Is there something wrong with the plant?"

"No, I'm so tired." She wiped tears with her arm.

He pushed Big over and sat beside Maggie, wrapping his arms around her. She leaned into his chest before she raised her head. "Ed, I'm pregnant. It worked."

He caught himself before he could say, "You're kidding." Somehow, he hadn't really thought it would happen. "Are you worried, Mags? Is that it? Worried about the pregnancy?"

"I guess I am."

Ed squeezed her tighter. "Me too. But it's what you wanted, and it will all work out." He smelled the familiar scent of her powder and felt a niggling regret because he would not be the father of this baby.

TWENTY-ONE

December 2018

A nother opportunity passed. She had failed, yet again, to tell Daniel about her pregnancy. She was a coward, and she was running out of time. Libby was arriving tonight. This morning, Daniel had been in a rush for work, and it seemed like a bad moment. Disgusted with herself, she tried practicing in front of the bathroom mirror.

"Daniel, I have something to tell you."

"Daniel, I'm three months pregnant."

"We need to talk."

Nothing sounded right, and she felt like an idiot talking to herself in the mirror. She *was* an idiot. She hiked up her shirt, pulled down her maternity jeans, and looked at her round, hard belly. She had to say something, and it had to be soon.

The lighted Christmas tree beamed at her when she went downstairs. They were Christmas tree Jews as were the generations before them. Charlotte and Daniel had bought and decorated the tree this past weekend, enjoying their time picking it out. Both loved going to the tree lot with its heavy scent of pine. Charlotte liked stomping about in the cold and assessing the merits or faults of each tree. They'd chosen an eight-foot Fraser fir, hauled it home on the top of Daniel's car, and then decorated it with the ornaments they'd collected over the years. Colorfully wrapped gifts were piled underneath. Tiny white lights framed the front door. Daniel even mentioned setting up Libby's childhood electric train but had not done it yet.

The tree cheered Charlotte a little. Maybe too much. Sometimes, she worried that objects were overly important to her, a reaction to a childhood of cluttered, dusty rooms and lumpy beds with faded quilts and old foam pillows. Her parents had rebelled against their refined and well-staffed childhood households by neglecting their own. They cared little about their surroundings. The only material things her parents considered important were books, which were piled all over their house. Charlotte was a reader, but her books were neatly shelved, her papers stacked on her desk. Disorder unnerved her.

As a child, she had longed for order, comfort, and beauty. She always looked forward to the yearly visits at her grandparents' house in Italy where the sheets were pressed, the pillows were filled with down, and the antique furniture was polished. Bougainvillea had draped the house. Lavender and roses bloomed in the yard. *Piccoli conforti*, her nonna had said when Charlotte admired these niceties. Little comforts.

Italy brought Charlotte the pleasures she had craved and filled her with something that had been missing. Now in her living room, she shut her eyes and tried to conjure up the scents of lavender and rosemary. The salt air she could almost taste as she ate dinner outside, where she could hear the splash of the water on the rocks below. If only she could wind herself through time and space and into the past.

She opened her eyes slowly and moved a potted white amaryllis from the coffee table to the marble fireplace mantel. Its stem formed an elegant curve against the pale blue wall. She dusted the coffee table with its tableaus: a small, shell-encrusted bowl from a shipwreck; a milky glass vase with a pale orange, overblown poppy bending at its neck; a small, oval red-and-gold antique Italian reliquary. These beautiful things, these little comforts, were meant to keep the world and its miseries at bay, but they failed her more each day.

After tidying, Charlotte retrieved a bottle of white wine from the fridge along with Daniel's Scotch from the kitchen cabinet and carried them downstairs. Since Libby had been in rehab for alcohol, Charlotte kept all the liquor in a locked basement closet when she was visiting. A removal of temptation. Interestingly, Libby had never mentioned the closet.

Charlotte opened the door with a thumbprint reader lock above the knob, and hurriedly—too hurriedly—set the wine on a shelf. She watched as the bottle teetered and crashed to the floor, breaking into shards and pooling all over. She knelt to collect the shards and cut her finger, which began to bleed. She started to cry out of frustration more than pain. Why was she even moving the wine? It made no sense. Libby could legally buy liquor and illegally buy Oxy.

She applied pressure with her other hand and went to get a Band-Aid. Once the bleeding stopped, she had to clean up the mess with rags and a dust buster. She went at it, furious with herself for rushing and for pointlessly locking up liquor, and furious with Libby for being an addict. The glass was completely shattered, and it took a long time before she was sure she'd found every piece.

While Daniel picked up Libby at the rehab clinic, Charlotte made her daughter's favorite dinner: wild mushroom lasagna with béchamel sauce, Caesar salad, and a pear tart. The food at the rehab was dreadful. It would be nice to welcome Libby with something celebratory.

She sliced the pears, trying to ignore the knots in her shoulders and stomach, trying not to anticipate tense meals and conversations. They would do fun things together. Go to movies and the ZooLights. Charlotte and Libby went every year to see the lights and displays in the park.

Daniel walked in the back door with Libby's duffel. "Smells amazing in here." Libby trailed behind him, her shoulders slumped, her eyes not meeting Charlotte's. They both dropped their coats on the nearest chairs.

"Welcome home." Charlotte gave Libby a hug, which she limply accepted. Charlotte couldn't help taking a deep inhale of the rose perfume Libby always wore on her neck and wrists.

"I'm not hungry," Libby said, as she removed her boots. She was wearing the same jeans she'd had on in the emergency room and an orange sweater Charlotte didn't recognize. Perhaps the girls swapped clothes in rehab just like in college.

"Just sit with us then. The table is set whenever you guys are ready."

"I'm starving." Daniel helped himself to the lasagna and salad Charlotte had placed on the counter. Libby took a small piece of the lasagna and a few pieces of lettuce. They sat down at the table. Charlotte served herself dinner and tried not to watch as Libby cut the lasagna into pieces and shoved them around her plate. Charlotte said nothing, but Libby looked up and glared at her.

"Is something wrong, Libby?" She probably shouldn't have said that, but she'd had it.

"You're trying to make me fat." Libby set down her fork and knife.

"Oh, come on, Libby. You know you don't have to eat if you don't want to. And you're far from fat."

"I'm done." Libby got up. "You're being a bitch. I'm going

back to New York as soon as I can. I hate it here." With that, she rushed out of the room.

Charlotte pushed her chair away from the table but didn't stand. She was trying not to be hurt. Or angry. She was both. Libby was often furious with her. Charlotte was the safest person to be angry at, the person who would never abandon Libby. But it was not okay. Libby was old enough to know better, and she was sick of being a doormat.

Daniel shrugged. "Maybe it's PMS."

"You could have said something."

"Like what?"

"Told her she was out of line. She called me a bitch."

"Libby will be Libby."

"You should have said something." She was trying hard not to scream.

"Like?"

"Like don't call your mother a bitch."

When Charlotte married Daniel, she'd thought of him as the person who would carry her out of a burning building. Hadn't he pulled her away from that flaming chair at the country club? In retrospect, she realized this was what she had been looking for in a man. The person who would, if necessary, save her. Protect her. Keep her safe. In her imagination, she'd bestowed this quality upon Daniel, who had never done anything again to protect her or even to cushion an emotional blow. Now, she thought he might leave her in the fire and run for it.

She got up to check on the tart, which was still in the oven and filled the house with its sweet, buttery scent. This should have been comforting, but it wasn't.

"Libby's always mad at you. You shouldn't pay attention."

"Don't justify it. She was mad over nothing. Over me making dinner, for God's sake!"

Since high school, Libby had hated her doctors, her meds, and being labeled with disorders. Libby thought Charlotte was responsible for all of this. Charlotte often wondered what it would be like after she was dead, and Libby would have no parent to blame and no parent to forgive. That might be both good and bad, although it looked as if she might, at least, have a sister. This responsible sister was currently the size of a prune. Bones and cartilage were forming. Tiny legs were developing knees and ankles. Arms could flex. Charlotte stood at the oven a moment and imagined the baby twirling and somersaulting inside her, kicking those little legs like mad. She hoped she was having a good time. That someone was happy.

TWENTY-TWO

 ED

December 2018

Around four in the afternoon, when it was beginning to get dark, Ed spotted Charlotte and another woman approaching the intersection.

Charlotte!

He was morphing into an overeager dog like Big. He wanted to run over. Hug her. Sniff her, if he was being honest. She smelled like orange blossoms.

Charlotte waved casually, as if embarrassed to acknowledge him. He wondered if she was embarrassed because he was a cop. Then he remembered he was not wearing a uniform. He was not allowed to wear one.

"This is Libby, my daughter." Her voice was high. Something was off.

It was hard to see the girl under her hat and scarf, but he noted a bit of resemblance. She had the same angular face, high cheekbones, and gold-green eyes. But there was something hard about her. A worn look he recognized. Eyes that wouldn't meet his, a set mouth. It was the look of someone who'd had trouble, who had suffered. He reached out his hand to shake hers.

She seemed surprised but offered her hand. "Nice to meet you."

Maybe Libby knew he was a cop. Kids didn't like cops much.

He remembered the time when about fifty Lowell students were hauled in for underage drinking at a party. The students' parents were furious at the officers for taking the kids in for something they considered harmless. He wondered if Libby had been there. The idiot parents who had thrown the shindig were arrested. It had made the papers because everyone wanted to hate on private school kids as well as their parents.

"We went for a walk, and now we're on our way to see the ZooLights in Lincoln Park." Charlotte put up the hood of her coat.

"I love the lights. One of the best things about Chicago. We know how to do Christmas."

Charlotte smiled. "We love them, too. It's our annual pre-Christmas ritual. We get hot chocolate, wander around, and take the whole thing in. It's magical with all those colors. The trees wrapped in lights look like enormous jewels."

"I take my grandsons. The boys go nuts there, especially over the animal sculptures."

Libby looked over at him. "Don't you wonder how the real animals feel about it? All the people and all the noise. The zebras hide, and the lions pace and look upset."

She was right. Ed shifted on his feet and glanced at Charlotte.

"It might not be great for them." Charlotte put her arm around Libby's shoulder. "Zoos, in general, are not so good for animals."

Libby looked like a disgruntled teen, but Ed remembered she was older than that. He wanted to ask Charlotte to stop back for a talk after they were done at the zoo. He wanted to tell her about Maggie and the IVF pregnancy. But it was getting late. He couldn't make this request in front of the girl who might think it was strange. He could tag along, but he might be imposing. He asked Charlotte anyway.

"Sure." Ed thought he detected uncertainty in her voice. He felt a sting of disappointment. He shouldn't have asked.

The path leading toward the zoo hadn't been shoveled, but foot traffic had tamped the snow down, and they were able to walk fast. It was cold, and both Charlotte and Libby had scarves wrapped around their faces. They trudged past the Farm in the Zoo. Ed could see over the gates that all the animals were inside their barns. They were so close he could hear the cows mooing. From here, the trio could see colored lights beaming into the sky. They were not far from the intersection where Sarah had been killed.

Charlotte pulled her scarf down. "Almost there." Her breath froze in the air.

They turned into the main gate. A light sculpture of Santa in his sleigh greeted them at the entrance, which was crammed with strollers. "Rudolph the Red-Nosed Reindeer" blasted over the intercom. Kids danced in the open area near the seal pool. Whiskered faces peered over the edge to watch. The place swarmed with children from babies to teens and couples with arms linked. "We Wish You a Merry Christmas" came on next.

They walked past two lions pacing on the rocks in their habitat. The tree lights blinked from pink to gold to orange and then from green to red. They passed an ice sculpture of a polar bear and three giraffe light sculptures.

Libby took a step back when they got to the giraffes. "Whoa, it's dizzying. I forgot how bright it is."

"This is only the entrance. Remember how much more there is to see? Why don't you get us some hot chocolate?" Charlotte reached into her pocket and handed Libby a twenty. "Get three, okay?"

"Can't carry three."

"They have those cardboard holders, sweetie."

Ed watched as Libby walked reluctantly to the stand and got in line. Despite the cold, he would have really liked a beer, which was also being sold at the stands. He looked enviously at some of the guys walking with froth-filled plastic cups.

"I'm glad you came by." Ed eyed Libby in the long line. "I was hoping I'd get to talk with you."

"What's going on?"

Ed bent toward her and lowered his voice. "I've been wanting to tell you something. Maggie's going to be a surrogate for our daughter. She had IVF, and she's pregnant. We just found out, and I'm sort of blown away by the whole thing."

Charlotte's hand traveled to her abdomen over her coat. She looked startled, as if she'd misheard. Ed wondered if he was conveying his unhappiness about Maggie's pregnancy.

"Blown away? In a bad or good way?" Charlotte stuffed her hands in her pockets.

Ed noticed how she glanced at Libby and didn't meet his eyes. He wondered if he'd said more than he should have. Overshared. "Not sure. I should be happy, but I'm not. It seems so strange to me."

"Because of her age or because it won't be your baby?"

"Both, I guess."

"Understandable." She hesitated, glancing again over at Libby, who was still waiting. "I'm pregnant, too. Almost three months." She said this as if it were perfectly normal news. "A girl." Her voice cracked as if this were the first time she'd said it out loud.

Ed's eyes widened. "Did you have IVF?"

"No. Affair." She laughed, which unnerved him.

"So, it's not your husband's baby?" What a dumb thing to say, but he had not pictured Charlotte as the affair type. He was good at reading people, but love was sneaky.

"No." Charlotte's face was flaming. "I haven't even told my husband I'm pregnant yet. It was a major surprise for me. I'm sure he won't take it well." She looked directly at him. "I mean, who would?"

"Wow." He needed a second to think. He moved closer to Charlotte. "What are you going to do? When will you tell him?" He realized she had hardly mentioned her husband. Ed wasn't even sure of his name.

"I've got to tell my husband. Soon. But I'm such a coward." She shrugged. Her parka slid up and Ed could see a tiny bump beneath her sweater. It dawned on him that he'd never seen Charlotte with her coat off.

"And the father?"

"We stopped seeing each other. He doesn't know." She looked down and toed the snow at her feet. Ed couldn't see her face.

"That's an awfully big secret."

"I've been slow in figuring out this whole mess." Charlotte glanced toward Libby at the concession stand. She cleared her throat and stopped talking.

Ed turned to see Libby heading toward them, three cups balanced precariously in her hands. He rushed to help her, relieving Libby of two of the cups, and handed one to Charlotte. He wished they'd had more of a chance to talk about her pregnancy and how she felt about it. She didn't seem particularly upset. He hoped, even though she must have been overwhelmed, that she was happy. He was astonished to find himself excited about her baby and surprised that he didn't judge her for what Maggie would surely define as the sin of adultery.

They walked farther on, Charlotte in the center, passing green and yellow monkeys hanging from the trees. Smoke from bratwurst stands gave off a delicious garlicky scent that made Ed hungry. The color of the trees flashed from purple to orange. Then to blue. The colors became violent. The blue began to throw out gang signs. A silver zebra liquified and slithered, becoming an enormous snake making its way through the snow. The trees shifted back to orange. Colors shot into the sky, sparked, and danced before his eyes. Then dizziness came. A panic attack.

When he felt the squeeze of his chest, Ed shut his eyes for a second. "I need to sit." He stumbled toward the nearest bench, hoping he wouldn't pass out.

"Ed, are you okay?" Charlotte's voice sounded far away. "What's wrong?"

"I'm fine." He made it to the bench and tried to slow his breath. He knew Charlotte would understand that he had PTSD.

"This happens sometimes. I need a minute or two of rest." He did not want to talk about his PTSD in front of Libby. There was something about this girl he didn't quite trust.

Charlotte leaned over him, looking as if she were ready to call 911. "Is it your heart?"

He smiled and shook his head. "Sorry," he exhaled. His heart began to calm. The world was steady again. "Much better."

"Are you really?" Charlotte bent over him.

"Yes." He murmured into her ear. "Panic attack."

"I understand." Her warm breath in his ear felt reassuring.

Libby threw out her empty hot chocolate cup and walked over to the bench. "I'm freezing. Let's go to the Ape House. That used to be my favorite."

Ed tentatively stood up. He was grateful he hadn't completely embarrassed himself.

Charlotte looped her arm through his. "Lead the way, Libs."

"It's right down here." Libby pointed to the path on the right.

Ed and Charlotte walked slightly behind her, and Ed moved ahead when they arrived, so he could pull open the heavy door. Inside the air felt warm and damp.

"It reeks in here." Charlotte held her gloved hand over her nose. Ed remembered how smells had bothered Maggie when she was pregnant. He glanced shyly at Charlotte. She caught him and smiled.

"You're such a delicate flower, Mom." Libby used a mean jokey voice that irritated Ed.

"It's pretty ripe." Ed hoped Libby would back off.

The Ape House was packed. People watched smaller gorillas swinging on ropes and mother apes crouching on wooden stumps with their babies. A few lay on the floor tangled in a pile of blankets, and in another exhibit, a large male clutched a fistful of lettuce and stared down the crowd.

"Oh my God!" Libby pointed to the male, who dropped the lettuce. "Look at that gorilla. He's huge."

Ed was not sure if it was a gorilla or an orangutan, but the enormous ape pressed his face against the glass and glared furiously at the people watching him. It was a gorilla, Ed decided. They were very smart. He had watched a show with Maggie about Koko the gorilla, who learned sign language and loved kittens. He was about to ask Charlotte if she knew about Koko when the gorilla grabbed his penis and began furiously masturbating. People were momentarily spellbound as his member grew.

"What's that monkey doing, Mommy?" a small girl asked.

"I'll explain later." The mother grabbed the girl's hand and headed to the door.

"Time to go," a father called to his children.

Teenagers giggled. "Do you think he'll get jizz all over the glass?" a pimply boy yelled to his two friends.

"Yikes." Ed was mortified. He could not believe this was happening in front of Charlotte and Libby.

Libby seemed fixated. "Gross. Think he's doing that on purpose, to drive people away?"

"Uh-huh." Charlotte laughed. "He knows exactly what he's doing. It's probably time to get out of here."

"Definitely time to go." Ed could not look at Charlotte, and he cringed all the way to the entrance.

"So much for G-rated zoos." Charlotte was still giggling.

They walked back to the entrance. Ed hesitated. He wished he could keep talking to Charlotte about her pregnancy. He thought about her going home with Libby. He hoped she had another friend to talk to, that she wasn't going home alone with her secret, but she hadn't mentioned telling anyone else. He could not begin to imagine what she was going through. It must be a roller coaster of emotions.

"Coffee soon?" Her voice sounded careful to Ed, emotionless for Libby's sake.

"Tomorrow would be good. Let's meet up and walk to Starbucks."

"Sounds like a plan."

Ed saw the strain in her face and the faint lines around her eyes. She waved and turned. He watched Charlotte and Libby walk toward Webster. They moved identically. From the back, it was impossible to tell them apart.

TWENTY-THREE  CHARLOTTE

December 2018

On Christmas Eve, Charlotte's father walked through her front door with bags of gifts hanging off both shoulders of his down coat. Charlie was seventy-eight and had a gorgeous full head of white hair. The rest of him was a little stooped and frail. Her mother, who was seventy-five, entered empty-handed and wore a strange, boiled-wool poncho and a vaguely dazed look on her face. Lucca was tiny, but there was nothing fragile about her.

The family dinner, traditionally at Charlotte and Daniel's house, would thankfully be smaller this year. One of Charlotte's brothers, Frank, was away with his family.

"You're looking good, Carlotta." Charlotte's dad enjoyed using her real name—her Italian name—which he knew she hated. Their mother was the one who had insisted on the Italian names. Her brother Sandro was the only one of the three who hadn't changed his name to an American one.

Charlotte's dad liked to needle Charlotte and throw her off-balance. She didn't know why. Perhaps it was because she was the only girl, but she suspected it was because she was like him. Stubborn. At least, that was what her mother said when she heard Charlotte's father teasing her.

"Thanks, Dad." She was careful not to let her annoyance show. "Let me take some of those bags."

"I'm fine, dear. I'll dump them under the tree." And that's exactly what he did. Dropped the gifts helter-skelter under the tree and across the living room rug.

Before dinner, Charlotte had tried on three dresses. None would zip. She had frantically gone through her closet, pulling clothes off the hangers, petrified that she had nothing left that fit. Her closet was almost empty before she found a baggy, plum-colored velvet dress with no zipper. She pulled it over her head and hung up the big pile of clothes she'd thrown on the bed.

Now she worried that her mother would notice her belly. Lucca didn't notice much, but she was skilled at homing in on insecurity and weakness. When Charlotte, who was the tallest girl in school, gained a few pounds during puberty, Lucca had hounded her with calorie counts until she lost the weight. Now, she brought up Libby's thinness even though Charlotte begged her not to talk about it.

"Hey." Sandro walked in from the street with his wife, Claire, and their kids, Luke and Lily. "We got a great parking space out front. The street's empty."

"Hey." Charlotte gave him a hug. Sandro was a year older, the brother she'd battled with as a kid. He'd broken her nose and chased her with knives but had miraculously turned into a nice, nonviolent adult. He was a psychiatrist, and Charlotte sometimes wondered what their chaotic childhood had to do with this.

"Come on in." Daniel rushed to the front door. "Let me take your coats. I'll put them in our bedroom."

Claire, who was one of Charlotte's favorite people, had made a Bûche de Noel complete with little meringue mushrooms. She produced a plastic squirrel from her purse to set on top.

Claire was a food stylist and carried blow torches, glue, spritz bottles, and skewers in her bag. With her cropped blonde hair and fine features, she reminded Charlotte of a sprite. Lily, who was twenty, and Luke, who was twenty-two, had Sandro's thick dark hair and high cheekbones, and their mother's hazel eyes. The best of both parents.

Lily and Luke joined Libby on the couch, which conveniently placed them in front of a platter of cheeses and olives. Sandro brought his kids glasses of Brunello, the red wine he'd bought in Tuscany last summer . . . the one he'd shipped from a vineyard, along with the olive oil he was always talking about, describing it as green, light, and fresh. Sandro liked to think of himself as sophisticated and worldly, which amused Charlotte. Sandro liked his luxuries, although she couldn't blame him. She certainly liked hers.

She watched as he hesitated and glanced at Libby, while setting the two stems on the table. Charlotte froze for a second, but Libby didn't look up. She was showing Lily her daisy chain bracelet from J. Crew, promising her one if she wanted it. Sandro leaned over Libby.

"Glass of wine, Libby?"

"No." The word loudly escaped Charlotte's mouth.

"No, thank you." Libby shot her mother a sour look.

"Okay, sorry." Sandro looked sheepish. "I forgot."

Charlotte's dad picked up the glass Sandro had brought him. "Hey, Libby, do you know all the ridiculous things your mother did when she was young?"

Charlotte, already ashamed, knew he was trying to lighten up the atmosphere, so she kept quiet.

"Like what?"

"She let one of her boyfriends paint a replica of the Sistine Chapel on her bedroom walls. It was really good. Amazing.

Then when they broke up, she splashed red paint all over it. It looked like a crime scene in there."

Libby laughed, and Charlotte was relieved that her father didn't mention that her mother had caught her having sex with this same boyfriend, when she was fifteen, in the painted bedroom.

"When she was older, and I tried to teach her to drive, she got mad at me, took her hands off the wheel, and crashed straight into a fence. Then she blamed it on me, saying I made her nervous."

Libby laughed. "Really, Mom?"

"Yes, and that's enough, Dad. You were making me nervous."

"You're still a terrible driver."

"You should have sent me to a driving school like everyone else."

Charlotte's mother placed a pink mound of shrimp and a bowl of cocktail sauce next to the cheese. She plucked one of the shrimp with her wrinkled fingers and offered it to Libby before she sat in the chair next to her husband and the fireplace. Charlotte was surprised when Libby accepted the shrimp.

"Thanks, Nonna. Do you want me to make you and Gramps a plate of cheese?"

"I'm going to hold off until dinner. There's always so much food. Your mother make her chestnut stuffing?"

"Yes, and it's delicious. I couldn't stop eating it earlier."

"A little more meat on your bones wouldn't hurt." Lucca ignored Charlotte's glare from across the room. "I'm going to go peek in the oven on my way to the yard to have a smoke." She got up and headed toward the kitchen.

Charlotte watched her. As Lucca had aged, she'd become even smaller. Not in a wasted way but doll-like, except for her leathery skin and the black hair shot through with a coarse gray that she knotted into a bun at the back of her head. Charlotte heard the oven opening and closing.

"Leave it alone, Mom. Or it won't cook evenly."

"It's fine." Lucca banged the back door as she went out.

Sandro came over and put his arm around Charlotte. "I'm so sorry about the wine. I guess I repress the overdose and her alcohol problem."

"It's hard to believe." Charlotte leaned into him. "I still have trouble. It doesn't seem real, more like a bad dream."

They watched their mother puff away on her cigarette, as she leaned against the wall on the outdoor balcony. Lucca had thrown Daniel's jacket over her black turtleneck, one of the many she bought in bulk from the Gap. The overhead outdoor light framed her against the brick. Smoke and breath became clouds in the frigid air. Charlotte thought she would probably outlive them all. Lucca claimed smoking was her ultimate pleasure, and she would rather die than live without it. There was not much Charlotte could say to that.

Scegli il tuo veleno, her mother had said. Pick your poison.

Lucca was indifferent to food, odd for an Italian, so Charlotte's food memories were from Italy and her grandmother. Some of these memories were hard to replicate. Elevated by their elusive status, they turned into longings. It was difficult, but not impossible, to find the perfect juicy peach in Chicago, but not her favorite fruit, wild strawberries. Tiny and sweet, they had to be eaten quickly before they rotted. Charlotte searched the farmers markets every summer, but even at these markets there were no wild strawberries.

Charlotte's nonna and her housekeeper, Gabriella, had taught Charlotte about tastes—salty, sweet, sour, bitter, savory—and which foods complemented each other. The salt of prosciutto with the sweetness of a ripe fig; the creamy burst in the mouth of a tiny tortellini spooned from fragrant, home-made broth; the proper amount of sea salt and rosemary to be rubbed into a chicken; how to sauté morels with shallots and make ravioli with freshly picked peas. This was a legacy for which she was grateful, even though her daughter shunned food and her mother preferred her cigarettes and books. It made Charlotte happy to offer up dishes she'd made, to see the full platters she'd produced lined up on the countertop. For her, it was a form of love, no matter how it was received.

Charlotte went into the kitchen, where she found Daniel basting the turkey. She sat on a counter stool. The glass of wine Sandro had poured for her was at her elbow. She was consciously not drinking it, but its crimson color and earthy smell tempted her to have a small taste. It was full and plummy and tinged with guilt. A sip would not hurt a baby. Still, she should not be drinking. And should anyone be drinking around an addict? She didn't know the protocol for this, but it seemed rude to ban drinking because her daughter had a problem. Or was it prudent and she was a bad mother? There were too many things to think about, too many things to go wrong.

"Turkey's ready." Daniel lifted the heavy pan onto the counter.

"Thanks, will you carve?"

"Sure. Hey, do you think you overreacted with Libby and the wine? You didn't give her a chance to say no."

"I did. But it was a reflex, like someone hitting my kneecap. I was worried."

"Maybe you should apologize later."

"I will. I didn't mean to embarrass her."

"Well, you did and yourself as well."

It took every ounce of her willpower not to let him have it. After years of barely parenting Libby, he had decided to take this moment, when she was already upset with herself, to lecture her about mothering. She blinked back tears as she rose to sprinkle almonds over the green beans and pour water into glasses. She waited for the moment she could call everyone to dinner, the moment when they would sit in a circle, and it would be clear that all they had to do was eat.

TWENTY-FOUR

 **ED**

December 2018

hristmas Eve at Ed and Maggie's was never easy. Liam and Teddy were what could be politely called energetic. Their mother, Ashley, was tightly wound, and Dawn was louder than everyone but the kids. Their adult children looked alike. Both Paul and Dawn had sloped noses, light blue eyes, and red hair. But Paul was compact and neat, while Dawn was always a bit undone, with a button missing or her hair falling out of the bun she wore for work. They had fought a lot as children and now maintained a polite, but distant, relationship.

Still, Ed and Maggie reasoned that, since the entire family would be in one place, it was time to tell everyone about the pregnancy. Dawn had complained she was not ready to discuss it with the others, and Ed had countered it was wrong to keep her brother and his wife out of the loop.

It was a fine line between protecting Dawn's privacy and excluding Paul.

Maggie and Dawn were closer than Ed and Paul. Ed regretted this, and he liked to blame it on Ashley. But the two of them had never had a tight bond like Maggie and Dawn. The men loved each other, but the closeness was not there.

"I think we should wait until after dinner," Ed whispered to Maggie in the kitchen. The counters were crowded with the side dishes and cookies Maggie had been preparing for days. Also set out were Ashley's green bean casserole, and Dawn's caramel cake, a cake so sweet it hurt his teeth. "Wait until Liam and Teddy are off playing with their presents."

"Sounds sensible." Maggie picked up the green bean casserole.

"So how do you explain to kids that their grandmother is pregnant with their cousin?" Ed suddenly wished he had not asked this.

Maggie put down the casserole and frowned. She was wearing a Santa sweater that Ashley had knitted for her.

Ashley, a lover of crafts and homemade goods, was a former flight attendant for United, and had been happy to finally get to stay at home. She was all-American pretty, with her long blonde hair and slender figure, but unfortunately, she had no sense of humor and was often shrill with the boys. Ed sometimes wondered what Paul saw in her. On the plus side, they had a basement full of jams and pickles.

"Dawn and I didn't talk about what to say to the kids." Maggie looked puzzled, and to Ed's relief, not mad. "I guess that will have to come later. Maybe when I'm big, and they can see it."

"Super Mario." Liam bounded into the room. "We want to play Super Mario now." He was wearing his new red Italian soccer jersey that said, "Motta."

Ed assumed that must be a soccer star. A friend of Paul's had brought the jerseys from Italy. Teddy was wearing one that said, "Pirlo."

Ed watched his family sort themselves while attempting to sit down for their traditional pineapple ham dinner. Big lay under the table to wait for the boys to drop food.

"Sit down while we say grace." Ashley steered the boys to the table. She wore a pair of bell earrings she had made, and they jingled when she moved her head.

"We're not hungry."

"I said sit."

They sat.

Maggie said a quick grace. Ed sliced the ham and started to pass plates down the table. Paul helped himself to some green beans and handed the bowl to Maggie.

"Have some mashed potatoes." Dawn walked around the table and served a scoop onto each plate.

Liam and Teddy mushed their mashed potatoes and blatantly fed pieces of ham to Big.

Ashley turned toward the boys, her earrings tinkling. "Okay, if you're not going to eat, scoot. Play your game." They rushed out of the room.

Ed glanced at Maggie. She chewed a piece of ham while wrinkling her forehead. He took a swallow of his Scotch.

Maggie set down her fork and knife on her plate, next to the ham. "Paul, Ashley, we have some news."

Paul looked up from his plate, and Ashley took a small sip of her wine. Maggie and Ed did not generally have news.

"I'm helping Dawn with her infertility."

"Great, Mom. Going to her appointments?"

"I'm going to her appointments . . . and I'm carrying the baby. I'm her surrogate." Maggie beamed.

Ed watched Paul's face rearrange itself, and thought he was hiding his shock well even as Maggie and Dawn explained the process.

Ashley was not hiding anything. She had an unhappy, prissy look as if she'd smelled something bad.

"I'm sorry we didn't tell you," Maggie said to Paul, as he helped her carry the plates to the kitchen. Ed and Ashley followed them. "We wanted to make sure it worked before we got everyone all excited."

"It's okay, Ma. I think we should wait to tell the kids, though. It will be hard for them to understand."

"I don't think we should tell the kids at all." Ashley scrunched up her nose. "We shouldn't discuss it with them. It's unnatural."

"Don't you think they will eventually notice?" Paul was beginning to look upset.

"Boys aren't that observant."

"Paul noticed way more than Dawn ever did." Ed was steamed at Ashley.

Maggie intervened by bringing in the cake. "How about we cross that bridge when we get to it? Let's cut the cake, move to the living room, and open the presents."

Ed had bought Maggie a Kindle, so she could get her books faster. He also gave her a small gold heart on a chain, which she put on immediately. It looked great on her, and she seemed happy with it. He was never sure about Maggie's gifts. He worried he would pick something she wouldn't like, and she would never let on.

Maggie gave Ed two comfy-looking flannel shirts, and a thick blue-and-white scarf she had knitted for him on the sly.

"I like keeping you warm. Even when I'm not with you."

Ed planted a big kiss on top of her head. "I love my gifts. Especially the scarf and the idea of you keeping me warm."

Ashley and Paul sat together on the couch; they were surrounded by a sea of wrapping paper. Ashley had a white terry-cloth robe on her lap, and Paul had a stack of the mysteries he loved to read. They were both quiet, and Ed hoped they were not fighting about telling the boys. He was worried Paul might have been hurt by the exclusion, but his son had never been one to share his feelings. Ed would never know what he was thinking unless he was prodded.

Ashley left the room and Ed, eager to be near Paul, got up and passed the cookies. Paul picked a raspberry thumbprint. Ed sat beside him.

"Good choice." It was lame, but Paul smiled, and he felt a surge of love for him. He knew most families had an Ashley, but he wished she weren't married to Paul, who was so inherently sweet. In some ways, Ashley was more like Maggie than he cared to admit. Controlling. There was that saying: Boys marry their mothers, and girls their fathers.

Dawn brought him a glass of her special eggnog. He sipped it and wondered if Charlotte and her family were opening presents now. If there was eggnog, and what she would tell him about her evening when he saw her. He had another sip and felt the rum warm his throat, but he also felt a pang in his gut, which took him a moment to identify.

Longing. He missed her.

TWENTY-FIVE  CHARLOTTE

December 2018

Two days after Christmas, Charlotte woke alone to a quiet house. Libby had, thankfully, not noticed her mother's growing abdomen and had flown back to her New York apartment and her job. Daniel was probably in the family room drinking coffee. She inched her long cotton nightgown up over her belly and ran her hands over the swell. Her girl.

This would be the morning she told Daniel. She would keep this promise to herself.

She pulled her carry-on suitcase out of the closet. She opened a few of the drawers in her bureau and stood there for a minute, gazing into them, deciding what to take. Only a few things fit her now. She hurriedly packed four baggy sweaters, her new maternity jeans, underwear, and socks. Then she went into the bathroom and added her makeup case, moisturizer, toothbrush, and toothpaste. She stowed the suitcase in the closet, tucked away behind her clothes.

The way she saw it, Daniel had two choices. She'd thought this part through. He would either tell her to leave, or he would offer to raise the baby as his own if his not being the father remained a secret. Most likely, he'd be furious and tell her to go. But whatever choice he made, he would certainly be shaken. And hurt. The hurt would be worse than the anger.

Pulling on her robe, she walked downstairs while trying to tamp down her terror.

She found Daniel in the family room, reading the front page of the *Wall Street Journal*. He seemed focused on an article. She stepped closer and read: *Retail: Bricks and Mortar Versus Online.* The other sections were spread on the floor by his chair. He was dressed for work, like every other finance guy, in his gray, pinstriped suit.

"Hi, do you want coffee?"

"Had some." He did not look up.

The sight of his hair thinning into a round pink spot on top of his head made her sad. There was something tender and vulnerable about it, something that made her turn and leave the room.

She had no appetite for once but wanted a cup of strong coffee. She needed caffeine before this conversation, which had to be soon. It was nearly time for Daniel to drive to work.

Standing at the counter, she spilled the milk as she poured it into the frother. She wiped the counter. And then had to wipe it down again after she poured in too much milk and it bubbled over. After the coffee was brewed, she added it to the milk, and then drank the cappuccino while leaning against the counter. The kitchen door was open, so she could see Daniel.

The room was freezing; her arms were pocked with goose-bumps. She tugged at her robe and drew it tight. There was no way to soften this news. She had to spit out the facts. She put her mug down and walked into the family room. She stood in front of the TV. Market news flashed and scrolled. "Daniel."

"Umm." He was now reading an article on interest rates, which he specialized in for work.

"I need to talk to you."

"In a sec. I'm almost done with this."

She waited, still standing. It was awkward, but she was too nervous to sit.

He looked up and pushed his reading glasses to the top of his head. "What?"

"I'm pregnant."

For a second, he looked puzzled, as if he were not sure if he should be happy or not. "How?" He put the paper on the floor. His eyes traveled to her abdomen.

"I had an affair. It's over, but I'm pregnant. He doesn't know." Her body prickled with anxiety. She was electric. This was what it must feel like to be bitten all over by red fire ants. Her heart, she thought, might explode, and burst through her chest.

"You had an affair? Who?" His face screwed into a question. He pushed the paper off his lap. She could see the muscles tense in his arms and face. The blue vein throbbed on his temple.

"You don't know him, and it's over." She was careful not to say this aggressively but to state it as fact. There was a baby. The father was gone. "I'm sorry. Really sorry."

But the thing was, she wasn't sorry. Not about the baby. She wanted her.

"You've decided to keep it?" His eyes moved away from her. He looked disoriented. Confused.

She couldn't blame him. "Yes. At first, I didn't know what I wanted to do, but I've realized that I want to keep her."

"You know it's a girl? How far along are you?"

"Twelve weeks. I had a test last week. She's healthy."

"And you're not going to tell him? The father? How long have you been sleeping with him?"

This was the part she would like to lie about. The red ants bit harder. Now her heart felt as if it would definitely leap out of her chest. The words, the truth, stuck in the back of her throat.

It took her a moment to speak. "About a year, and I'm not going to tell him. We're done." The truth was she was no longer sure what she would do, but she wasn't about to admit to that.

"Christ, Charlotte."

He got up, walked to the powder room, and slammed the door. She leaned against the door, not knowing what to do. She knocked softly. "You okay? Can I bring you anything?"

"Go away."

As she was about to go upstairs, she heard a sob. This was the last thing she had expected. She waited outside the door, but he didn't open it. Finally, she climbed the stairs.

Shaken, she circled the bedroom and opened the curtains to look at the street. She watched parents and their down-suited children walking to school. The boxwoods in the yard were smothered in snow, with bits of green poking through. The small one near the sidewalk looked as if it was dying. An orange plastic bag was stuck against the ironwork fence. She pulled on a pair of leggings and a sweater, then sat on the end of the unmade bed and inched backward until she was propped against the pillows. The stinging feeling had stopped. Sorrow had taken its place. Her marriage was over.

She could not hear Daniel from here. The silence lasted for an impossibly long time, during which she reminded herself that she had never changed a ceiling light bulb, fixed a flat tire, or taken the garbage out late at night. She had never even lived alone, and she was afraid. She wished she could evaporate and dissolve into the air. But she was too solid, too busy growing this baby.

She heard the trudge of his steps—the creak of stairs, the creak Daniel had always wanted to get fixed. He was in the doorway. His eyes were red. "Don't leave me, Charlotte." His voice was faint, but clear. "We can get through this." It was his old voice, the one that had loved her.

She realized how much easier it would have been if he had thrown her out. She let herself sink into the pillows. He sat down next to her on the bed. He took her hand and enclosed her fingers in his. His hand was warm and smooth and familiar. It was a hand she would miss. "I'm so sorry." To her dismay, she started sobbing. She couldn't stop, but she knew she could not stay here. "I have to leave."

"I'll help you raise this baby. She'll never know."

"It's too late, Daniel."

"Please, Charlotte. We can go to counseling. I'll do better this time. Stay with me."

"I can't."

"But I forgive you."

"Forgive me?"

"You're the one who had an affair."

"It's not about forgiveness."

"I don't get it."

"It's about the fact that I had an affair in the first place. And now I'm going to have a baby. I've already gone. I can't go backward."

"Can't you give me a chance? I only want to be with you. Please, stay."

She hesitated, and then her body took over. "I can't, I'm so sorry." She withdrew her hand, slowly got up, and pulled the suitcase from the closet. She could feel his eyes drilling into her back.

"It's not like you have anyone else." His voice had turned cold. Metallic, she thought.

She could almost taste it.

"No, I don't."

She looked back at him when she got to the door. His eyes had narrowed.

"How could you do this to me?" he said. She was not sure if he meant the baby, having an affair, or leaving. She shut the door behind her.

Outside, it was obnoxiously bright and cold. Charlotte caught her breath and tried to make herself stop crying. She wiped the tears from her face before they froze, too agitated to dig for her sunglasses or gloves.

The glare from the snow hurt her eyes. She blinked all the way to the corner where she waited for two lights, clutching her suitcase before she found an available taxi. The driver, a bald man with black glasses, greeted her with a nod as she set her bag on the ripped seat.

"O'Hare?"

"Thirty-one Magnolia, please."

Her parents' house was dark. She let herself in with her key.

"Anyone home?" she called loudly, standing in the foyer, knowing her father, who refused to retire from his law office, would be at work. She wanted to make sure her mother heard her and would not be startled when she appeared.

"Carlotta? In here," her mother yelled. "The living room."

Charlotte removed her snowy boots, placed them on the mat, and left her suitcase in the front hall.

She found her mother lying in her usual spot on the green velvet couch. She was reading, dressed in her robe. An ashtray was balanced on her stomach, a cigarette in her hand. A cup of espresso sat beside her on the floor. The heavy green curtains were still drawn, and the room was dark, except for two lamps on the end tables.

"*Cara*, what are you doing here?" Lucca sat up. "Would you like a coffee? We got that fancy machine you have." Her mother used a battered stovetop espresso maker.

"No thanks." Charlotte thought about all the secondhand smoke she was inhaling.

The air stank of it.

"Everything okay? Is it Libby? Nothing terrible is going on, right?"

"Libby's fine. I'm fine. But I've left Daniel." Even saying this was exhausting.

Lucca dragged on her cigarette and exhaled a raspy note. "Hmm."

"That's all?" Charlotte squeezed onto the end of the couch near her mother's bare, un-manicured feet, which still had their elegant arch.

"It was a long time coming, *cara*."

"I've been married for twenty-four years." That was all she could think to say.

"And you've seemed unhappy for most of them. He was never one of my favorite people. I tried to keep my mouth shut, but you know what I thought of him."

Charlotte did know and even though she'd left Daniel, she felt the sharpness of her mother's criticism. A fresh pain. "I know, Mom. But there's another thing. I'm . . . I'm pregnant."

"No. Really?" Lucca looked toward Charlotte's middle, which was still covered by her coat. "That's a big complication. Have you thought about this? Having a baby alone?"

"The baby isn't Daniel's." Charlotte talked fast. She wanted the explanations—her sorry story—over with. "I had a relationship with someone. An affair. We broke up before I knew I was pregnant."

Lucca pursed her lips and shook both her hands in her *mio dio* way. "How far along?"

"Twelve weeks. I had a test. It's a girl. She's healthy."

Lucca reached to get another cigarette from the pack beside

her. Charlotte flinched, thinking again of all the secondhand smoke and the baby. "You know this will be hard. No husband. No help. One income."

"I do."

"Sure this is something you want? You can still terminate. You don't have to go through with it."

"I'm sure. It's all I've been thinking about."

"You're made of strong stuff."

"Thanks, Mom." She unbuttoned her coat. Lucca liked the house hot. Charlotte was sweating.

"You're certain you don't want the father involved? That's not good for a child. Not to know who their father is."

"I don't have a choice. I broke up with him, but he was about to dump me, so it was self-defense."

"Did you love him? The father?"

"I did. I do."

"Oh, *cara*, I'm sorry."

"I don't think I meant all that much to him."

Lucca shook her head. "Don't be so sure about that. Who knows how he felt? You're not a mind reader."

"He's also married with kids."

Lucca shrugged. "What if Daniel fights you? Decides he wants the baby?"

"Daniel and I haven't slept together for more than a year. He must know a simple DNA test would show it's not his baby." Charlotte struggled not to fidget, to remain still at her mother's feet. She had never told her mother about Daniel's lack of sexual interest. One more reason she felt less than what she should be in the desirability department.

Lucca shifted on the couch toward Charlotte, her arms out, her bathrobe sagging open and exposing her wrinkled chest. Even though her mother had always ignored her beauty, it must have been a hard thing to let go of. "You'll stay here with us, of course."

"I'll find a place, Mama, but I'll stay until then." She felt as if she'd already traveled far, although she'd only begun.

Charlotte hugged her mother, crunching Lucca's bird bones beneath her arms. She was the big to Lucca's small. She'd grown up with the worry that she had been too much of everything for Lucca. Too big, too demonstrative, too bourgeois. Lucca was reserved. Some might say cold, and Charlotte was comforted by this rare warmth. She suddenly felt her mother's shoulders heave. Lucca was crying.

"I'll be okay." Charlotte leaned back, surprised. She took her mother's hand, running her finger over its network of veins. "Don't worry."

"I can't help it. You've had to go through so much. Libby, Daniel, a breakup. Are you sure about this baby? It's one more way of being alone. Another prison to put yourself in."

"Positive."

"As long as you're sure." Lucca looked up at Charlotte and gave her a quick kiss on her chin, which was as high as she could reach. She smelled of cigarettes, newsprint, and coffee.

Charlotte had read babies developed taste and smell in utero. Even though it was doubtful the baby could sense anything beyond amniotic fluid, she hoped her baby could smell Lucca. That she was imprinting this moment, and her grandmother's hug, in her budding memory.

TWENTY-SIX

 ED

December 2018

E d stood next to his Jeep. It was a Friday afternoon, and he stared at the dirty slush covering the intersection. He was trying to ween himself away from the intersection and was down to filming twice a week. Today was so dreary, he felt as if he might never see the sun again. He was thinking about buying one of those special lights, when his phone chimed with the pleasing new bell sound he had installed last night. His last message alert, a whistle, kept alarming him.

Coffee?
Yes, ru coming?
Be at intersection in 15.

Something was up. Charlotte never came by on Friday anymore. She had Pilates or yoga or something. He thought of Dawn's miscarriages and hoped, for Charlotte's sake, nothing had happened to the baby. However, he secretly thought it might be a blessing not to have a fatherless child. That was going to be one tough road. He'd even (shamefully) fantasized about being single and stepping in to help her raise the baby. Heroic and all. He had not gotten past picturing himself holding the baby, but still the thought was there.

What an old fool he was. His own wife was having a baby.

The problem was, he was having trouble picturing hers, but he could picture Charlotte's baby.

The wind chill was minus ten. He got back into the car to wait.

Charlotte approached, looking uncharacteristically inelegant. Depleted. She wore baggy jeans tucked into her rain boots and a man's brown parka. Her hair was a mess, her face pale, and she had purplish blotches under her eyes.

"Hey there. This is a nice surprise. Everything all right?"

"I left my husband." She brought her mittened hand up to her mouth, the gesture of a person watching a horror movie.

"Are you okay?"

"Not really." She leaned against one of the big oak trees as if she desperately needed propping.

"Where are you staying?" What if she needed a place to stay? Could he ask Maggie and bring a strange pregnant woman home? He could end up with two middle-aged pregnant women under one roof . . . his roof!

"With my parents."

He was relieved to know she had parents. Caretakers. Up until now, he'd never thought of her as alone. "How did your husband take it?"

"At first, he wanted me to stay. He got angry when I said I couldn't."

"He was willing to raise the baby?"

"Yes." She rocked back and forth in her boots.

"You'd rather raise her alone than with him?" He tried to keep the surprise out of his voice, reminding himself he knew almost nothing about her marriage.

She nodded.

He'd run out of words. He wanted to do something, but he didn't know what. "How about I buy you a coffee?" he said to break the silence. "We'll go to Starbucks. Hop in the car. I want to hear all about your apartment search."

Charlotte settled into the passenger seat for the short ride. Ed parked directly in front, which was a miracle in the city.

"You have a seat." Ed held the door for her. "I'll bring the coffee. Do you want a fancy one? One of those lattes? There's chocolate you can sprinkle on top."

"No, a regular. Decaf, please." She sat at a small table in the corner.

When he returned, he handed her the coffee. "Did you tell your daughter yet?"

"Yes, I gave her that stupid 'We've been drifting apart for a long time' speech. She kept saying she didn't get it. When I told her I was pregnant, she said she really didn't get it. Didn't understand how I could leave her dad now. I left it at that. She's coming home tomorrow, so I can talk to her in person. I rented an apartment a few days ago. It'll be bare, but I'll have it by then."

"Where's your new place?"

"On Cleveland Avenue. It's tiny, but it'll do."

"Anything you need? Or that I can do to help?"

"Thanks, but no. I bought two beds that'll be delivered tomorrow. The rest I'll do slowly. It'll come together. Eventually. Just not in a couple of days."

"Well, let me know if you need any help."

"Thanks, Ed."

They sipped in silence.

Finally, Charlotte looked up from her coffee at Ed. "Did you have a good Christmas?"

"It was complicated. We used Christmas dinner to tell my son and his wife about Maggie's pregnancy. My daughter-in-law, Ashley, was a prig about it. Said it was unnatural and all.

Luckily, Maggie and Dawn were so happy they basically ignored her."

"That was mean of her."

"Yeah, she can be like that. I feel sorry for Paul. He's stuck with her all the time. We keep our interactions brief. But we love the kids and Paul, of course."

"You've talked about everyone's feelings but your own." Charlotte stretched her legs out in front of her. "How do you feel about the pregnancy?"

"The truth? I never wanted her to do this, and I'm scared to death."

"Oh, Ed. I'm sorry."

Ed looked down, slightly ashamed, but what good was a friend if you couldn't tell her the truth?

TWENTY-SEVEN  CHARLOTTE

January 2019

Charlotte waited outside the security area so she'd be sure to spot Libby. It was after nine, and the airport was quiet. She could see travelers lingering at the bar with their carry-ons and their beers. There was no line at the McDonald's, only a lone pilot.

Libby came into view, a tiny figure walking rapidly past the lingerers, her wheelie gliding behind her. Her sticklike limbs looked as if they could be easily snapped in two. Her eyes were focused on the floor. She seemed so vulnerable.

Charlotte jumped in front of her and waved to get her attention. "Hi, sweetie. Here."

Libby looked up and her eyes landed on Charlotte's belly.

"How was the flight?" Charlotte tried to wrestle Libby's carry-on from her.

"Fine." Libby would not yield the suitcase.

"I got here early, so I parked and came in. We need to go to the garage."

Libby followed her up an elevator and then through the maze of hallways to O'Hare's outdoor garage. "Get ready for a cold seat. The car's been parked here for a while." Libby sat slumped and silent in her seat. Charlotte chattered as she sped down the highway, which was mercifully free at this hour. "I think you'll like the new apartment. It's small but cozy. Once I get furniture, it'll look a lot different."

This apartment was the third rental Charlotte had looked at with Missy Briggs, a realtor. Missy appeared to be about fifteen, but she must have been in her twenties. Charlotte was doubtful when she first saw Missy. How could she have any expertise? Initially, it seemed she did not. The first two apartments were dark, cramped, and depressing. One smelled of greasy hamburger, the other of cats. But then Missy had brought her to this small, sunlit apartment with a decent-sized bathroom shared by two bedrooms and a pretty view of the street and treetops.

Charlotte had only taken the small suitcase of clothes, which were growing tight, and not much else. Her few purchases had been sheets for the new beds, towels, and a Nespresso machine. The oddest part was she didn't want anything from the house except her computer, files, and storyboards. She never wanted to see the couch, the coffee table, or her stove again.

The thought of all the possessions she had cherished—the marble eggs, hand-blown glass vases, heavy silverware—made her stomach hurt. She was done with all that and hoped never to have to go back to the house. She wondered how she could have her office ferried over by some hired stranger.

Daniel had used these possessions as a threat in one of his angry calls. He could not say, "You'll never see your daughter again," so he said, "You can say goodbye to all your things."

For once, she'd said the right thing. "Keep them. Except for the clothes. They won't fit you." Then she'd hung up on him, infused with a new and wonderful sense of limitlessness. She could ignore, or at least try to, his nastiness, and would not have to suffer through any painful division of plates, books, and paintings. Let him keep it all. She would rather have nothing.

Even though Daniel disliked his mother, he had learned

his excellent withholding skills from her. Kiki was the queen of doling out: vacations, money, inherited antiques. She dangled these temptations in front of Daniel, but ultimately gave them to his sister, Kathy, and her children, the beloved grandchildren. Kathy's family accompanied Kiki and Henry on safaris and to island resorts. Her children had their private school educations paid for and were gifted the family jewelry. Not that Charlotte would have wanted to go on a vacation with the elder Oakeses, wear their jewelry, or be indebted for an education or a monetary gift. She didn't care. But Daniel was hurt over and over, and Kiki continually salted that wound. Daniel was punished because he had married her, and now he would like to make her pay for it.

She never had to see Kiki again. The thought made her giddy.

"Exactly how small is the apartment?" Libby drew circles in the frost on the car window.

"It has an open kitchen, two small bedrooms, a living room, and one bathroom." She did not mention the linoleum floor in the kitchen, which she was trying to ignore.

"Are you going to take some furniture from the house? From Dad?"

"No. Fresh start."

"Can you afford that on what you make? You're not making Dad pay you, are you? Are you taking him to court and suing him for all his money?"

Charlotte felt her face go hot with fury. Her hands tensed into a death grip on the steering wheel. "Nothing has been sorted out yet. And I work, too. It's our money, not just his."

"When I was in school, it was always the dads who left. I remember eating chicken fingers and spaghetti from the kids' menus in the hotels and watching TV with my friends. Their dads let us order whatever we wanted and buy movies on TV. I thought it was fun. I didn't realize what it meant."

"Well, you were a kid." Charlotte wondered if Libby was reminiscing or being nasty. She turned the car onto her street and pulled into her space behind her building. The motion detector lights went on and cast eerie shadows onto the snow marked by tire treads. "Here we are."

"They should plow." Libby pulled her suitcase out of the car, frowning in disapproval.

Charlotte was also frowning because Libby was being a spoiled brat. And they'd only just arrived.

They plodded through the dirty snow to the building's back door. A gray hallway led to the lobby, which contained two small chairs and a round wood table topped with a fake orchid. They stepped into the elevator. When they reached the third floor, they followed the long, brown-carpeted hallway.

Charlotte was painfully conscious that the building smelled of Indian food—garlic, cumin, and curry. Not altogether unpleasant but not exactly fresh. Libby wrinkled her nose but didn't comment.

Charlotte opened the door and saw the apartment through Libby's eyes. The living room was bare. The walls still had nails from the former tenant's art. The only place to sit was on two brown leather stools she'd bought on sale earlier that day and hauled home in a cab. They were pushed against the laminate kitchen counter. Libby stared blankly into the kitchen and then blinked.

"You should see it in the daylight. It's sunny and a lot cheerier. Let me show you your room."

Charlotte had taken care with Libby's bedroom. She'd spent her day and an excessive amount of money on it. The full-size bed was made up with contrasting sheets patterned with flowers and stripes and a fluffy duvet. A small, mirrored nightstand her father had brought from their basement was the only other piece of furniture. A vase of white hyacinths rested on the stand along with a purple box of Libby's favorite chili chocolates from Vosges.

"Hangers are in the closet. Unpack. Freshen up if you want. I'll make us a snack. Did you eat dinner? Are you hungry?"

"I'm not really hungry."

LaGuardia was a food desert. Libby had to be hungry. Charlotte took a salad out of the fridge and added the vinaigrette she'd made. In addition to this new salad bowl, she'd also bought six white plates. Two were on the counter with red-and-white cloth napkins and the silver flatware she had borrowed from her mother, who never used it. She laid a baguette next to a plateful of runny Camembert cheese.

These were her offerings. She desperately wanted Libby to like something. Anything.

Libby was taking a long time in her room.

"Come sit down," Charlotte called.

Libby emerged and perched on a stool. She broke the tiny end off of the baguette and cut herself a sliver of the pungent cheese.

Charlotte cut a large triangle of cheese and broke off a chunk of the baguette. She plopped a heap of arugula onto each of their plates. "Would you like some herbal iced tea?" She pointed to a full pitcher on the counter. "It's mint. No sugar."

Libby studied her plate for a minute as if unsure. "Okay."

Charlotte poured from a pitcher into an empty wine glass.

Libby took a sip. She was quiet for a minute. She spread a bit of cheese onto the bread and put it back on the plate. She shook her long hair away from her head and fixed her eyes on her mother. "So, what exactly is going on with you and Dad?"

Charlotte was in the middle of a bite of bread and cheese. She balled up her napkin and put it on the counter. "We've been moving toward this . . . the separation . . . for a while." She kept her voice steady, thinking of the show-no-fear approach when faced with mean dogs and wild animals. "We were married young, and we've both changed into very different people."

"That must happen to a lot of people. Some work it out."

"Well, we don't have a lot in common anymore." It was unfortunate, she knew, that she still sounded like a Hallmark after-school special, but Libby's comment surprised her. She did not want to say that she was the one who had not been willing to work it out.

"But you have me in common, and now you're having another baby." Libby's eyes were fixed on Charlotte again, and she was frowning.

Charlotte concentrated on her crumpled napkin for a moment. "Your dad and I do not have this baby in common. She's not his."

"I don't understand." Libby stabbed her cheese with her knife.

"I'm not proud of it, but I had an affair. I thought I was too old to get pregnant but apparently not."

Libby curled her lip and looked at Charlotte as if she were repulsive. There was nothing worse than being judged by your child and found to be disgusting. "What about the baby's father? Who is he? Are you going to marry him?" Her voice filled the empty room as she pushed her plate away so violently that Charlotte thought it would slide right off the counter.

"No." Charlotte's hands moved to clasp the edges of her stool.

"Doesn't he want to be with his baby?"

It was Charlotte's turn to hesitate. She inhaled deeply.

Libby was hunched over the counter waiting for an answer. She looked, for a second, like a small child. "He doesn't know about the baby, sweetie. And I'm keeping it that way. We stopped seeing each other before I knew I was pregnant."

"I can't believe you were this stupid, Mom. No birth control. After all your talk about condoms with me. Was it that guy, that cop?"

"Of course not!" Her body tingled with rage. It had to be all the hormones. "It was stupid, Libby. But you could be a little nicer. You're not the only one in the world with problems. And who the baby's father is does not have to be anyone's business."

Libby scowled and looked down at the counter.

"I'm trusting you to keep this a secret."

"Do you think that's fair? To the baby?" Libby was staring her down again and Charlotte's rage kept rising.

"This is my choice. I'll reevaluate later. When she's older. This is all I know how to do now."

"Does Dad know it's not his baby?"

"Yes."

Libby got off her stool. "You had everything, Mom. Now you're throwing it all away. If you'd wanted another baby, you could have had one with Dad."

"That's enough, Libby." She was shouting now, which surprised both of them.

"I'm going to sleep." She left Charlotte and stomped into the bathroom. Charlotte heard the water running. She imagined Libby looking at the cracked but pretty original black-and-white tiles. Libby was probably thinking about the difference between the apartment and the house she'd grown up in, the house where her father was still living. She tried not to feel embarrassed. This was a choice she had made.

A few minutes later, Libby appeared. "Night, Mom." She

was wearing a large T-shirt, and her face was pink and scrubbed.

"Night, sweetie. I'm sorry I yelled." And she was sorry . . . terribly, terribly sorry. But Libby was old enough now to think of others and have some empathy. There was no excuse for her mean behavior. She had been tiptoeing around her daughter for too long.

"See you in the morning." Libby walked into her room and shut the door.

She had kept her vow not to tell Emory. In a way, it pleased her to deprive him of this knowledge—the fact of his baby. But it didn't help her erase him from her thoughts.

She had looked Emory up on the Internet more than once to see his picture. In most of the photos, he was at fundraisers standing with groups of people: Greater Chicago Food Depository, the ACLU, Chicago Children's Memorial Hospital. She'd scrolled through the photos, unable to stop. She looked at the one where he was wearing a khaki suit with his wife on his arm. There was his blue sports jacket . . . one of his favorite T-shirts. She ran her finger over his face, over the smooth computer screen. Perhaps she had a touch of Libby's OCD. No sane person would do this, especially with the way he had treated her. It was sad and silly to love someone who did not love you back. And no matter how hard she tried not to be, she was still in love with him.

Still, Libby had made her think about the baby having no father. Charlotte wrote him an email.

Emory,

I've no idea how you will feel about this, but I'm pregnant. It's a girl, and I am certain you're the father. It was a big shock. We both thought I was too old, didn't we? I've left

*Daniel and am living on my own. I'm not expecting or ask-
ing for anything from you, but I thought you should know.
I'll understand if you don't respond.*

Best,
Charlotte

But why was she expecting nothing? Why was it okay for him
not to respond? Low expectations were emotionally safer. She
knew that much, so she wrote it again and deleted the last two
sentences. Then she worried he would think she might be trying
to trap him into child support, so she put them back in. She read
and reread, went to push send, and pressed delete instead.

"You look pregnant." Libby observed her mother as she made
her a bowl of yogurt, fruit, and granola. "You have a tummy and
actual boobs."

"Uh-huh, and both will get bigger."

"What is it?" Her mouth was full. "Do you know?"

"A girl. A baby sister."

"For sure? How did you find out?"

"I had a test to make sure the baby was healthy. It showed
the sex."

"When's she coming?"

"Around July 8."

Libby stared at Charlotte's belly, which was covered by her
robe. "I'm getting a sister." She reached down tentatively and
patted her mother's bump. "Hi in there. Hi, little sister." She
had one more bite of her yogurt, pushed the bowl away, and
went back in her room.

Charlotte sat down on the stool, astounded.

TWENTY-EIGHT

 **ED**

March 2019

E d pulled into his driveway and shut off Dr. Phil, who was probably right about a person having the power to determine how they feel and then using that power for positivity. Maybe he should work on feeling more positive. He was in a perpetual state of dread about Maggie, and he needed to calm down and accept this pregnancy. He opened the front door of their house and removed his coat. Big ran out to greet him, but the house was strangely silent.

"Maggie."

"In the bathroom. Come here." He could tell something was wrong.

Maggie was standing near the toilet, pants off. She had a towel around her waist and was wiping blood off her legs.

"I think I'm miscarrying." Her face was gray.

"Does it hurt?"

"Some cramping."

"God, I'm sorry." As he said this, he was overcome with relief.

"Me too. Dawn will be heartbroken. I feel like a failure."

He took the washcloth from her, placed it in the sink, and put his arms around her. "You're not a failure. You've done your best. This is nature, not you."

She pressed her face into his shoulder, and he felt his shirt dampen. They stood like this for what seemed like a long time. She finally lifted her head. "I should call Dawn."

"I'll do it if you like."

"Thanks." She put on a pad and her underwear and flushed the toilet.

Ed saw bloody water with clumps of what must be tissue swirling down and was overcome with a disgust that embarrassed him. Together they sat on the couch. Ed picked up the landline and dialed.

She answered on the second ring. "Hi."

"Hi, honey."

"Everything okay?"

"Actually, not. Your mom miscarried."

Dawn was silent for a minute.

"How is she?" He could hear the tremble in her voice.

"Shaken." Ed hoped Dawn wouldn't start crying.

"Can I come over?"

"I think she needs to sit with this for a little while."

"Okay, okay. I'll call later."

He did not want Dawn here weeping and making Maggie feel worse. He patted Maggie's hand when he hung up. "Can I get you anything? Some tea or juice? A heating pad for the cramps?"

"No, do you think I should call the doctor? It's after hours."

"Wouldn't hurt. Give me the number. I'll call and talk to the service for you. Then you can talk to a doctor when one calls back."

Maggie sat, her shoulders rounded in disappointment, listening to him leave a message. The phone rang about five minutes later. She picked up the phone and knew Ed had picked up the line in the kitchen and was listening.

"I'm Dr. Reed." It was a woman's voice. "The doctor on call. I hear you miscarried. I'm so sorry. Your file says you're a surrogate."

"Yes, my daughter's surrogate. Is there anything I need to do? Should I be checked?"

"Did you pass some clumpy tissue with the blood?"

"Yes."

"It's nothing to worry about, but I'm going to schedule you for a D&C just to make sure the miscarriage was complete. It's very common. Call the office in the morning, and they'll give you a time."

"Thank you." Maggie hung up.

"You stay put," Ed told her as he came back into the living room. He covered Maggie's legs with a pink blanket she'd crocheted. "I'll go in the kitchen and scare up some dinner. I know we have frozen lasagna. Sound good?"

"Yes, thanks, hon." She propped herself on a pillow and lay prone on the couch.

In the kitchen, Ed let himself feel his relief. He let it flood into him. Visions of pregnancy disasters had been torturing him. He'd been worrying that Maggie could get preeclampsia. He'd googled it constantly. He'd read that the risk goes way up after forty. Her blood pressure might have soared. She would have had to abort to save her own life, despite her pro-life beliefs. Or worse, she could have refused an abortion, choosing to risk her life and possibly have a stroke. He'd been envisioning her being incapacitated, drooling, and speechless in a wheelchair. Lost to him.

He put the lasagna in the microwave, then boiled water for the green beans he'd also found in the freezer. He checked the directions and added salt to the water. He was not used to cooking. While he waited, he poured himself a whiskey, fed Big, and monitored the stove, using the timer on his phone. He heard the TV. Maggie must have turned on the news as a distraction. Maybe she wouldn't try in vitro again, although he knew she would do anything for Dawn.

When dinner was ready, he put their plates onto two trays and carried them to the coffee table. The whiskey had mellowed him a little.

"Looks delicious." She sat up a little higher on the couch.

"Wouldn't go that far." Ed positioned the tray in front of Maggie. She ate a bite of the lasagna and put her fork down.

"Is it okay?"

"I was thinking. If this had to happen, I'm glad it happened early. I hate to think of Dawn going through hope and disappointment over and over again. I'm beginning to wish that she would consider adoption."

"Me too." He exhaled loudly. He couldn't believe he was hearing this.

The news flashed. Twenty-three shootings in Chicago this past weekend. Eleven deaths. Gang wars on the West Side. Maggie was looking at her plate, and he thought she didn't notice, but he was wrong.

"It's time to get out, Ed. It's crazy. Your best friend was killed. You were shot. Enough is enough. I mean it."

He picked up the remote and switched to *Seinfeld*.

"Bon appétit."

He used a high voice, pretending to be Julia Child, which usually made Maggie laugh. This time, all he got was a small, sad smile.

TWENTY-NINE  CHARLOTTE

March 2019

It was a cold, snowy night, the kind where one was thankful to be inside. Charlotte was under her quilt in bed reading when the downstairs buzzer rang. She got up and picked up the intercom phone near the front door.

"Mom."

It was Libby. She was visiting for the weekend and staying with Daniel. Charlotte had not seen her since the visit in January, but she called Libby every day.

Charlotte went to the door and opened it.

Libby stumbled in. Her unbrushed hair was covered in snow. Her limbs were loose.

"Dad's got some lady living in the house. Monica." Her breath reeked of booze.

"Are you okay, Libs?" Charlotte's heart and head pounded. This could not be happening again. "You smell . . . you smell like alcohol."

"Did you know? Know about the girlfriend?" Her voice was belligerent, as if she'd been wronged. "She's walking around the house in your robe."

"No. I didn't know. But I can see you're upset. Is that why you're drinking?"

"I'm fine."

"I'm not so sure about that, honey."

"You even tell me how I should feel. You're so controlling."

"I'm worried about you. You seem drunk."

"It's all about you. Always, Mom." Libby shot her mother a sharp look. It landed on Charlotte's large belly. "And you're no one to talk about right and wrong."

Charlotte attempted to keep her voice calm, despite being plenty alarmed. "Why don't you sit down? Discuss what's upsetting you."

To her surprise, Libby sat. "I'm not drunk."

"Okay, you're not drunk. What's going on?"

"Nothing." And with that she stood up, walked out, and slammed Charlotte's front door.

Charlotte opened it. "Take a cab," she called, before the elevator door shut.

She was too shocked and tired to stop her. Instead, she went back inside and called Libby's New York psychiatrist, Dr. Nichols, and left a message. "This is Charlotte Oakes, Libby's mother. Libby's relapsed. She's drinking. A lot. I can smell it. She denies it, and I'm really worried. I don't know what to do."

She texted Libby: *Call me when u get home.*

She hoped Libby had the sense to listen to her and take a cab. Danger lurked in all Chicago neighborhoods at night. A drunk girl was a perfect target.

Dr. Nichols called back in ten minutes. "Do nothing. She must be the one to tell me. In order for her to conquer something she's abusing, she needs to bring it up on her own. Take control."

"I'm frightened. She was in bad shape. What if she starts taking Oxy again?"

"I know it's hard, but she needs be the one to fix herself. That's the only way it works."

"I'm guessing she's stressed about the divorce. I'm sure she's told you."

"Life is always going to hold a lot of stressors. She needs to learn to cope. If she has relapsed, would an alternative treatment be okay with you? I don't think a twelve-step rehab is the best place for her. She'd do better with an addiction specialist recovering at her own pace."

"Well, traditional rehab sure doesn't seem to be working."

His voice softened. "Most rehabs aren't good with dual diagnoses, like the addiction and the OCD. It's not a surprise. Thanks for giving me a heads-up. Take care."

Charlotte thanked him and hung up. It was dark in her bedroom. Only the bedside lamp was on.

U home? she texted.

Yes appeared on her phone screen.

She let her book drop onto the floor and shut her eyes, but couldn't sleep. Listening to the wind howling, she kept seeing Libby's furious face. What made her so angry all the time? Would Libby ever be able to have a life? Be happy or at least content? She was beginning to doubt it. Hot, fat tears rolled down her cheeks, and she wiped them with the corner of her pillowcase.

The next morning, Charlotte got Daniel's voicemail when she called. She did not leave a message. She pressed her face against the cool pane of her living room window. Outside, a garbage truck barreled up the salt-pocked street. A man walked by with an Australian Shepherd; two squirrels raced up a tree. She watched the squirrels and wondered if Daniel really was unavailable or not answering because she was on the other end. Part of her was relieved, despite the fact that she needed to talk to him while Libby was still in town. She didn't want her to head back to New York without a plan in place. She wished her daughter wasn't going back at all and would stay in Chicago where she could keep an eye on her.

Her phone rang. It was Daniel. The baby gave a big kick. Maybe she felt her mother's nervousness. Charlotte headed to her new couch and sat down.

"You called." Daniel's voice was cold. Impersonal. She pictured him on his chair in the family room. The TV on mute. The girlfriend, probably a young blonde, curled up in the other chair since she'd been there last night. Maybe she was still wearing Charlotte's robe, a camel-colored cashmere that Charlotte wished she had taken with her. It was her favorite robe.

"Yes, we need to talk about Libby. She came over last night, and she was completely smashed."

"You're sure? I was out, and she was in bed when I got home."

Charlotte heard him taking a sip of something, probably coffee.

"Positive. I talked to her doctor last night. She's going to need treatment." This was going well so far. He wasn't yelling.

"Can she go back to the rehab?"

"Her doctor said we can't do anything until she asks for help. But he thought it might be better if she worked one-on-one with an addiction specialist and went at her own pace." Charlotte stroked the soft, brown velvet of the couch.

"Why would we do that?"

"Because she's probably not the right fit for a twelve-step program. She hated the prayer and the God aspects of it. And she's already relapsed twice."

"How would this be different?" His voice was getting testy.

"She would not be locked up, and she'd see a specialist along with her doctor. She'd get help with her OCD and with her addiction. He says they're intertwined. A rehab uses a one-size-fits-all formula. It's not individualized."

"Constant therapy sounds expensive."

"The other way didn't work." She was digging her finger-nails into the couch. She could not tell Daniel that Libby might have even more issues since the hit-and-run. She didn't trust him.

"Plenty of people have relapses and get it right the third or fourth time around. We heard them talk about that during the family meetings. We shouldn't assume it won't work." His voice was getting louder.

"That's true." She tried to add some sweetness to her voice. "But I think we should give this way a try. Go with a system that addresses all her problems. The OCD and anxiety proba-bly cause the drinking."

"Twelve-step is the tried-and-true program. We'll be hand-ing her over to one more doctor if we go the other way, which will cost a fortune. It's ridiculous. Most of rehab is covered by insurance."

"Please, Daniel." She could hear the begging in her voice.

"I won't pay for another shrink."

She knew she had lost. Knew she would have to figure out a way to pay for it, which would be impossible with what she made.

THIRTY  CHARLOTTE

March 2019

She found Ed sitting at a small table looking out the window. He didn't see her. He seemed mesmerized by something.

"Hi." It came out a little loud, and he looked startled. "You seemed deep in thought."

He pushed a cup toward her. "I got you a decaf cappuccino."

Now that she was closer, she could see something about him was off, and for a second, she was worried he'd somehow found out about Libby. He had dark circles under his eyes. The lines around his mouth and eyes looked deeper, as if he'd suddenly aged ten years.

"Ed, is something wrong?"

"Maggie miscarried." He took the top off his cup and smooshed it in half. "She had to have a D&C."

Tears sprung into Charlotte's eyes. Her hands involuntarily traveled to her abdomen. "I'm sorry. How awful."

"I'm sad for her and relieved for me, which makes me a horrible person."

"Oh, Ed, you're one of the best people I know." She leaned across the table, without thinking, and grabbed his hand. It was their first physical contact, and it did not seem weird. He did nothing to remove it. They were close enough that she smelled a mix of Tide and Old Spice, which seemed exactly right.

"Thank you."

"How's Maggie?"

"Fine. I guess it's early enough so that physically, it's no big deal. But she's upset. She feels like she failed, let Dawn down."

"What will Dawn do?"

"Not sure. I get the feeling Maggie doesn't want to go through this again."

"Have you asked her?"

"Well, no. Not directly."

"Maybe you should ask her, you know, directly."

"We've been talking about having Dawn and Jake over for dinner this weekend to bring up adoption."

"So, Maggie did mention adoption."

"Yeah, but I don't know what will happen if they don't want to adopt. It's not like they don't know that option exists."

"It'd be hard on both Maggie and Dawn to keep this up."

"I never want to do this again. Never want to see another fertility doctor's office, and I've only been twice."

"Don't blame you." She was edgy and hot, so she unwound her scarf and unzipped her parka. "I feel bad about my healthy baby who was a complete surprise. It seems unfair."

"That's silly. You're feeling fine, right?"

She was not fine, but she didn't want to burden him when he was upset. "Pretty well. I'm a little tired probably because Libby visited."

"How did it go?"

She caved. "Badly. She came over drunk and stormed out. She's relapsed, and I'm really worried about her."

"What did you do? Tell Daniel?"

She sipped her coffee.

"I called her doctor. Daniel has a girlfriend, and Libby's upset about that, among other things. The doctor said I should wait until she brings the drinking up since she's denying it. He eventually wants her to do one-on-one rehab with an addiction doctor."

"That sounds like some sort of plan."

"Daniel refuses. Says it's too expensive. It's not really a plan yet, and she's already back in New York."

"That's a tough one." He added a packet of sugar to his coffee that, Charlotte saw, already had cream in it.

"Ed, there's cream in your coffee! I can't believe you lied to me all these months about not taking milk in your coffee. Why didn't you tell me?"

"Didn't want to hurt your feelings. I'm fine with sugar."

"I would have happily added it, you sneak."

Ed laughed. It was good to see him laugh. A relief. And for a second, Charlotte could see through that hidden window in his face all the way back to when he was a boy.

When they finished their coffee, and Charlotte thought Ed was at least a little better, she knew she needed to head home. On her desk was a $4,500 bill from Libby's new addiction doctor. Insurance had paid for her detox at NYU but would not cover this new therapist, who saw Libby five days a week at $450 a crack. Daniel was still refusing to help. Charlotte had gone through her small savings and had $2,800 in her account, barely enough to cover her food and rent.

She looked at the diamonds sparkling on her hand. Tomorrow she would sell the diamond band and her engagement ring. That should cover a few weeks of Libby's private treatment. Eventually, Charlotte would get her divorce settlement, and then she'd be able to pay. This was shitty of Daniel, but it did no good to dwell on it.

The guard buzzed Charlotte into Blackburn's Jewelers. The store was empty and silent. She walked past cases filled with rings, earrings, and brooches. A small gold snake with emerald eyes glittered in the corner of the case near to where Charlotte stood waiting.

Julie, the owner, stepped out from the back. She was a tall, California-blonde type. Her skin was golden, and she radiated health.

"Charlotte, hi! How can I help you? Is it that time of year? Are you picking out a bracelet?" She reached into a case and produced a tray of gold bangles. When she looked back up, her gaze fell directly on Charlotte's belly. Her eyes widened, and her brows shot up.

"Actually, no." Charlotte was mortified. Ashamed of having to sell her rings, ashamed of her pregnancy, ashamed of not being who she was expected to be. She hadn't realized it would be this hard. "I need to sell you back my engagement and wedding rings." She wished she could drop through the floor.

"You do? You know the resale value isn't the same as what you paid?"

"I don't know anything about it; I need to sell." She removed both rings from her finger and placed them on the counter. They looked dull against the sparklers below.

"We buy our diamonds from diamond dealers." Julie moved the rings onto a velvet tray. "You'll only get about thirty percent of what you paid."

"Really? Even for good diamonds? From here?"

"Yes, that's how it goes." Julie put on her lighted jewelers' glasses and closely inspected the rings. She did so in a way that made Charlotte feel as if she had somehow damaged them.

She picked up the phone and pressed a few numbers. "Margaret, please bring me the receipts for Daniel and Charlotte

Oakes." Margaret, who always dressed in black and had a perfectly symmetrical bob, came in with a pile of receipts.

"Nice to see you, Mrs. Oakes," she said, and left immediately.

Julie put on her reading glasses and shuffled through the receipts. "Daniel bought these rings a long time ago. He paid $8,000 for your engagement ring and $10,500 for the diamond band. They're good stones."

Charlotte watched as she punched numbers into the calculator. She needed to become a person who didn't care that she had to sell her rings. She would feel much better not wearing them. She already did.

"That comes to $5,500. I could give you $7,000 if you're willing to take a credit."

"No, I need to sell."

That amount would not go far. And she would be getting another bill soon. Charlotte had never not been able to pay. She made enough from her job to cover her minimal expenses, but nothing like these huge medical bills.

Julie picked up her phone again. "Margaret, will you please write a check to Charlotte Oakes for $5,500?"

Charlotte looked at the jewelry case to avoid looking at Julie. Margaret quickly came down with a check in an envelope. Charlotte thanked the women and fled the store, disappointed in the end that Julie, whom she'd known for all these years, didn't care enough to ask about her well-being.

THIRTY-ONE  ED

May 2019

Maggie was still grieving. It was as if she'd gone down a dark hole, and he didn't know how to help. He also felt guilty about his relief when she was miserable. He needed time alone tonight, so he headed to the Green Mill for an early set of jazz and a whiskey. It was the place he went when he needed an escape.

"My buddy Nick wants to talk," he told Maggie over the phone. "We're going to grab some ribs." He now felt bad about his lie as well as his need to be alone. He drove through the Green Mill's Uptown neighborhood with its bustling check-cashing places, dollar stores, and cheap Chinese restaurants and found a parking spot near the bar.

"Hey, Ed," Frankie, the bouncer, greeted him. "It's been a while. The place is all yours right now. The guys will be glad someone came to listen to their set."

He sat on the slightly sticky stool, ordered a drink, and tried to give himself over to the music. The band played some of his favorites: "Goodbye Pork Pie Hat," "Take Five," and "Lush Life." None of the songs cheered him up.

A few office workers came in and ordered beers, followed by a trio of older men who were warmly greeted by Frankie. Ed's stomach rumbled, but it was too early to go home since he'd said he was having dinner with Nick.

He walked down the block to Demera, an Ethiopian restaurant he'd always wanted to try. Maggie disliked foreign and spicy food, so this was the perfect time. With the waitress's guidance, he ordered an Ethiopian beer and a spongy bread to scoop up the food—spicy beef stew and a split pea dish. It was delicious, and for a bit, he was able to simply concentrate on scooping small, fiery bits into his mouth and washing them down with the beer. By the time he finished, it was eight. He decided to drive to the intersection before he went home.

When he arrived, he got out of the car and stretched. His back hurt. He needed to exercise. The intersection made him miss Charlotte, so he walked the few blocks to the lakefront.

Lake Michigan was dark gray and full of enormous chunks of ice. Its expanse always amazed him, a lake that looked like an ocean and could be equally cruel. There were rip tides that killed swimmers every summer when the beaches were packed with people trying to cool off. During winter storms, enormous waves crashed over the seawalls flooding the Outer Drive, closing it to traffic, creating commuter chaos. Tonight, the lake was still. Even the clouds seemed frozen in the sky.

He walked back and passed the white apartment building that reminded him of a birthday cake. He got in and turned on the radio. Dr. Phil. Something about not having any more excuses and being honest with yourself about your behavior.

He pressed off. He did not need to hear this tonight. He knew what was going on. There was no traffic on the highway, and he sped along in silence. He pulled into the driveway and didn't bother with the garage.

Big greeted him at the front door. He could hear Maggie in the kitchen and the clatter of pots. She shouldn't be cooking.

He should have brought her something to cheer her up or suggested they go to the movies tomorrow. God, he was lame.

"Hi, Mags. I'm going to jump in the shower."

"Take a look on the coffee table. There's an official-looking letter from the department."

His stomach was queasy as he slit the envelope open. He quickly read it, then read it again.

> An internal ballistics report has determined that the bullet that struck Officer Thomas Malloy in the head September 3, 2019, was from Officer Ed Kelly's gun. The bullet ricocheted off the suspect Tyrone Jackson's gun before hitting and killing Officer Malloy. Officer Kelly is cleared of any wrongdoing in Officer Thomas Malloy's death.

He allowed himself a moment of consolation. The letter exonerated him, but his guilt would never go away. He would go back, but it would be brief. Tommy was dead. He didn't deserve to be a police officer.

THIRTY-TWO  CHARLOTTE

May 2019

There was no way she could keep paying for Libby's therapy. She should speak to the addiction therapist, Dr. Gruber, about her financial situation and reassure the doctor that she would pay in full when her divorce was final and she got her settlement. This might require a trip. It was always better to talk about dicey situations in person rather than over the phone. If she went to New York, she could also see Libby and talk to her again about her car and the hit-and-run. Her guilt over Sarah's death constantly weighed on her, and soon, she wouldn't be able to fly. Then she would be busy with a newborn. Time was slipping away. She had to address the accident now and quit hiding from what might be the truth.

Sitting at her computer, she cashed in miles for a round-trip ticket. She would have two days in New York. She emailed Dr. Gruber for an appointment and called Libby.

Lately, despite her looming question, her conversations with Libby had been easier. It was either the distance or Libby was improving. "How would you feel about a visit, while I can still fly?"

Libby hesitated a moment. "I guess that's cool."

Charlotte hated to ask, but she had to. A New York hotel would be a fortune. "Can it be a slumber party where I sleep on

your couch?" Life would be easier after she got her divorce settlement, but she would always have to be careful with money.
She was still on Daniel's insurance, which would cover her
pregnancy and the baby's birth. After they divorced, he would
have to pay for her insurance for the next three years. At least
her business was doing well and would pick up even more in
the spring.

"Sure. When are you coming?"

"Thursday. I arrive before you'll be done with work. That
okay?"

"I'll leave a key with the doorman."

"See you soon, sweetie. I'm excited." Excited and appre-
hensive. She hadn't seen Libby since the night she'd been
drunk. She rifled through her closet trying to figure out what
to pack. She'd gained almost thirty pounds, and her wardrobe
was limited. She'd bought another pair of maternity jeans and
some large men's oxford shirts. At least now there were stylish
maternity clothes as opposed to the hideous tents she'd worn
the first time around. But they were expensive, and she hated
to spend a lot on clothes she knew she'd never wear again. Her
belly wasn't the only part of her swelling. Her feet were so swollen, she couldn't fit into her shoes comfortably and she'd had to
buy some wide sneakers and large snow boots. Both were ugly.
She had a moment of nostalgia for the sky-high pumps she'd
worn the night she'd fainted. After folding her shirts and putting them into her carry-on, she texted Ed. *Going to visit Libby
in New York for two days on Thursday.*

Have fun! he wrote. *I got my uniform back. I start again next
week but have decided it will be brief. Retirement is in my near
future.*

Fantastic! We need to celebrate when I get back.

Writing Ed, she had another jolt of shame over Libby's

possible crime. She wondered if she should tell Daniel she was leaving, but he wasn't helping to pay for Libby's treatment, which was why she was going to New York. Screw him.

Emory.

If she died in a plane crash (which was what she expected every time she flew), Emory would never know about the baby. But if she were killed, the baby would be, too. Telling him now would seem like an excuse to reach out—a way to justify talking to him. Planes were certainly safer than cars and much safer than the taxis she took. She told herself this every time she had to fly. She also kept a close watch on the flight attendants to see if they looked scared. That, she figured, would be the time to panic.

It was odd to walk into Libby's apartment alone. There was the couch they had chosen together and the table she'd helped to assemble. The apartment smelled of Libby's rose perfume. She set her suitcase down by the couch. She had forgotten how tiny the place was, compared to any apartment in Chicago.

She used the bathroom, which was pristine. Libby's bed was in an alcove. A small nightstand was next to it, and Charlotte reflexively opened the drawer. A printout of the *Chicago Tribune* article about the hit-and-run was on top. It was folded in half, and Sarah's face beamed up at her. Charlotte's heart sped up, and the baby elbowed, then kicked. She shut the drawer and sat down on the bed. If Libby hadn't been driving, why would she keep an article about an accident she hadn't seen?

The day of the accident, Libby had refused to answer her about the car, and the next time Charlotte asked, she'd denied it. Maybe she'd looked up the hit-and-run because Charlotte had basically accused her of taking her car. Still, it made her anxious, especially since she'd grown so close to Ed.

It was only three, and Libby would not be back until seven. Charlotte's appointment with the therapist was the next morning. She was too agitated to sit. She had to get out of the apartment. Walk. Think. She would go buy food and make dinner. This neighborhood was devoid of normal grocery stores like Gristedes. Whole Foods was expensive, but her only local choice. If she wanted to make a nice dinner for Libby, that was where she would have to go. She put her coat back on and walked past piles of garbage bags to the Whole Foods on Houston. She had forgotten about New York and garbage . . . how the city didn't have nice, neat alleys like Chicago.

It was a damp, gray day, but one of the good things about being pregnant was that she was never cold. She wore her too-small parka unzipped. She passed the old knish place and Russ & Daughters, with its odd but tempting window display of dried fruit and smoked fish exhibited side by side, as if apricots and smoked salmon were a delicious combination. The smoked fish did tempt her. Pregnancy made her constantly hungry, and she loved Russ & Daughters' fish, especially on an everything bagel with tomato and red onion. Too expensive and indulgent. She kept walking.

The sameness of Whole Foods was soothing. When she walked past the flowers, she hesitated but then reached for a bunch of blue hydrangeas. She bought a whole organic chicken, herbs, butter, greens, blue cheese, pecans, and eggplant. She would roast the chicken and eggplant for dinner, maybe throw in the potatoes she'd found in Libby's fridge. The apartment would smell of home when Libby walked in. She wasn't sure if that was good or bad.

She stopped at a French bakery and picked out miniature

éclairs and fruit tarts and croissants for breakfast. Another splurge, but she wanted this time to feel special to Libby, to make sure she didn't feel displaced by the baby as well as to smooth the way for the questions she would have to ask. She carried the pink bakery box carefully in one hand, the shopping bag in the other.

It took her a few minutes to find cooking tools and a vase. The roasting pan she'd bought for Libby had clearly never been used. The electric oven, with its computer panel, confused her for a minute. Soon, she was chopping, her phone streaming Mozart piano sonatas. Both were calming. She needed that. Her life was upside-down. And the thought of bringing up the accident made her jittery all over again.

"I could smell dinner all the way down the hall." Libby tried to hug her mother and ended up bouncing off her belly. It had been months since Libby had hugged Charlotte. "Your stomach's huge."

"Gets in the way of human contact," Charlotte joked, happy for once to make light of her pregnancy. Libby's hair had grown, her eyes were clear, and there was natural color on her cheeks. "You look wonderful, sweetie. How are you feeling? You like your new therapist?"

"I'm good. I really like Dr. Gruber. She's young and gets what it's like for me. She doesn't make me feel bad. She says addiction is like having diabetes or any other disease you need to manage."

"That's terrific." Maybe Libby had brought up the hit-and-run with her doctor. "How's work?"

"I like going there. J. Crew is much better than being in group rehab therapy or hanging out in that awful cafeteria and drinking soda all day." She fake shuddered.

"That cafeteria was greasy and disgusting. Did you tell anyone at work about your treatment?"

"Only my boss because of my time off. I'm friendly with a couple of girls, but there's no reason to tell them, especially since their favorite activity is going to bars. There's no way I would do that. God, I never want to go through detox again."

"I hope you meet some friends you can be honest with. That must be lonely."

"It is what it is," she said with a shrug. "That's what most people my age do."

"There must be people who like to do other things. Maybe you could take a class or join a writing group. Meet some people with similar interests." She knew this sounded like typical motherly advice and hoped she didn't sound lame.

"That's not a bad idea. I would like to take a writing class. New School has some."

"That sounds fun. You should do it. Dinner's almost ready. Hungry?"

"Starving. And you bought flowers. They're so pretty."

When she looked at the flowers again, she thought of the ones she brought to Sarah's memorial. Her hormones kicked in, and she felt her eyes begin to brim. Nearly everything, including commercials, made her cry these days. She turned away to hide her face and pulled the chicken from the oven. The scent of rosemary floated through the room. The chicken was brown and crisp. The eggplant and potatoes sizzled. She blinked away the tears and regained her composure.

Libby walked over to the cabinets. "I'll get plates. We'll have to eat at the coffee table."

Charlotte piled the plates with food, and they carried them to the couch. "I poured water, but it's in the kitchen."

"Got it." Libby fetched the glasses.

"How does it feel being pregnant again?"

"A little weird. But the thing about pregnancy is that it keeps changing."

"Changing? How?" Libby seemed genuinely curious.

"At first, I was sick, and that was miserable. Now I feel fine, and I'll get bigger and bigger, and then it will be over. The fun part is she's moving all around now." She pulled her sweater tight over her abdomen. "There's her foot."

"Wow," Libby said. She tentatively touched her mother's belly. "She's kicking! Is that her elbow over here?"

Charlotte nodded. "She's pretty active. Especially this time of day."

"I don't know if I ever want to have kids," Libby said, her hand still resting on her mother.

"There's no law that says you have to. A child should be wanted." Charlotte couldn't help but think this might be for the best. She wondered if Libby was thinking of Sarah.

"So, you really want this baby? Even though there's no real father?"

She wasn't sure how to answer that "real father" comment. There was one; he just didn't know about his baby. Thinking of Emory, she was hit with both sorrow and anger.

"At first, I wasn't sure. It was a surprise and daunting." She was embarrassed to be confessing this to her daughter, but thought it was important to tell her the truth.

"What changed your mind?"

"Love, I guess. I loved this baby's father. Even though it didn't turn out well, it made me fall in love with her."

"That's . . ." Libby stopped for a second. "That's awesome, Mom. Who's the father?"

"You don't know him. He's someone I met through work.

He's married, so that makes the situation even worse. That's one of the reasons I'm not telling him about the baby."

Charlotte was quiet for a moment. She knew she had to ask about the car. She couldn't pretend that everything was okay. "Since we're talking, Libs, I want to ask you again about the accident. I keep thinking about it. Were you driving? It's important for both of us that you tell me."

"I told you, no. And I don't think it's fair to the baby not to know her father."

"You may be right about the baby. I'm taking all this slowly. Not making any rash decisions."

"Did you pick a name yet?"

"I was hoping you'd help." She knew this was a ploy for Libby to avoid more questions. Still, she went along with it.

"Really?"

Something about the way Libby said this—her surprise at being included—made Charlotte sad. "Any ideas?"

"How about a flower name? I've always wanted one."

"Which ones do you like?"

Libby thought for a moment. "Hyacinth, Lily, Poppy, Violet . . ."

"Violet and Poppy are beautiful. Poppy sounds stronger. Violet makes me think of that old phrase, 'shrinking violet.' What do you think?"

"I like both. Poppy goes better with Libby, though."

"I kind of love it," Charlotte said.

"Me too." Libby ate a bit of chicken and put down her fork. "I've been feeling a lot better recently. And this dinner is delicious."

"That makes me happy," Charlotte said. She didn't know how she could bring up the accident again without losing the ground she had just gained. She did know she had to stop being a wimp.

"I'm glad you came to visit," Libby said. "I didn't realize how much I miss you. I think when I'm done with my therapy, I want to move back to Chicago. Maybe in the fall."

"That would be wonderful." She had to plow forward. Ask the question.

"I'm going to look for a job with animals."

"You've always loved animals. That's a great idea. Maybe you could work for a vet. Or become a vet."

"That would be cool."

"I think you'd be a great vet if you're willing to put in all that time. But Libby, we need to talk about the car and the accident. You keep saying you didn't take the car, but it wasn't there when I got home. I went out and looked. After you came home, it was back. With a dent."

"I told you, Mom. I didn't take your car. Stop asking me." Her belligerent look was back. Her eyes narrowed and the color drained from her face.

Charlotte got up to get the pastries from the fridge before Libby could see her face, which also must be ashen. She arranged the miniature pastries on a plate and carried them to the coffee table.

"I'm full." Libby's face was still clouded with anger.

Charlotte was now certain that she'd hit Sarah. She didn't know what she'd do with a confession, but she needed Libby to tell her what she'd done. If only she could rewind and somehow do things differently. Change the outcome of Libby's life. But that was magical thinking. She had to deal with reality, and the reality was looking worse and worse.

THIRTY-THREE  ED

May 2019

"We should get a bird feeder," Ed said to himself. It was a bright Sunday afternoon in May, the first decent day in a long time. He had been organizing the garage, spring cleaning, and listening to the birds chattering through the open door. He hoped they would have a robin's nest in the maple tree again this year. He walked around a pile of tools and returned to the house.

"Wipe your feet," Maggie said, before he even got in the door. Just then, the phone rang. Maggie picked up and listened. "Great," she said. She hung up and turned to Ed. "Dawn and Jake are coming over."

"Nice," he said, and wondered if there was a specific reason. Sometimes, Jake liked to sit and watch a game with him while Maggie and Dawn chatted. "To hang out?"

"She didn't say. I'll make some iced tea." Maggie arranged some molasses and sugar cookies on a plate. When Ed snatched one, she smiled. "Take these to the coffee table, and guard them from Big."

It was so quiet outside that Ed could hear the beep of Dawn and Jake's car alarm when they pulled up. Big heard it, began barking, and rushed to the door.

Dawn was wearing a Michigan T-shirt, and her hair was wet from a shower.

"Hi, honey," said Ed, giving her cheek a kiss. He got a whiff of the coconut shampoo she'd been using since she was a teenager.

"Come and get some iced tea," Maggie called out.

Jake came in behind Dawn, who was headed to the kitchen.

"Want to watch the Cubs?" Ed asked.

"In a bit," Jake said, as he settled into the armchair.

Dawn and Maggie put the tea in front of the men and sat down. Big was lying on the floor at their feet.

Dawn opened her phone and silently handed it to her mother. It was a picture of a pretty blonde teenage girl in a soccer uniform.

"Who's this?" Maggie asked, her forehead wrinkling in confusion.

"Her name is Kayla, and we think she's going to be the birth mother of our baby," Dawn said with a huge smile.

"Oh, my lord," Maggie said, staring at the screen. She handed the phone to Ed.

He stared at the phone in disbelief. "How did you find her?"

"Through my doctor," Dawn said, taking the phone from Ed. "Kayla's only fifteen. Her parents are very Catholic, so she agreed to have the baby, a girl, and give her up. We've been talking to Kayla for about a month. This is her boyfriend, Jeremy." She scrolled to a picture of a handsome, red-haired boy. "The baby might even have red hair like me!"

"Does she . . . Do they . . . want to give the baby to you?" Maggie's voice trembled, and she took a sip of her tea.

"She's interviewed four couples, but says she's the most comfortable with us," Jake said. "She gave us the okay today. We've also talked with her parents, who are thrilled about the religious part."

"We're thinking along the lines of modern Catholic," Dawn said. "Kayla liked that."

"What about her boyfriend?" Ed asked. This was incredible, and he didn't want Dawn to be crushed if it didn't work out.

"He's on board with whomever she chooses," Jake said. "They're both sweet kids. He will also have to sign the papers."

"What about their medical backgrounds?" Maggie asked. "You don't really know what you're getting into. What if there's mental illness or a terrible genetic disease?"

"Since we know the parents, we can check all that out," Dawn said. She looked happier and more relaxed than Ed had seen her in a long time.

"You should probably talk to their parents," Maggie said, her voice high with what Ed recognized as anxiety. "The kids are too young to know. And some families hide medical issues. There's that."

"When is she due?" Ed asked. He was sensing this was headed in the wrong direction. Maggie did not seem happy about the adoption. This puzzled him.

"She's six months, and we know she's had excellent medical care because she's one of my doctor's patients."

"What if she changes her mind?" Maggie asked.

"She can't sign the adoption papers until seventy-two hours after she gives birth," Jake explained. "Then, it's final. But she could change her mind before then. It happens."

"But usually not with someone this young," Dawn said. "She has high school to finish. A whole life ahead of her."

"You know, maybe you should rethink this," Maggie said. "I would be willing to try surrogacy again. It seems as if that's more of a sure thing. No one could take the baby from you, and you wouldn't have a medical background issue."

"Mom, we don't want to put you through that again,"

Dawn said. "And I don't think we're going to have either one of those issues."

"But I'm willing." Maggie was beginning to look frantic to Ed.

"We don't want to lose another baby again, Mom," Dawn said. "It's happened over and over to me, and it happened to you. I think this baby will work out."

"You're sure?" Maggie swiped her hand through the air and hit her glass. Both glass and tea went flying, but there was no breakage. Only a big spill. Maggie jumped up to get a towel.

Ed followed her into the kitchen. "What's going on?" he asked. "You don't seem happy about this."

"I think it would be better if they had a genetic child. Adopting could open a can of worms."

"They seem to have come to terms with this," he said. "Maybe you should back off a bit."

Maggie picked up a clean towel, turned her back on Ed, and walked out of the kitchen.

"How would this work with the parents?" Maggie asked, as she continued wiping the tea. "Would you keep in touch?"

"We're open," Dawn said. "It's up to them. Everything I've read says it's good to have a relationship with the birth parents. Imagine how it would be to have a baby and think you'll never see her again."

"Devastating," Maggie said.

"It would be," Dawn agreed, taking a bite out of a sugar cookie. "And the baby may have questions as she gets older. It's better for everyone to be open and honest."

"How about visits?" Maggie asked.

"We talked about that," Dawn said. "We think it's a good idea. We know we'll be the parents. She's not in a position to be a parent, and too much love never hurt a child."

"I hope the parents don't regret their decision when they visit," Maggie said. "That doesn't sound like a good idea to me."

"I can't believe how perfect this is," Ed said, petting Big, who was nudging in to snatch a cookie.

"I still think you should be careful," Maggie said. "People do change their minds."

"How about we celebrate," Ed suggested, wishing Maggie would stop putting up obstacles.

"Something stronger than this tea," Dawn said, raising her glass.

Ed went to the liquor cabinet and got out a bottle of Bailey's, along with four small glasses. He poured and passed the first glass to Maggie, knowing it was the only liquor she might drink.

"To your new daughter, our granddaughter," he said. They clinked glasses and even Maggie had a sip. Out of the corner of his eye, Ed saw a large tear travel down her face. She quickly brushed it away.

THIRTY-FOUR  CHARLOTTE

May 2019

Charlotte was seated at her new farm table surrounded by storyboards and a large pitcher filled with cosmos from the farmers market. It was almost summer, and her clients wanted new clothes, so she was pairing dresses with shoes and bags. She stopped only to inhale lunch, a turkey and tomato sandwich and some grapes. Work, at least, helped keep her mind off Libby.

Libby was finishing up her addiction therapy and would soon be moving back to Chicago. Her biggest plan so far was to get a dog. She'd already found a pet rescue where she could volunteer and stake out potential candidates. But the question of Libby's guilt weighed on Charlotte. She felt as if she was betraying Ed, even though she had no outright confession. What she would do with that confession, she didn't know.

It was mid-afternoon when Ed texted: *Meet me at Starbucks?*

Desperate for a break, she was quickly out the door. Charlotte waddled down Dickens Avenue, her protruding belly button visible through her cotton T-shirt. The air smelled of cut grass and newly laid mulch and even though the baby was uncomfortably perched on her bladder, it was wonderful to be outside.

She turned onto Clark Street, where parents were lining up their cars for school pickup at Lowell. This was something

Charlotte had never done since they had lived two blocks away. It was the end of the school year, and the students were in high spirits. The girls on the field hockey team were streaming out the school entrance and getting on a bus, sticks in hand. It seemed so long ago that Libby was a student there. She'd never played field hockey or anything else, claiming a hatred of sports and uniforms. Charlotte paused for a minute to listen to the girls' laughter as they goofed around on the sidewalk.

At Starbucks, she was suddenly nervous about seeing Ed. She bought a coffee, a decaf cappuccino, and two lemon cookies, then found a table where she could watch the street. As soon as she sat, Ed came hustling down the block in his blue police jacket and shirt. He saw her and waved.

As he neared the table, she picked up her coffee. "Cheers to your uniform." Then she remembered that this meant he could arrest her, as well as Libby, which is probably what they deserved.

"I have even bigger news," he said, even before he was seated across from her.

"What? What?" Charlotte slid his coffee and cookie across the table.

"Dawn and Jake are adopting." He was grinning.

"How? Who?" She leaned forward, and her belly butted up against the table.

"The baby's mom is a patient of Dawn's doctor, and he introduced them."

"That's incredible!" Charlotte took a sip of her coffee. She had to focus. Ed in his uniform *was* making her nervous. He looked much more intimidating.

"I'm so excited. Dawn and Jake plan to keep in touch with the birth parents. Visits and everything. It's a whole new age. Maggie thinks it's a little much."

"The keeping in touch?" she asked, taking a bite out of her cookie.

"She's not happy about the adoption. She even offered to be a surrogate again, saying a genetic baby would be better. It was a little bizarre."

Charlotte wrinkled her forehead. "That does seem a bit strange. When's the baby due?"

"A month or so after you. The girl is only fifteen, so it's nice she's giving birth in the summer. She won't miss any school. Do you want to see their pictures? Dawn sent me screenshots." He passed the phone. "That's Kayla, and that's the father, Jeremy."

"This will be a beautiful baby."

"She will. It's a girl," Ed said, sipping his coffee. "We'll be on pins and needles until she's born and the papers are signed. How's Libby, speaking of girls?"

Charlotte willed her face not to heat. "She's good, and she's planning on moving here in August. I'm helping her look for an apartment." Charlotte glanced out the window and saw a group of teenagers. "Look at that. I can't believe kids still smoke."

He laughed. "Kids continue to be stupid."

They were quiet for a minute, watching the street and the students.

"One more thing," he said. "I'm going to file for retirement. After Tommy's death, I don't want to work in the department anymore. And I promised Maggie. But I'll work until the end of August."

"I guess I expected this, but I'll miss you." She had to stop herself from giving a small sigh of relief.

"I'll still come see you."

"I've got an idea," she said, smiling. "I'm dying to meet your family. How about you all come to dinner before I have this baby. It can be a retirement party."

She was shocked at her own suggestion. It was possible the baby had made her lose her mind.

"Do you really think that's a good idea?"

She did not, but there was no polite way out of the invitation now. "It's my last chance to have people over."

"We're a big family. It's too much for you," he said, shaking his head.

"Not at all. I love to cook. Will you think about it?"

"Of course," he said, but his face looked as if it were saying, *No way.* Charlotte suspected he was worried for some reason about her meeting Maggie.

Maybe the dinner wouldn't happen.

THIRTY-FIVE

 **ED**

May 2019

E d opened the car windows on his way home from coffee with Charlotte. He let the exhaust-filled wind blow on his face as he mulled over the idea of a dinner and the Charlotte/Maggie situation. He'd never mentioned Charlotte to Maggie and had no idea how he would bring up a party.

The problem was that he'd been deceptive for months. Maggie would not be happy. She might be furious, touchy as she was about his being around other women. When Tommy had been away for a few days, and another officer, Louise, filled in for him, Maggie had been batty. That is, until she'd finally seen Louise's photo, which like Louise, was not particularly attractive.

But Charlotte was not Louise. He needed to tell Maggie he had a female friend, and he was not looking forward to it.

When he walked in the back door, Maggie was frying pork chops with onions, one of his favorite meals. The house smelled delicious, but his stomach contracted with stress. Big ran into the living room, butted his head against Ed, and licked his hand.

"Hey, honey," he called as he made his way straight to their small liquor cabinet. "Any chance you want a drink? I'm pouring myself a whiskey."

"You know I don't want one, Ed, but you go ahead."

He poured himself a glass, took a gulp, and then carried it into the kitchen, which smelled sweet and earthy like baked potatoes. He sat down. Big settled at his feet. "I need to tell you something, Mags." His arm felt heavy as he lifted his drink.

She turned to face him, her eyes swimming with worry. "What? No one's died, right?"

"No, no. I didn't mean to scare you. It's only that I have something, well someone, I've been meaning to tell you about. A friend. Her name is Charlotte, and she was with me when I found Big. She came up with the name Profiterole. I didn't know what a profiterole was, either."

"What are you saying? I don't understand." The kitchen was warm, and a few stray hairs stuck to Maggie's forehead.

"I have a friend, Charlotte, who I haven't told you about."

"What? You're having an affair?"

"No. Not an affair. Not at all. She's a friend. I met her at the intersection. She left flowers every week, and we started talking."

He had made a terrible mistake by bringing Charlotte up. He should have said no, but he wanted her to meet his family. So stupid!

"Why didn't you tell me about her when you met?"

Ed knew this was the question that would lead to all the problems he was about to have.

"At first, I didn't know we'd become friends, and then I was afraid to tell you because I thought you might not like that I have a woman friend." He was over-explaining.

"I don't. I don't like it at all."

"She's a friend, Mags. Have I ever given you a reason to distrust me?" Sweat was running down his back. He'd always prided himself on being a truth-teller.

She plopped down in a kitchen chair. The pot holder was still in her hand. "Not up until now. But this is a doozy. How often do you see her?"

"When we first met, once a week at the intersection. But then we started talking, and now we have coffee at Starbucks a couple times a week." He realized how bad it sounded as the words left his mouth.

"How old is she?"

"Around forty-five. She loves your cookies." Ed could feel the beat of his pulse in his wrist. It was leaping around like a crazed animal.

"How am I supposed to feel about this? Is she married?"

He gulped his drink. Heat streamed down his throat to his stomach. Thank God for whiskey. "She's getting a divorce, but she's pregnant."

"Why on earth would she divorce now? Pregnant? And at forty-five?" Her face was scrunched, and she looked interested, confused, and angry at the same time.

"The baby isn't her husband's." He held his breath, waiting.

"Whose baby is it?"

"A man she'd had an affair with. He doesn't know. But she told her husband before she left him. She's having a tough time."

The pot holder in Maggie's hand flew at his face. She got up and stalked out of the kitchen without looking at him. Big raced after her.

He knew enough not to go to her immediately. She needed time alone when she was upset, but this was going way worse than he had expected. He sat drinking his whiskey. The plates for dinner were on the counter, and he set the table. He filled two glasses with ice and water. Big wandered back in. Ed gave him a bowl of Maggie's dog soup before he went to knock on the bedroom door.

"Can we talk, Mags?"

"Go away," she said. "That woman sounds like trash."

He knew enough not to defend Charlotte. It would only make Maggie angrier, and Charlotte's story wasn't a pretty one. He turned the doorknob and poked his head in. She was lying on top of the bed with a pillow over her head. He walked in and sat down at the foot of the bed, near her feet.

"You know how much I love you, right?" he said. She pulled the pillow from her face.

"Why didn't you tell me at the beginning when you met her?"

"I was afraid you'd be mad. And you are." He said it softly, knowing it was not much of an excuse, and that no matter what he said, he would sound guilty as hell.

"Decent people don't behave like she does, Ed. I don't much approve of divorce, and I definitely don't approve of affairs. And a baby on top of all that. I don't understand how you can be friends with her. Is she pretty?"

"I guess she's pretty, but that doesn't matter. You're the one for me. My very own Julia Roberts, who doesn't hold a candle to you, by the way."

They sat in silence for a minute. "Why did you tell me now?"

Ed could feel his face reddening. "This might sound ridiculous."

"What?"

"She invited the whole family for dinner."

"She what?" Maggie sat up. "Why?"

"Charlotte thought you knew all about her, and she wants to have a family retirement party for me before she has her baby. She wants to meet you. She wants to meet the whole family. I've told her about everyone."

"Lord," Maggie said. "When did she ask?"

"Today. I saw her. She's huge. She invited all of us. The whole family."

"I don't know what to think," she said, shaking her head as if the dinner invitation might be one more count against Charlotte.

"Maybe we should eat tonight's dinner before it spoils," he suggested. "One thing at a time."

He watched as Maggie sat up and slipped her feet into her pink fuzzy slippers. On the way to the kitchen, he refilled his whiskey glass. He knew he was drinking too much but gave himself an extra splash anyway. By the time he got to the kitchen, she had the pork chops, a baked potato, and a broccoli-cheese vegetable on his plate. He sat down. The whiskey had gone to his head, pleasantly muting his feelings. Big was already under his chair.

Maggie clasped his hand, and they bowed heads while she said grace.

He shook out his napkin. "Looks delicious, hon." His plate made that painful squeaking noise when he cut into his pork chop, which had cooled and toughened. Maggie cringed. "Sorry," he said.

The pork chops tasted like cardboard. They were hard to chew and even harder to swallow. He gave up on them, afraid of another squeak, and reached for some sour cream for his potato. He offered the container to Maggie, who gave him a silent shake of her head. He knocked over the salt shaker when he tried to pick it up. The little shaker made a loud crashing sound in the quiet room and startled Big, who looked up from under the table.

"Sorry," he said again. Maggie did not respond.

He ate his potato and watched her pick at her broccoli. He tried to think of something to say but couldn't.

Maggie had stopped eating. She'd left her pork chop untouched and had only taken one bite of her potato. She stared at her plate. "I guess I'm finished," she finally said.

"I'll do the dishes. You go relax."

Maggie walked out of the room. He cut up a few pieces of meat and fed them to Big, which was not allowed. The dog stood behind him and whined for more.

"Go lie down, boy. You're going to trip me. You've had enough."

Big gave him a pathetic look with his big brown eyes but went to lie down under the table.

He found Maggie on the couch. She was sipping ginger ale out of a plastic cup. She kept a bottle of flat ginger ale in the bar for those times when her stomach acted up.

"Your stomach bothering you?"

"A little," she said.

"Sorry I upset you." He tried to take her hand, but she shook it away.

"I still don't understand any of this, Ed."

"I get it. I would hate it if you'd sprung this on me. I should have told you sooner."

"I don't want to talk about it anymore. Let's watch the *National Geographic* documentary on Cuba. I've been wanting to see it."

A show would be a welcome break from this discussion. "Sure," he said, taking the remote from the coffee table.

They sat silently, watching people dancing in tiny kitchens, strolling near the ocean, and peering out the windows of once-majestic houses.

Halfway through, Maggie said she was tired.

"You go on to bed," he said. "I'd like to watch the rest of this program." They usually went to bed together, but he sensed

Maggie might need time. He turned down the sound and listened to the water running in the bathroom sink and to Maggie brushing her teeth. He heard her shake out her daily vitamin before he turned the sound back up. When he saw the light in the bedroom go out, he tiptoed to the cabinet and poured another whiskey. His head would hurt tomorrow. Staring into his glass, he thought of Dr. Phil saying honesty is one of the most important components of a successful marriage.

Maggie did not stir when he finally got into bed. He wondered if she was pretending to be asleep but knew he would have to wait and continue his apologies in the morning. He pulled up the covers and fell into a deep, drunken sleep.

When his alarm woke him, his head ached, and his mouth was dry and gummy.

Served him right.

He turned to look at Maggie. She was gone. He sat up in shock. The first thought that ran through his mind was that she had been kidnapped.

And then the truth struck him. She had left. Left him.

His thoughts careening, he prowled around the house and took inventory. She'd taken some clothes, her toothbrush, her cosmetic case, and her car. He had no idea what to do, so he made the bed and pulled the sheets tight the way she liked them. After he was done, he sat on the edge of the bed.

Two birds in the tree outside the window were making a scolding sound. Or perhaps he just thought that because he felt so down. And lonely. And guilty. It was not that he didn't know where she'd gone. He assumed she was at Dawn's house. What gnawed at him was the realization that this was the first time she'd left him after more than thirty-five years together. That was what made him feel so panicked.

He called in sick; he felt sick. And then he drove to Dawn's.

Standing on her front steps, he saw Maggie through the window. She was seated in a chair reading a magazine. He rang the bell.

Dawn was still in her robe. "I was wondering when you'd get here. You'd better talk to her." She stepped back to let him in. "What happened?" she asked in a furious whisper. "What is this about another woman?"

"There's no other woman. Could you let us have some privacy?" He sounded snappy and was vaguely sorry about it.

"Honestly, Dad," Dawn said, but she left.

He walked in, and Maggie wouldn't look at him. She stared down at the floor. He sat on the couch, propping himself with a pillow. His mind went blank. What finally came out of his mouth was, "Dawn and Jake should put down some carpet now that they're about to have a baby."

She looked at him as if he were nuts. "They like the floor," she said. "They ripped out the carpet that was in here and refinished it."

At least it was a conversation opener.

"Look, I'm so sorry, Mags. I know that I hurt you, and I didn't mean to. I shouldn't have kept the friendship a secret. It was wrong."

"I'm not sure I'll be able to trust you again. I don't know why you came here. I don't want to see you." She looked up at him, then past him. With her lips pursed and white, she looked ugly to him for a second.

"I came here to say I'm sorry. Will you come home? We can talk more there."

"Go away, Ed."

"Maggie, listen, please. Charlotte is really only a friend."

"I don't keep secrets from you, Ed."

"I know."

"We can't have a marriage if you behave like this."

He was beginning to understand that Maggie would always see this as cheating. Keeping Charlotte's existence a secret was a form of cheating. "Sorry," he muttered again.

"Your friend is getting a divorce and is knocked up by another man. That doesn't say much about her moral character. And you choose to spend a lot of time with her."

"It sounds bad, but she's really a nice person. I think you'd like her if you met her."

It did sound bad now that he was hearing it from Maggie, who might not like Charlotte at all.

"She's everything I don't believe in. And you picked her, even if she is only a friend. Now go home."

Ed walked down Dawn's steps and got into his car, glad to be heading away from Maggie's fury. He drove home and wandered around the house, wishing he'd gone to work. He hated being home alone with nothing to do. He tried one of Maggie's crosswords but gave up halfway through. He stared out the window at their small lawn. He watched a robin dig around in the grass and thought about driving to Target and finally buying that bird feeder he'd been thinking about. The phone rang. It was Dawn.

"Okay, Dad, talk to me. She's out for a walk."

"I don't know what to do," he said. "I still can't believe she's this angry about me having a female friend."

"It's hard to tell exactly what's bothering her. Your friendship or the friend or that you kept it a secret."

"Any ideas?" he asked.

"I think she'll calm down. Give her some time."

"She's never done anything like this. She up and left."

"She feels betrayed. You hurt her."

"I honestly didn't mean to. I feel awful."

"This woman is really a friend? You've never had a female friend."

"Yes, a friend." He gazed out the window. A worm dangled from the robin's mouth.

"What if Mom wants you to stop seeing her?"

"That wouldn't be fair."

"Would you stop seeing her?"

"I guess so."

"You don't sound sure."

"You sound like a lawyer." His head still hurt. He couldn't bear the thought of never seeing Charlotte.

"I am a lawyer."

There was a pause. "I see her coming down the block, bye," Dawn said. The phone went dead.

Ed paced around the house until he felt the walls closing in on him. When he couldn't stand it anymore, he got in the car and drove to Old Orchard Mall.

He went into a store named Lush he'd heard about from Dawn or Maggie. It was filled with bright soaps and bath products that made him sneeze. He bought a purple lump called a bath bomb and a green one in the shape of a turtle. He passed Vineyard Vines and wondered who would want clothes with smiling whales.

Then he went to Nordstrom, which seemed safe. He wandered around, looking for gifts to buy Maggie. It was hard to think among the endless racks of purses, jewelry, and cosmetics, which all looked cheap and shiny to him. The word *trinket* popped into his mind. There were too many trinkets here. And too many salespeople saying, "May I help you?"

He pushed open the store's big glass doors and went into the central courtyard. It was a beautiful day, and the place was bustling. He sat for a while and watched shoppers who were young mothers and retirees, all looking either determined or happy. He felt miserable and wandered into Barnes & Noble, where he picked out a book called *Mrs. Everything* for Maggie, then put it back and bought *Where the Crawdads Sing*.

Walking back to the car, he thought about how he'd first agreed to retire to make Maggie happy. Now he was afraid he would be sucked into her small world, that he would shrink to fit into it. With church off the table, Maggie's main interest was Dawn. He was certain she still wished she were carrying their daughter's baby. It had bound the two of them together, which Maggie seemed to desperately want or need.

Charlotte had offered Ed a glimpse into a bigger and messier but more interesting world. One where all the rules weren't necessarily followed. A world he might or might not be happy in. A world that made him realize how little he knew about himself.

He stopped at Dawn's with the Lush bag and book. No one was in the living room. He rang the bell, and Dawn answered. She was in her work clothes, but she must have taken the morning off.

"Sorry, she doesn't want to see you."

"I brought her these." He handed Dawn the gifts.

"Nice. I'm sure she'll like them." She closed the door and left him standing on the steps.

He got back in the car, drove home, decided he did not want to go in, and drove to Target. As soon as he went through the big doors, he knew it was a mistake. The red-and-white signs were overly cheery, the air was too cold, the lights hurt his eyes, and the cosmetics and drugstore aisles reminded him of Maggie.

He made his way to the outdoor section and found a bird feeder. He paid, drove home, and emptied the parts onto the floor. It took him most of the afternoon to assemble it and hang it on the tree in their backyard. He realized he'd forgotten all about buying bird food, so he went inside, got a loaf of bread, ripped it into little pieces, and went back into the yard and put them in the feeder.

He sat in the kitchen and watched, waiting for the birds, but squirrels got to the bread and soon the feeder was empty again.

He watched the news around six and took his first sip of whiskey, hoping that it would help his still-aching head, when Maggie pulled up and parked in the driveway. He watched as she wheeled her suitcase through the back door. He was afraid to ask what had changed her mind.

"I ordered some Chinese food. It should be here soon." She acted as if nothing had happened.

"Thanks. I'm glad you came home."

She nodded and took her suitcase into the bedroom. He could hear her unpacking and brought her a glass of orange juice.

"Is everything okay, Mags?" He held out the juice as if she might strike him.

"No. Not really. Things aren't okay."

She let him circle her with a tentative hug for a second, then pulled away. "I suppose I should meet this woman and see what I think."

She took the packet of bath bombs out of her suitcase and carried them, along with her cosmetics bag, into the bathroom.

"You want to meet her?" he asked. "Really?" This no longer seemed like a good idea.

"Yes. I want to see what this so-called friendship is all about."

Ouch, he thought, but said, "Does that mean you want to go to her dinner? At her home?"

"Yes, but it doesn't mean I like the situation." She frowned. "And I need a little time. Let's plan for some time in June, and I'll bring dessert."

INTERSECTIONS

The doorbell rang, and he welcomed the interruption. He escaped to the front door, where he retrieved the Chinese food. The paper bag was still warm. Comforting. He held it to his chest for a minute before he unpacked the egg rolls, chicken chow mein, and moo shu pork onto the kitchen table along with plates. He did not call Maggie. Instead, he drank water and waited, hoping for some peace. He would phone Charlotte tomorrow. Best not to tell Charlotte about Maggie's fury. It would only make her nervous when she was trying to give a nice dinner, which he now dreaded. He was keeping secrets from everyone.

THIRTY-SIX  CHARLOTTE

June 2019

Five days before Ed's retirement party, Charlotte woke in the middle of the night with a dull pain. She wasn't due for another two and a half weeks, but the sheet beneath her felt wet. When she stood, she saw liquid trickling down her legs. Then another pain.

She did not bother to time the contractions. Her age made her high-risk. Her water had broken, and she needed to get to the hospital. She pulled on her maternity jeans and a cotton Indian shirt, one of the few shirts that still fit. Her suitcase was packed. She phoned her doctor, ordered a taxi, and took the elevator down.

It was three in the morning on what was now Sunday. The streets were empty. The air smelled faintly of last night's barbecue smoke. The taxi drove down the Outer Drive, passing the beach. The streetlamps cast shadows on the sand. She couldn't make out the lake. The dull pains continued, but she was not worried. They were close to Northwestern. She could see the bright lights of the hospital. The driver, an elderly man, pulled into the entrance, and she paid him.

"Good luck," he said.

"Thanks. That's kind. I need it."

The hospital was a small, efficient city. Doctors walked by, their white coats flapping. Nurses gathered around computers.

"Do you have a partner with you?" the woman at the admissions desk asked.

"I'm alone."

"Do you want to call a friend?"

Charlotte's hand crept into her purse to feel the comfort of her cell phone. She was hit with a contraction. "No, maybe later."

"May I have the number in case you change your mind?"

Charlotte wrote Claire's number on a Post-it. A nurse led her to a room and hooked her up to machines and an IV. Charlotte watched the waves of her contractions on the monitor to her left—how they rose, crested, and fell. She rode them out. The pains sharpened. Outside, the sunrise tinted the sky yellow and red. She saw the lake through the window. The boats started to appear.

"Are you sure you don't want me to call your friend?" a different nurse asked. Charlotte thought about Claire. Her brother might come to the hospital if she called Claire, and she didn't want that. She wanted Ed. The comfort of Ed, if Maggie didn't mind, which she might.

"I'm going to call a different friend," she said, reaching for her cell phone on the nightstand.

"I'll wait," the nurse said. "I can give directions. People get confused coming in here."

He picked up on the first ring. "Hold on," she said, as a contraction rolled through her. "I'm at Northwestern having the baby. Do you think . . . do you think Maggie will mind if you come? I'll understand if she does."

"I'm on my way," he said. "I'm at work, but I can leave."

"Wait one sec." She handed the phone to the nurse, so she could give Ed directions.

Ed was taking a long time. Maggie might have minded and told him not to come. Or he was lost wandering down the wrong hallway. Nurses and residents came in and out.

"You are three centimeters."

"You are five."

"You are seven."

"This will help with the pain," a nurse said, and a warm liquid streamed through her veins and carried her away.

She swam through the cold lake. Her legs scissored, and she glided away from the pain, past Daniel, who turned away, bobbing up to the surface. Past Libby, who offered her a hand. "My darling," Charlotte tried to say. Her words were bubbles. Libby's hand was warm. Emory appeared. His eyes were open, blue as the water. "I have to go," she bubbled. She surfaced. Emerged into the sky.

Pain cleaved her in two. There was nothing else.

"It's time to push."

She shut her eyes against the room, against her doctor who had appeared at the end of her bed. She was peering down between Charlotte's legs.

"Push, Charlotte," she said. "You can do this."

When Charlotte opened her eyes, Ed was beside her. He smelled like fresh laundry. Charlotte was aware now of her own sour smell, of how her hair was plastered to her head.

"Squeeze my hand tight," he said. A nurse sponged Charlotte's face with a cool cloth.

"Please don't leave," Charlotte said to Ed.

"I won't. I'm here." His hand was solid and strong. "Squeeze," he said again. "You won't hurt me."

Charlotte squeezed. Bore down. A scream shattered the silence. A wail.

Charlotte opened her eyes to a dangle of arms and legs above her.

"She's beautiful," Ed said.

The doctor placed Poppy on Charlotte's chest. She reached to stroke the slick of her daughter's hair, to look at her daughter's astonished eyes, enormous and baby gray.

"Wow," Ed said.

"You're here," Charlotte said softly to Poppy. "You're with me now." She was sure Poppy understood. She took her tiny hand in hers, marveling at the little perfect fingernails.

"I have to borrow her for a few minutes," the nurse said. "To clean her up and run some tests."

Charlotte watched as Poppy was carried across the room. Ed squeezed her hand. "Congratulations," he said. "It was an honor to be here."

"Thank you for coming."

Together they watched as Poppy was gently washed, weighed, and wrapped in a pink blanket. Charlotte could not take her eyes off her baby.

THIRTY-SEVEN

 ED

June 2019

E d was glad he'd been at work when Charlotte called him from the hospital because he didn't have to immediately explain to Maggie where he was going. He drove home in silence replaying the birth in his mind. The little pink bundle, the smitten look on Charlotte's face. He was flattered Charlotte had wanted him to be there and relieved that she had delivered a beautiful, healthy baby.

Big met him at the door, shimmying with pleasure at his return.

"Hey Mags," he called, wondering if he should tell her about his afternoon and the baby. She had seemed resigned to going to Charlotte's dinner party, and now he would have to tell her it was off. He would tell her about the baby but not about being at the hospital with Charlotte. That might stir up Maggie's anger again.

"In here, Ed." As usual, she was in the kitchen. He sniffed. The kitchen smelled rich, of tomatoes, onions, and beef. She'd made his favorite—spaghetti with meatballs. "Can you open this for me?" She handed him a container of parmesan.

He opened the container and went to pour himself a drink. Best not to spring the news as soon as he walked in the door. He carried his whiskey back to the kitchen and set the table.

Maggie carried two plates piled high with the spaghetti over, and Ed retrieved the container of cheese.

He waited until he was one drink in, and they were about halfway through their dinner, which he would have enjoyed more if he hadn't been nervous.

"I got some news today," he said.

"Good news?"

"Yes. Charlotte had her baby, a girl she named Poppy. That means no dinner party this week."

"I was kind of looking forward to meeting this woman. I'm curious about your friendship and what she's like since you've never had a female friend before. It's always been other male officers."

"I'm sure you'll get a chance." He was surprised.

"Will you go visit her when she's out of the hospital?"

"I expect so. Do you want to come along?"

"No, but I'll eventually knit something for the baby."

This was a shock. He studied her face for any hints of resentment, but it was placid. He didn't know what had changed for her, but whatever it was, he was thankful.

"Would you like some dessert?" Maggie asked.

He patted his stomach. "Too full."

"Why don't you pour yourself another drink, and I'll come sit with you for the news."

He exhaled in relief as he left the kitchen. He was off the hook . . . at least for now.

The next morning, Frank was already at his desk when Ed arrived. "Hey Ed, look at this." Frank slid a fuzzy photo over to Ed.

It was a Prius, like the one from the hit-and-run. Navy blue.

There was some sort of decal on the back. Orange. A flower, maybe.

That's right. There had been a decal, and it had been orange. "Where did this come from?"

"The mail. An anonymous source."

"I thought there were no witnesses."

"We all did."

Ed ran his finger over the photo. His heart was beating so fast, he was having trouble concentrating.

He squinted at the photo but couldn't make out the license plate. The car must have been moving.

"Can you make out the plate, Frank?"

Frank bent over the photo. "Nope."

"Our only clue, and it does us no good."

"I shouldn't have shown you that photo. Most hit-and-runs don't get solved. And the department is about to stop investigating this one. There's no viable evidence."

"Maybe if I went to Prius dealers, I could find some more evidence."

"Try and let it go, Ed. I know it was awful, and that kid died. But it looks as if it will never be solved."

"I can't."

"You know, I checked, and we only solve a small percentage of these. Even of the fatal ones. Something between two and ten percent if I'm remembering right."

"That's a terrible record. It's hard to believe we're that bad at it."

"Yeah, I know. But even when there are witnesses, people don't trust the police."

"True." But Ed wasn't ready to give up yet.

The next afternoon, he went to one of the two Prius dealers in the Chicago area. He would have gone sooner, but he felt more legitimate now that he was back in uniform. He couldn't imagine this information would be handed to anyone who wanted it. This dealership was in Highland Park, a well-to-do suburb about forty minutes north of Chicago. The manager came up to him, looking alarmed.

"What can I do for you?"

"Do you have a list of all the people who have bought Priuses? We're looking for a car that was involved in a hit-and-run."

"Of course. Let me print it out for you." The manager disappeared into his office and returned about five minutes later with a sheet of paper.

"Thanks, I appreciate it."

Ed took the sheet back to his car. The third name on the list was Charlotte Oakes. A navy-blue Prius. He blinked in disbelief, staring at the paper. He knew she couldn't have been driving, but had it been someone she knew? Her daughter? Had she been lying to him this whole time?

THIRTY-EIGHT  CHARLOTTE

June 2019

I t was an awkward moment.

Ed walked into her hospital room as a nurse was help-ing Charlotte with breastfeeding. To be specific, she was attaching Poppy to her engorged breast. Even though Ed had been at the birth, he turned beet red. Then he stammered, "Excuse me," and left.

She called to him, but he was already gone and down the hall.

"Men are so weird," the nurse said.

Charlotte nodded, wondering what was going on with Ed, but she was too enamored with Poppy to dwell on it. It was hard to believe Poppy was actually here, and that she remembered what to do with a baby. How to cradle her tiny head. How to wrap her like a burrito. How to do the baby bounce walk when she fussed. It was all coming back.

When she left the hospital the next day, it felt surreal to be back in her apartment, even though she'd been looking forward to it. She'd set up a bassinet in her bedroom, so the baby could sleep next to her for a few months. She fed Poppy, and she sat on the armchair in her bedroom, patting Poppy's back until she burped and fell fast asleep on her shoulder. She carefully placed the baby in the bassinet and was shocked when she did this successfully and didn't wake her.

INTERSECTIONS

She was still sore, and it hurt to walk. She slowly went into the living room and poured a glass of the Perrier that Claire had so kindly left her. Claire had stocked the fridge while she was at the hospital. There was milk, coffee, a rotisserie chicken, peaches, a homemade plum tart, and even a bottle of her favorite white wine.

A note on the counter said, *Call me for anything!*

Claire had also put together a basket of lavender-scented bath products. *You will appreciate the effort it takes to get clean now,* she wrote in her note. This made Charlotte smile. Claire was the best.

Her parents were bringing over dinner tonight, but Libby was arriving to see the baby in three days, and she would need more groceries. She caught her face as she walked by the antique mirror she'd hung in the living room. It was horrifying. Her long hair was a tangled mess, and she had enormous purple smudges under her eyes. She walked quickly past her reflection and sat on the couch to make a market list.

One minute she was writing, and the next she awoke to the sound of Poppy crying. The list and pen had fallen to the floor. She was sprawled in a contorted position on the couch and drooling. She wiped her mouth with her hand and rushed to get a red-faced Poppy. Charlotte had slept for nearly two hours. Poppy was wet and stopped crying when Charlotte changed her, using something called a Snappi Cloth Diaper Fastener because she thought diaper pins were a bad idea—sharp and dangerous. Charlotte managed to both fasten the diaper and put a waterproof diaper cover over it. The hospital had used disposable diapers, so this was her first try with cloth. She was sweating by the time she finished.

Just as she'd settled back on the couch to nurse Poppy again, there was a knock on the door.

"One second." It was probably her neighbor Caroline. She hastily draped a baby blanket over her bare breast and answered the door. Ed was in the hall. In his hand was a foil-covered casserole dish.

"Your neighbor let me in the front door when she was walking in. Dawn wanted me to bring this to you. We need to talk, Charlotte." His eyes drilled into her. She tightened her grip on Poppy. Whatever was going on wasn't good.

"Come in and sit down." She motioned him inside.

Ed put the casserole on the counter and sat down on one of the armchairs facing the couch.

"Would you like a drink? I have juice, water, and coffee."

"I know it's only two thirty, but I could use a real drink right now. Do you have any whiskey?"

Rattled, and with Poppy over her shoulder, she got the whiskey bottle down from the cabinet and poured a drink for Ed. "I can't bend down easily with the baby. If you want ice, you'll need to get it."

"It'll be fine neat."

She handed him the drink and settled on the couch, the blanket still over her left breast. "I need to feed her. I hope you don't mind." At least she was reminding him that she was a new mother with a completely dependent baby.

"Not at all." He took a big sip of his whiskey.

This was a surprise, as he'd bolted out of her hospital room when she was nursing the other day. She let Poppy attach and re-covered her breast and a bit of Poppy's head. When she looked up, Ed was staring right at her face.

"I went to the Prius dealership in Highland Park to get a list of people who had bought cars. Your name was on it. Navy blue. Like the one in the hit-and-run."

"I do have a navy-blue Prius." A chill blew through her body.

"May I see the car?"

"Yes. It's out back. If you take the elevator to the basement and walk out the door, it's parked right there."

He stood up silently and walked out the door.

She pressed her nose to Poppy and inhaled her baby scent. If Ed arrested her, what would happen to Poppy? With trembling hands, she placed the baby back in the bassinet, ran to the bathroom, and vomited.

He knocked on the door right after she'd retrieved Poppy again. His face was steely.

"It just dawned on me that you were at the accident that day. That's why you looked familiar when we met at the intersection. You were there, and you never told me."

She nodded, waiting.

"I saw the outline of the decal. It's like the one I saw on the car involved in the hit-and-run. Is there anything you want to tell me about the car? I know you weren't driving, but was someone else driving it? Did you tamper with it?" She had never heard him use this tone. She was being interrogated.

She leaned back into the couch pillows. "I honestly don't know if anyone else was driving it. When I came home that day, the car was gone. I asked Libby, but she denied driving it. She doesn't even have a license. It expired."

"But you looked for your car that afternoon."

"Yes."

"When did you notice it was back?"

"When Libby got home."

"And that's when you asked her if she'd taken it?"

"Yes."

"And after that. You must have gone back to the garage."

"I did, and the car was there."

"Was there any damage?"

"A very small dent."

"But it's not there anymore, right?"

"I had it fixed."

"And the orange flower?"

"I scraped it off. Well, as much as I could."

"So, you suspected something."

"Libby has not always been completely honest with me. You know that. I asked her several times."

"I think we both know that Libby was driving that day."

All she could do was nod.

"Why didn't you say something to me, Charlotte?" He looked stricken. "You never even let on you saw the hit-and-run."

"I was afraid you'd have to turn us in. That we'd both go to jail."

She thought she might cry but didn't. She had to handle this as the grown-up she should have been all along. "I need to talk to Libby. She's coming here this weekend."

Ed nodded.

"Will you turn us in?"

"I don't know what to do. Libby could get up to fifteen years for leaving the scene of a fatality. Do you think she was high?"

"I have no idea. She might have been."

"Well, she can't be tested now."

One relief.

"Charlotte, she killed a child. There has been no answer or justice for that family. Do you think that's right?"

"Of course not. But I also want to protect my daughter. How could I not?"

Ed got up, washed his glass, and put it away.

"You have to talk to her this weekend. Get the whole story.

261

No more lying. I'll talk to you on Monday after she leaves." And with that, Ed was out the door.

Charlotte sat there holding Poppy. What would happen to her baby if Libby and she both ended up in jail?

THIRTY-NINE

 **ED**

June 2019

He felt as if he'd been transported to an alternative reality as he opened the door of Charlotte's building. The person he'd been searching for all this time was Charlotte's daughter. On top of that, Charlotte had been a witness, so she must have seen her car. He understood denial, but this was crazy.

Ed stepped outside, and the sidewalk shimmered in the heat. It was dizzying, and he had to walk slowly back to his car. The enormity of Charlotte's secret overwhelmed him. He did believe she'd repressed (at least partially) the fact that Libby could have been the driver, but it was still an enormous betrayal, especially since she'd had the wherewithal to fix the dent and remove the decal. The outline of the daisy was what made him certain he was right.

He sat in the Jeep, with the air-conditioning turned on high, trying to sort it out. His first thought was that he didn't really know Charlotte at all. But this wasn't true. He did know her, and on some level, he understood why she would lie to protect Libby. He ran his hand over the steering wheel and thought of his oath.

"On my honor, I will never betray my integrity, my character, or the public trust. I will always have the courage to hold myself and others accountable for our actions. I will maintain the highest ethical standards and uphold the values of the community, and the agency I serve."

Libby had left the scene. Charlotte was an accomplice. If he did his job, they would both be in a great deal of trouble. If he didn't report Libby, he would be breaking his oath and going against everything he had always believed in. He was at a loss. There was absolutely no one he could discuss this with, and he was facing a decision that could ruin Libby's life along with Charlotte and Poppy's. He wasn't fond of Libby, but Charlotte was the most important person in his life other than Maggie and the kids. And it was also true that Sarah had darted into the street. He still felt the shame of not being able to somehow save her, but he also didn't know if, under the same circumstances, he would have been able to stop in time.

He turned the key and pulled out of his parking space. Day camp buses were dropping off kids. A woman walked by with a stroller and a dog. All familiar, but not. In the space of a few minutes everything had changed. He had lost his footing.

FORTY  CHARLOTTE

July 2019

Libby was due at her apartment any minute, and Charlotte was a mess. She'd lost Ed and ruined their friendship with her secrecy. She was out of options. She had to confront Libby. A child was dead, and both Ed and Sarah's family deserved to know the truth.

This is what being a wimp gets you. A wave of self-loathing and anger at Libby ran through her.

The buzzer rang just as she'd put Poppy down. She'd managed to make a big garlicky Caesar salad for Libby, but she'd run out of time and energy and ordered a pizza from a new fancy pizza place.

"Come in." Charlotte gave Libby a big hug. Libby looked great. Glowing.

"Can I see my sister?"

"Yes, but quietly. I just got her to sleep." She was struggling to keep the nervousness out of her voice.

"How long does she sleep?"

"She'll probably be up again at eleven and two. Then again at five."

"That doesn't sound fun."

Charlotte did not tell her how much worse she'd been as a baby. "It's exhausting."

They snuck into Charlotte's room, and Libby leaned over the bassinet. "She's beautiful. Look at those perfect rosebud lips. What color are her eyes?"

"A grayish blue for now, but they might change."

"But maybe not."

Emory had blue eyes. There was a chance.

Libby set her things down in the room where she still had a bed, now crowded by Poppy's crib.

"Are you hungry?"

"Starving."

Charlotte was trying to figure out the best way to bring up the accident. She poured two iced mint teas and got the pizza out of the oven, where she had been keeping it warm. Just as they sat down and Charlotte took a sip of her tea, Poppy let out a loud newborn cry.

"I guess she decided to get up before eleven. Maybe she wants to meet me." Libby helped herself to a slice of mushroom and fontina pizza and some salad.

"She's probably wet. I'm going to change her."

When Charlotte returned with Poppy, Libby said, "She's pretty cute." Libby studied her new sister, who was cradled in her mother's arms, and Poppy was looking up at Charlotte with her wide eyes.

"If I bounce her a little, she may fall back to sleep again. You go ahead and eat."

Charlotte got up again and did her baby dance. Poppy complied by falling sound asleep on Charlotte's shoulder. Charlotte reluctantly put her down. She would have to dive into questioning Libby. Tell her the truth that Ed knew. There was no other way. She had to stop treading so carefully around Libby. She'd committed manslaughter—involuntary but still manslaughter.

Libby was on her third slice of pizza. Charlotte sat down across from her and braced herself.

"Libby, Ed traced the car from the hit-and-run to me. He also remembered that I was at the accident. I never told you or Ed."

Libby's face went white. She put down the pizza.

"He questioned the Prius dealer and got my name. Identified the car."

"What did he say?"

"He was very upset and asked me if I'd had the car repaired and removed the decal. I'd done both, and I told him. He knew I was not in the car, so he assumed you were driving. I've been a coward for not pressing you to tell me the truth. You hit that little girl, didn't you?"

Libby looked down at her lap. Then she shoved her plate away, put her head down on the table, and covered her head with her hands. Charlotte got up and stroked her back. Then she reached down and enclosed her with her arms. Libby's back started heaving.

She sobbed for a long time, and Charlotte continued to hold her.

Libby slowly raised her head from her arms. Her face was blotchy and tear-stained. "It was an accident."

"How did it happen?" Charlotte kept her voice soft.

"I shouldn't have been driving. I'd taken some Oxy. I was going to go to the dentist, but then I decided that I was too high. I was heading home. Speeding. I didn't see her until it was too late, and I couldn't brake fast enough. I was scared to stop. I killed her. I'm a murderer." She started to sob again.

"You did kill her, but it wasn't intentional. It's tragic, but you're not a murderer. You were high and fled the scene, which does make it even worse. Legally, that is." Charlotte reached over to stroke her arm.

"What should I do?"

Libby looked so lost and frightened that Charlotte grieved for her as well as Sarah and her family. She would have done anything to take this pain away from Libby. To suck it into herself and let Libby go free.

"I think the best thing to do is for me to talk to Ed. He knows you're here this weekend."

"I want to talk to him."

"You do?"

"I want to confess. I can't stand feeling this way any longer."

"You know that confessing won't change the facts."

"I'll feel better about myself if I turn myself in."

FORTY-ONE

 ED

July 2019

M aggie was making spinach balls and five-layer dip for their annual Fourth of July family party, and Ed was about to go to Target to buy birdseed and a small flag for the front yard.

"If you see some red, white, and blue napkins, pick them up, okay?" Maggie loved all holidays and believed they should be celebrated to the fullest. Ed loved that about her.

He was looking through the napkins at Target when his phone rang. Charlotte. He froze. He'd thought they'd agreed to talk after Libby left. Maybe he didn't have to answer. But he did. He couldn't not answer.

"Hello." He could hear the sternness in his voice.

"Hi Ed, I wonder if you could come over today. Libby is here, and she would like to talk to you. To tell you what happened. We would come to you, but it's hard with the baby."

"She suggested this?"

"She did."

"How about if I swing by this afternoon. Say around two?"

"Perfect. Maybe Poppy will be napping, but it's still hard to tell." Her voice was high and nervous.

"See you soon." He grabbed some red, white, and blue paper napkins, birdseed, and a bigger flag than he'd meant to buy. He could feel acid at the back of his throat. Libby was the person he'd been looking for all this time, and now he wished he'd never found her.

"Come in." Charlotte's apartment was a mess. Clean laundry was piled on the couch, mainly baby clothes and diapers. Libby's clothes were spilling out of the suitcase in the middle of the living room floor. "Would you like some iced tea?"

"Sure. Is Poppy napping?"

"She is, but who knows for how long. She's still in that unpredictable stage. At least she doesn't have days and nights mixed up." She was talking too fast.

Charlotte went into her kitchen, brought three iced teas on a tray to the coffee table, and headed toward her bedroom. "I'll get Libby."

Ed sat on the couch and sipped the tea closest to him. He was hoping to get rid of the acidy taste in his mouth. Libby came out of the second bedroom with Charlotte. Her long hair was pulled back, her face freshly washed and makeup-free. She wore blue jean shorts and a plain white tee. She looked about fourteen.

She sat in the chair across from him, and Charlotte passed her a tea.

"I'm looking forward to what you have to say, Libby." This was untrue, but he had no idea how to start this conversation or confession politely.

Libby looked at her lap, and Charlotte looked at Libby.

"I took my mom's car that day. I hit that little girl. She appeared so quickly, I couldn't stop. When I realized I hit her, I was scared and just kept going. I didn't know what to do. It was wrong. Terrible. I'm so ashamed. I still can't believe I killed her.

A little kid. That I'm a murderer." She looked up at him. Her lips quivered, and his heart broke a bit for her.

"I saw her dart into the street, and I get that you couldn't stop. It's the fleeing that makes it serious."

She nodded. "I know."

"Were you on anything, Libby?" He saw her flinch.

"I took some Oxy. I was on my way to the dentist, but I decided I was too high, and that I should go home. I was trying to drive back when it happened."

"Driving high makes it even more serious."

She nodded again.

"If it happened again. If you had a second chance, what would you do?"

"Stop. But I don't ever want it to happen again."

"And the Oxy?"

"I'm in recovery. I'm an addict, and I can't promise I'll never take Oxy again. I don't plan to, but I can't promise. But I can promise that I'll never ever drive when I'm high."

He looked over at Charlotte and saw that her face was wet. Awful as this was, he wanted to hug her.

"You're not a murderer, Libby. It was an accident. And it may or may not have happened if you were sober. We'll never know."

"Are you going to take me in?"

"No."

Both Libby and Charlotte looked astonished. Charlotte took a swipe at her eyes.

"Really?" Libby stood up and threw herself into Charlotte's lap. Tears now streamed down her face.

Ed leaned over to talk to her. "We can't bring Sarah back. You didn't mean for this to happen. You could go to jail for fleeing the scene, and I don't want to ruin your life. I know you've had a lot of struggles, but you have to promise me that you absolutely won't ever drive while high or drunk again."

"I promise."

With that, Poppy started wailing. Charlotte sat for a minute looking stunned before she got up to get her. She brought the baby back into the room and handed her to Libby.

"Ed, even though it's early, I'm pouring you a whiskey." She found a highball glass and wine glass in the cabinet and poured them both a drink. She walked over and handed the whiskey to Ed.

"I know your decision goes against all of your principles, and we will never be able to thank you enough."

His decision violated both his morals and the oath he had taken, but he knew that, in the end, he might be saving another life. Libby was young. She had time to redeem herself.

FORTY-TWO  CHARLOTTE

October 2019

C harlotte and Ed had an unspoken agreement not to talk about the accident anymore. Ed had retired, and Charlotte wheeled Poppy to Starbucks at least once or twice a week to meet him. Sometimes they walked through the park and the zoo. He had begun tutoring inner-city kids in an after-school program at Fourth Presbyterian Church. They were like the kids who had originally been on his beat. He talked about the thrill he got as he watched their amazement when they sounded out a word or solved a math problem. Maggie, he said, was busy knitting gloves and hats for his three students as well as for Dawn and Jake's new baby, Cory, whom she adored.

"Cory looks so much like Dawn that I think Maggie has almost forgotten she was adopted." Ed scrolled from one adorable picture to another on his phone. "She's smiling already. Can you believe it?"

"She is a beauty."

Ed glowed with grandfatherly pride.

Neither Charlotte nor Libby told Daniel about the accident or Libby's confession. Libby was part of Daniel's life, and it was up to her if she wanted to share her story. Charlotte also kept quiet about Daniel's refusal to pay for Libby's therapy. She was still furious with him about it, but she wanted Libby to have a good relationship with her father. Or at least, a decent one.

Libby moved back to Chicago and found a job at a fancy pet supply store in the Gold Coast and a therapist she could see on her lunch hour. On a Monday, Libby's day off, Charlotte walked Poppy to Libby's apartment on Dearborn Street. It was October, Charlotte's favorite month. The air had a slight chill, and the leaves had turned. Giant spiders and cobwebs decorated the iron gates, and pumpkins were everywhere.

It had been nearly a year since Sarah had died. Charlotte stopped, for a moment, at the intersection. Poppy began to fuss, and she moved on. Charlotte phoned Libby when she was in front of her building. Libby, dressed in a corduroy coat and a beanie, came dashing out.

"Hey, Pop Pop. What's up?"

Charlotte believed Poppy, who was three months old, looked at Libby with a special intensity, a knowingness. Libby seemed both surer of herself and humbler. Hopefully, she would make peace with what she'd done, but at the same time, never get over it. Sarah should have a permanent corner in Libby's mind.

Libby leaned over the stroller, making funny noises. Poppy waved her arms in excitement and babbled. The women strolled through Libby's neighborhood past the stately buildings and brownstones. Libby liked to push the stroller. Her apartment was near Emory's office, and even though Charlotte was careful to stay off his street, she wondered if she would run into him. A small part of her hoped she would. She still occasionally daydreamed about a life with him—about Poppy having a father, especially now with Halloween coming up. That holiday had belonged to Charlotte's father. He was the one who took the kids trick-or-treating, carrying a flashlight to light their way.

Not that Poppy was old enough to trick-or-treat. She was a soft baby blur, covered by a white blanket scattered with gray elephants. Emory wouldn't have suspected anything if they'd run into him. But it would have been odd. Uncomfortable. Still, she liked the possibility, the small frisson of pleasure she got when walking through his neighborhood.

"Have you bought Halloween candy yet?" Libby asked.

"Yes, I'm hoping to have a lot of trick-or-treaters."

"Reese's Cups?"

"Of course."

"I'll come over. We can have our own little Halloween party. Look what I got Poppy." She pulled a tiny bee costume out of her purse.

"That's adorable. We'll have to take a lot of pictures. First Halloween and all that."

Libby stopped on the sidewalk still gripping the stroller. "Mom, I know I haven't been easy. Thanks for sticking it out with me."

"Of course. I'm your mother, and I always worry I never did enough. Or the wrong thing. That I was responsible for your troubles."

"I was unhappy, but there was not anything you could have done about that. I hated school. I hated myself and my thoughts. My OCD. I didn't have many friends or get asked out by boys. I was weird and that made me angry because I couldn't help being me. And I worried I was unlovable, which I might have been. Drinking and drugs were a good escape until they weren't anymore. I still can't get over that my selfishness killed a child."

"You were never unlovable, Libs. I wanted you more than anything. And I desperately wanted you to be happy, but there seemed to be nothing I could do about your unhappiness. I felt completely helpless. I was sure I was a terrible mother."

"You were never a terrible mother. You didn't give up on me. I wouldn't have made it through school without you or succeeded in becoming sober. Did you want other children? Was I too much to handle? Was that why you and Dad never had more?"

"I couldn't get pregnant again. Your dad was against fertility treatments and in vitro. I think he was happy with one. So, you were it. That's why I was so surprised when I got pregnant with Poppy. Besides being old, I thought it was completely impossible."

"It seems like some kind of fate. She was meant to be, and I'm so happy about it."

"Me too. I'm not religious, but she is a blessing."

"I get to have a sister who I can watch grow. It'll be so much fun."

Charlotte thought again of Sarah, and she was certain Libby was thinking about her, too. The little girl who didn't get to grow up. She gave Libby a big hug, and Libby hugged her back. She was with her two girls, and she couldn't remember ever being this happy.

November 2023

While Libby was taking a vet-school prerequisite course at the University of Illinois, Charlotte and four-year-old Poppy were walking Libby's rat terrier, Milly.

"I want a sprinkle cookie," Poppy said, as they passed Windy City Bakery, the café where Libby took Poppy for treats. The bakery had an old-fashioned counter where sundaes, sodas, and milkshakes were served. A case, filled with muffins and cookies, was in the back next to a long communal table. Small tables for coffee drinkers were scattered about the rest of the place, which was busy. It still felt celebratory to be out again after the pandemic.

"But we have Milly," Charlotte said. "Dogs aren't allowed."

"I'll hurry. It'll be fine," Poppy said, with an authority that shocked Charlotte, who was afraid to tie Milly up outside or let Poppy go in by herself. She nervously walked Milly in with her and hoped for the best.

"Be quick," Charlotte said to Poppy.

She led Poppy over to the bakery case, and that is when she saw Emory. He was sitting at a corner table. His battered, brown leather briefcase rested next to a pile of papers he was marking up with a green Sharpie. She froze for a second before she felt the surge of adrenaline that told her to grab Poppy and flee.

It was too late to escape. He reached for his coffee and spotted her.

"Charlotte." He waved. His voice was both familiar and not.

She had no choice. Her heart lurching, she walked with Poppy and the dog toward his table.

"Oh my God," he said, as he stood up. "A grandchild?"

"No, this is Poppy. My daughter."

"A daughter," he said slowly. He wrinkled his forehead and looked confused. "You have another daughter?" He chewed on his lip, which Charlotte remembered he did when stressed or surprised.

"Yes, I do. Libby's in graduate school now. She wants to become a vet." She saw him glance at her unadorned hand. He wore a wrinkled blue shirt and jeans and looked much the same as always except for a small pooch in his midsection, which pleased her.

"Nice to meet you, Poppy," he said, holding his hand out. Poppy, who was clutching her cookie, looked puzzled and did not take it. She stared at him and chewed on her lip. It was a shock to see Poppy and Emory side by side with their blond hair and identical blue eyes. Poppy's light coloring had surprised Charlotte.

"How old are you, Poppy?" Emory asked, smiling. His dimple showed, and Charlotte realized Poppy had the same one, along with his corkscrew of a smile.

"Four," she said. She ducked behind Charlotte, then popped back out. "I go to Lowell school."

Emory's face paled when he heard "four."

"Wow, you're a big girl." Emory's mouth was still smiling,

but the rest of his face was not. His dimple disappeared, and his features tightened in concentration. Charlotte knew he was doing the math. He looked up at her. She refused to meet his eyes.

"Have a seat," he said, gesturing to the table.

"We can't," Charlotte said. "We're in a hurry."

Emory turned back toward Poppy. "What kind of cookie do you have?"

"Yellow sprinkle," Poppy said, as she took a nibble. Milly jumped up and tried to snatch a bite.

"Milly, down," Charlotte said too loudly. "We should really get going. I'm breaking the rules by having a dog in here. She's Libby's dog." Her heart was still wild in her chest. It seemed impossible, after all her agonizing, that he was actually here with his child.

Seeing Emory and Poppy together reminded Charlotte about how daddies were a topic of conversation at school. Shortly after Poppy started junior kindergarten, the questions had begun.

"Camille says everyone has a daddy, even if he doesn't live with you," Poppy said one day on their walk home.

"That's not true," Charlotte said. "You don't have a daddy."

"You sure?"

"Very sure."

Poppy let it go for a few days until they were in a crowded elevator in the Bloomingdale's building. "You need a mommy and a daddy to make a baby. Miss Jackie said so."

Charlotte felt the heat start at the bottom of her feet and shoot through her head. The elevator was silent.

"We'll talk about this later, sweet pea," Charlotte said, as calmly as she could. A man gave her a wink. When the elevator opened, she rushed Poppy to a bench at the far end of the floor and sat her down.

"Honey, I wanted you so badly, I went to a special place where I could get the daddy parts to make you. The parts from this place, though, didn't come with an actual daddy."

"You can go to a place and get daddy parts? Do you buy them?"

"Yes. It's called a sperm bank. The daddy part is called sperm. It takes an egg and a sperm to make a baby." She might, she thought, end up in some special kind of hell for lying mothers, but she couldn't think of another reasonable explanation.

"Oh, okay." That was all Poppy said. Charlotte hoped the questioning was over for a while.

"That's terrific about Libby and school," Emory said. He had not taken his eyes off Poppy. Finally, he looked up, directly at Charlotte. "I think we should chat sometime soon."

She did not want to chat. She wanted to run. All the fantasies she'd had about becoming a happy family evaporated.

He picked his iPhone up from the table and opened it, scrolling through contacts. "Do you still have the same number?"

"Yep," she said. "We have to get going. Can you say bye, Poppy?"

"Bye," Poppy said. "Bye, poo-poo head."

Emory laughed.

"Sorry," Charlotte said. "It's school."

She took Poppy's soft little hand and led Milly toward the door. "You can't call people poo-poo head, Poppy."

"I didn't like him."

"Why?"

"He looked funny."

"You still can't call people names, especially if you think they look funny," she said, firmly. But then she couldn't help asking, "Why did he look funny?"

Poppy shrugged and chewed her lip some more. Charlotte wondered if Poppy sensed a connection and somehow intuited Emory was her father. They walked past the long communal table, the case full of cookies, and the blackboard listing specials. He would call, and she would lie. He did not want another child. She did not want him. She was not sure if Poppy would want him or not. When the time came, she would let Poppy make that decision.

Charlotte listened to the hiss of the espresso machine, to the clatter of a spoon against a cup, and to a hum in her head. A chair scraped as she neared the door. She heard footsteps behind her. Every nerve in her body snapped to attention. Then she saw it was a young man. A stranger. He held the door open for them, and they walked out onto the crowded sidewalk.

The sun had just set, and for a brief moment, the sky was amber before it darkened. She was stunned, as if she'd surfaced from a dive too quickly. She gulped the cool air and felt the adrenaline trickling out of her body. Her heart stilled. Poppy skipped alongside her in her pink puffer coat. Cookie in hand. Oblivious to darkness.

ACKNOWLEDGMENTS

I owe huge gratitude to:

All the writers who have helped me along the way at Bread Loaf Writers' Conference, Tin House Summer Workshop, New York State Summer Writers Institute, One Story Summer Conference, Sirenland Writers Conference, and Bennington Writing Seminars, especially Brian Morton. Without Sigrid Nunez's and Cheryl Strayed's encouragement at Bread Loaf, I might never have applied for an MFA.

My patient early readers—Pam Carroll, Linda Strauss, Andrea Leeb, Elizabeth Ziemska, Alexander Uhlmann, Elizabeth Briggs, Nancy and Tom Florsheim, and Susan LeVine.

Chicago Police Officer Elizabeth Briggs for help with police technicalities and for her enthusiasm. Rachel Berger for introducing me to Elizabeth and making me laugh.

She Writes Press, especially Lauren Wise, Brooke Warner, and Lindsey Cleworth.

Simone Jung and Layne Mandros at Books Forward.

Lorraine Saco-White for her excellent editing.

I have worked on this book in many places, but *Intersections* will always be a Chicago story.

ABOUT THE AUTHOR

Karen F. Uhlmann observed a police officer, who had been on the scene of a hit-and-run death of a child, return to the intersection four or five afternoons a week to videotape and ticket cars. His grief and dedication were heartbreaking—and became the seed for *Intersections.* Karen received her MFA in fiction from Bennington in 2010 and has published short stories and book reviews in *Southern Indiana Review, Story, Whitefish Review,* and *The Common* among others. She won the 2016 Rick Bass/Montana Fiction Award, and the 2012 Northern Colorado Writers Award judged by Antonya Nelson. She was recently shortlisted for the Lascaux Prize in Short Fiction and longlisted for a collection of short stories by The Santa Fe Writers Project. A long-time Chicago resident, she now lives in Los Angeles.

Looking for your next great read?

We can help!

Visit www.shewritespress.com/next-read
or scan the QR code below for a list
of our recommended titles.

She Writes Press is an award-winning
independent publishing company founded to
serve women writers everywhere.